PRAISE FOR *THE VERY BEST OF CARE*

"*The Very Best of Care* is an emotional roller coaster that transports readers into the world of neonatal intensive care through the eyes of a terrified but tenacious new mother. A story of the highest stakes and shocking betrayals that will keep you rooting for the timey family and riveted
through the very last page. An excellent debut. I look forward to more from Julie Hatch!"

—Tammy Euliano, physician, researcher, professor at the University of Florida, and author of *Fatal Intent and Misfire*

"Julie Hatch uses her extensive knowledge to weave a believable and exciting plot featuring the care of premature babies. *The Very Best of Care* takes the reader behind the scenes into the fascinating world of hospital life. With illegal and illicit experiments going on behind the scenes, it is an exciting page-turner that . . . leaves you breathless. A great read well worth five stars."

—Readers' Favorite, 5-star review

"A fast-paced novel that immerses readers in the high-stakes world of hospital NICUs, where tensions between doctors, nurses, and expectant parents play out amid the pressures of for-profit healthcare. With sharp insight into the tangled relationships between hospitals, pharma, and insurance, Hatch crafts a gripping story that builds to a powerful crescendo."

—Francesco Paola, author of *Left on Rancho*

THE
VERY BEST
OF CARE

A NOVEL

JULIE HATCH

SPARKPRESS

Copyright © 2025 Julie Hatch

All rights reserved. No part of this publication may be reproduced, distributed, or transmitted in any form or by any means, including photocopying, recording, digital scanning, or other electronic or mechanical methods, without the prior written permission of the publisher, except in the case of brief quotations embodied in critical reviews and certain other noncommercial uses permitted by copyright law. For permission requests, please address SparkPress.

Published by SparkPress, a BookSparks imprint,
A division of SparkPoint Studio, LLC
Phoenix, Arizona, USA, 85007
www.gosparkpress.com

Published 2025
Printed in the United States of America

Print ISBN: 978-1-68463-314-2
E-ISBN: 978-1-68463-315-9
Library of Congress Control Number: 2025903039

Interior design and typeset by Katherine Lloyd, The DESK

All company and/or product names may be trade names, logos, trademarks, and/or registered trademarks and are the property of their respective owners.

This is a work of fiction. Names, characters, places, and incidents either are the product of the author's imagination or are used fictitiously. Any resemblance to actual persons, living or dead, is entirely coincidental.

NO AI TRAINING: Without in any way limiting the author's [and publisher's] exclusive rights under copyright, any use of this publication to "train" generative artificial intelligence (AI) technologies to generate text is expressly prohibited. The author reserves all rights to license uses of this work for generative AI training and development of machine learning language models.

For the mothers and fathers
of the thousands of preemies born every year

CHAPTER 1

"Stop! Sophie, stop!" Carol was yelling at her. "Close your legs!" Sophie fought to squeeze her legs together while she clutched the oxygen mask tightly to her face. Her heart pounded. Her abdomen was on fire. What the heck was happening? She clenched her legs together as if her life depended on it. Something was terribly wrong.

"Sophie!" Carol shouted again. "Just breathe. Keep your legs together and breathe."

She heard Carol's voice through the fog and had a hazy realization that she was in labor—fourteen weeks early. This wasn't possible. Her obstetrician had given her and her baby a clean bill of health just yesterday. Her mind flashed over the past twenty-four hours. What had she done? Why was she here? She started to hyperventilate. *Oh no, please, God, don't let anything happen to Danny.*

Before one contraction ended, another one mounted in such intensity that Sophie couldn't help but scream out. She started to panic. *This can't be happening.* Then another contraction mounted. Yes, in fact, this *was* happening.

"Oh my God—Carol, help me! What do I do?" Sophie cried.

"Sophie, take little panting breaths like this," Carol instructed. She demonstrated short, blowing exhalations while she rushed around Sophie's gurney, dragging a cart behind her. She yanked on a little plastic lock, breaking open the drawers filled with emergency supplies.

Sophie started panting, which worked for thirty seconds before her eyes popped wider and a wrenching contraction ripped through her lower body. Sweat dripped down the side of her face. She grabbed Carol's wrist. "What is going on? What's wrong? Promise me Danny will be okay. Please save him." Sophie felt the heat of terror and labor burning her face.

"Sophie, you're going to be okay. And so will your baby." Carol turned and yelled out, "I need some help here!"

Nurses crowded around her gurney, bumping into each other as they hurried to tear open packages of supplies. They ripped off pieces of tape to hold Sophie's IV in place. Two IV bags hung precariously from the pole that extended above Sophie's head. Needles, syringes, and vials of medications littered the counter. The noxious smell of alcohol permeated the air.

"Sophie, we're doing everything we can to keep that baby inside of you," Carol explained in a tight, controlled tone. "Just keep panting." She dropped the head of the gurney down, laying Sophie flat on her back.

Paralyzed with fear, Sophie stared at the brown water-stained ceiling tiles above her. *I haven't even met him yet. He can't die now.* Then another agonizing cramp gripped her belly. "Nooooo!" She tried to sit up, but the pain was unbearable, forcing her to stay on her back. Tears ran down her temples and collected in her ears. She'd never felt so helpless. She started to pray. *God, please don't let him die. I've tried so hard. He can't just die now.*

The beeps from the monitor slowed, no longer reassuringly steady and strong.

"The baby's heart rate is dropping!" Carol shouted. "I need another IV started right now. She needs a fluid bolus. Someone check the baby's position." Carol's eyes were fixed on the fetal monitor. "The baby's heart rate is sixty, and it's not coming up. She needs to deliver. Someone get Dr. Wagner."

"I'm right here." Dr. Wagner was standing behind her. He put a hand on Carol's shoulder and asked her to move.

The commotion around Sophie grew: more noise, more pieces of equipment wheeled to her bedside. Panicked, she yelled, "Where's Adam? I want my husband here."

She felt Dr. Wagner's hands between her legs as he prepared for the delivery. Sophie swatted him away. At another excruciating stab to her abdomen, she screamed.

"Sophie, just relax," Dr. Wagner instructed. She tried to kick his hands away. A moment later, in a firm voice, Dr. Wagner said, "Okay, Sophie. Now. Push!"

The head of her gurney jerked up, forcing her into an upright position. Dr. Wagner propped her legs open with his elbows. She gave one little push, and just like spitting out a slippery watermelon seed, her son slid out. Sophie reached for him.

Before her hands got near him, a team of nurses and doctors waiting in the periphery moved in, picked up her baby, wrapped him in a blanket, and put him in a waiting transport incubator made of plexiglass.

"Give me my baby. Let me have him!"

One of the nurses pulled out her miniature-size stethoscope and placed it on Danny's chest. Another member of the team put little oxygen tubes in his nose. A third connected him to the transport heart monitor and temperature probe. Once he was in the preheated incubator and connected to the temperature probe, they unwrapped Danny. Sophie was shocked at how tiny and fragile her little son was. She watched as they prepared to wheel him away.

One of the nurses stopped to explain to Sophie. "We're taking your baby to the NICU. One of the doctors will be back to explain everything to you, but right now we have to get him upstairs."

"Okay, let's go."

"Wait! Please, can't I just see him for a minute?" Sophie pleaded.

"N—"

Dr. Wagner interrupted. "It's okay, let Mrs. Young see her baby for just a second. Open the porthole and let her touch him." The nurse opened a door in the transporter just big enough for Sophie to put her hand through. She stepped aside and gave Sophie and her baby a chance to do what little bonding could be done in thirty seconds. The NICU team regathered and wheeled the transporter out of the room. Sophie struggled to sit up to catch one more glimpse of her son.

"Try to relax, Mrs. Young." The triage nurse gently pressed another mask over Sophie's face as she heard voices fade into the distance. Then everything went dark.

CHAPTER 2

Sophie woke a while later—minutes? Hours? She couldn't tell. Her stretcher was up against the back wall of triage, tucked out of the way from the main part of the room. She was chilled despite the warm blankets piled on top of her. She felt the restrictive tug of an IV line taped to her arm, tethering her to an IV pole.

Once fully awake, it all came rushing back. Sophie touched her doughy belly with her baby no longer inside her and grasped the gravity of the situation. Danny had been born too early to survive without the neonatal intensive care unit. How could that be? Her own doctor had told her she was a picture of perfect pregnant health. And even though she'd felt some twinges walking to the hospital, she felt better by the time she got there. What happened?

She chewed on her lower lip as she thought over the past three hours.

She had been running errands on her lunch break, making her way through the crowded sidewalks of Midtown Manhattan. The weather was typical of late December—cold, raw temperatures; gray skies; and week-old dirty slush on the city streets.

She'd bought a new Kong for Blu, her and Adam's Portuguese water dog. Blu had been there for the two of them through the years of failed attempts at starting a family. It was their last try at IVF that was finally successful.

With the Kong tucked under one arm and her pocketbook slung over the other shoulder, Sophie headed uptown to her

Madison Avenue office. The first twinge hit when she stopped short to keep from bumping into the man waiting for the traffic light. At first, it registered low on her panic radar. She went another three blocks and felt another twinge, more like a cramp in her lower abdomen. But when it happened a third time at the intersection of Fifty-Seventh and Lexington, she had to decide—go left back to her office or go right to New York Metro Hospital. She had to be sure Danny was okay. She wondered, were these twinges of cramping normal? One minute she was confident everything was fine; the next minute she doubted herself. How was she supposed to know if something was wrong? She was no obstetrician. She had known this little guy inside of her for over six months—shouldn't she know if everything was okay? She stopped to call her obstetrician's office and left a message for someone to get back to her as soon as possible. Was it really necessary to go to the hospital?

No way was she taking any chances. Work would just have to wait. She chose to go get checked out—a decision that would haunt her for years. Second-guessing herself all the way, she hurried to the hospital.

Sophie entered the two-hundred-year-old lobby of Metro Women's and Children's Hospital. Another cramp hit her. She hurried through the crowded lobby to the information desk. Holding her belly, Sophie asked, "Where's maternity triage?"

The woman behind the desk pointed to her left. Overhead were signs that read ONCOLOGY, MATERNITY, FERTILITY CLINIC, PEDIATRICS, NEONATAL INTENSIVE CARE, DAY SURGERY, and MATERNITY TRIAGE. Sophie hurried down the hall to triage. She couldn't help but notice the wall that extended the full length of the hallway, lined with black-and-white photos of hospital physicians wearing starchy white lab coats.

She arrived at maternity triage to find a small crowd of

women waiting at the desk. A couple of them yelled for someone's attention. Another cramp seized Sophie. Remembering instructions from her doctor's nurse, she sat down and pulled out her water bottle.

"If you feel cramping, drink lots of water. That's probably the problem. And for God's sake, sit down and take a break." Sophie recalled the strict advice from her obstetrician's nurse.

She drank the entire bottle, filled it up again from the water dispenser against the wall, and continued to drink. After a brief sit-down, she got up to stand in line at the triage desk. Her cramping had subsided.

Behind Sophie stood a petite young woman, holding her stomach and wincing slightly. Sophie turned to her and smiled.

"Hi, I'm Sophie."

The young woman's name was Anna. Waiting to be called into triage, the two women chatted and compared notes—both were twenty-six weeks pregnant and here at Metro for a quick check of some minor abdominal pain. Seeing that Anna was still wincing, Sophie moved behind her and told her she should go first. Then she offered her a drink from her water bottle.

Anna shook her head. "No thank you. I'm okay."

When Anna's turn came to step up to the triage desk, her soft brown eyes looked at Sophie questioningly.

"Yes, you go. I'll be in right behind you."

"Thank you."

Sophie gave her a wink and said, "Good luck, Anna. See you in there."

Sophie checked her phone—it had been twenty minutes since she felt the last cramp. *Maybe it's all a false alarm.*

Sophie's turn came. A nurse in her fifties, Sophie guessed, with graying hair and smile lines that radiated from the corners of her eyes, greeted Sophie. Sophie read the hospital badge clipped to her scrubs breast pocket: CAROL BENNETT, CHARGE NURSE.

"Come with me." Carol led Sophie into triage.

"Actually, Carol, I feel much better now. I think I can go back to work." Then came a faint cramp, accompanied by that little voice in her head: *Don't you dare let anything happen to Danny.*

Carol studied her. "Well, since you're here, let's just check to make sure everyone's okay. No need to be nervous. You're probably right. More than likely everything is fine."

"Okay. Maybe a quick check would be good, just to be sure."

Sophie followed Carol through the door into the busy triage unit. She looked for Anna but couldn't find her.

Carol led her to a space with a gurney behind a curtain. The curtain didn't close completely, leaving a large gap that caused Sophie to feel exposed. Carol got busy as she untangled monitor wires, pulled apart the Velcro of the blood pressure cuff, and stuck a digital thermometer under Sophie's tongue. "Sorry, we're out of the skin temp thermometers."

Sophie looked up at her and offered an "It's okay" smile.

"Are you having a boy or a girl?" asked Carol.

"A boy," Sophie answered around the thermometer in her mouth.

"That's wonderful. What's his name?"

"Daniel."

"I love that name. Is it a family name?" Carol continued with light conversation as she settled Sophie in for her stay in triage. Her chattering helped to ease Sophie's nerves.

Five minutes later, Sophie lay with wires attached to her chest and abdomen that connected to monitors on the wall above her head. An IV dripped into her left arm. Carol had done a brief physical exam and confirmed her gestation of twenty-six weeks.

"Your uterus is just a little irritable, nothing serious. It happens all the time around twenty-five to twenty-eight weeks. Not so much a sign of early labor, more a sign you need to relax and hydrate."

Carol adjusted the IV clamp, speeding up the drip of the fluid.

"I'm going to give you a small dose of progesterone, a medication that will help keep your uterus from cramping." Carol injected the medicine into her IV.

Sophie took some deep breaths and allowed herself to believe that everything would be okay. She and Adam had worked so hard to conceive. No way was she going to let any harm come to this little treasure inside of her. He'd never survive being born this early.

She took in the busyness of the crowded triage unit. The air was charged as doctors and nurses bustled from patient to patient, checking monitors, taking vital signs, examining bellies, injecting IVs, writing notes in charts, and typing on laptops, all the while talking among themselves and with their patients.

The clock read two thirty. She'd been gone from the office for over two hours. When Carol came back around to check on her, Sophie asked if she'd be able to leave soon.

"I've got a pile of work waiting for me at the office and two impossible deadlines," she smiled as she explained.

Carol looked at her monitor and felt her belly. "If you don't have any more cramping in the next fifteen minutes, you should be good to go."

That's a relief. Sophie considered calling Adam but decided against it. She wasn't going to interrupt him and his class of high school sophomores just to tell him she and the baby were okay. She could wait until dinner to tell him about her afternoon.

Adam. He'd been the one to rescue her six years ago from the rigid, restrictive confines of her own making. Safety and security for Sophie had always come in the form of planning and controlling. The tall, dark-haired, blue-eyed Irishman had reached in and touched her heart. Adam had rescued her from a marriage that had gone sour as soon as she'd taken her vows. The marriage she'd been so careful about, to choose the right guy and plan the perfect ceremony, was over in under a week. The guy turned out to be a monster. Adam, who was a friend at the time, had stepped in to help. He'd cracked open her rigid exterior and shown her how to let go, lighten up, and trust that the world was not out to hurt her. She'd come a long way in learning to calm down, but she knew she was still a work in progress.

Sophie sat up and swung her legs over the side of the gurney, looking for her clothes. It was time she got going. She scanned the room for Carol. She needed help getting rid of this IV, then she'd be out of there. Fifteen minutes had passed, and she felt back to normal. She examined her IV, figuring out how exactly she should disconnect from it.

"Mrs. Young?" A voice pulled her from her concentration. "I'm Dr. Wagner."

Sophie looked up to meet a tall, rather handsome doctor. He smiled and politely offered his well-manicured hand. She shook it and smiled up at him. He was dressed in blue scrubs and a white lab coat with his name embroidered on the front. He leafed through her paperwork as he spoke. Hanging behind him was a nurse with a hospital ID clipped to the front of her scrubs top. AMANDA, Sophie read.

"You're thirty-seven," Dr. Wagner read off the chart.

Sophie nodded.

"Ah yes, I see here. Says you're twenty-six weeks."

She nodded again.

Dr. Wagner jotted something down on a folded piece of paper that he'd pulled from his scrubs pocket. He turned and handed it to the nurse. "Could you hang on to this, please, Amanda? Why don't you lie back down, Mrs. Young. I'd like you to stay just a little longer so I can be sure you and your baby are okay."

Reluctantly, Sophie got back under the covers. "Is there something Carol missed? She said I should be good to go, and I really need to get back to work." Feeling queasy with the idea of staying in triage any longer and missing any more work, she added, "Please, I'll check in with my regular doctor first thing tomorrow. I'm *fine*." She wanted out of there. This Dr. Wagner was probably just dotting his *i*'s and crossing his *t*'s before letting her go.

"I know I'm not your regular doctor, but I need to make sure everything checks out with your baby. I can't just let you go without an exam and a chance to monitor your baby. Relax, this won't take long." He gave her a reassuring smile.

"Okay, I'll try." She took a deep breath.

"Good." He gave her hand a quick pat, then took a minute to adjust her IV before turning to check on the next patient. He and Amanda moved from patient to patient as a pair.

Triage was getting busier. The wails of one very pregnant woman reverberated off the triage walls.

"Let's get her upstairs to deliver," yelled one of the doctors.

Sophie watched as two nurses ran to push the laboring woman out of the room. She put her hand on her belly, silently telling Danny to settle down and behave until she could get them both out of there.

CHAPTER 3

That had been before the storm of her labor and the blur of her own chaotic delivery. Now here she was, a new mother, nearly four months early. Unbelievable. What in God's name had happened? Hardest to think about was whether her son would survive. She tried not to let her mind go there but couldn't help thinking the worst. She needed Adam. Where was he?

An antiseptic smell hung in the air. She read TRIAGE written backward on the window of the door at the other end of the room. There were no windows, and the beige linoleum and fluorescent lighting made for a bleak backdrop. This was supposed to be a happy place where new lives were born. Instead, Sophie was depressed—she felt empty both physically and emotionally. Her baby was somewhere upstairs in the intensive care nursery. Her life had turned inside out in a matter of minutes.

Carol had called Adam's school, and he was on his way. He'd missed the birth of their son. Disappointed and exhausted, Sophie closed her eyes and drifted off. She heard babies crying, then the voices of nurses soothing them. She heard Blu barking, then saw Adam wearing two surgical masks—one over his mouth, the other on his forehead.

Rousing from her twilight doze, she realized it was all a dream. She heard loud voices coming from the next gurney over, bringing her fully awake. Before a nurse yanked the curtain closed, Sophie caught a quick look at the woman lying there. It was Anna.

Beneath the curtain, Sophie could see the legs and feet of

the triage staff moving quickly around her gurney. She heard the edgy voices of doctors and nurses talking loudly over each other. An alarm sounded. Someone silenced it, only for it to immediately start again. Two people with tourniquets hanging from the pockets of their white coats ran in behind the curtain. An ultrasound tech rolled her portable machine behind the curtain, forcing staff to move aside. There was too much activity. Anna was in trouble. Carol's voice rose above the din of noise. "Stay with me, Anna. It's going to be okay. Just stay with me."

Sophie listened as the commotion grew. Puddles of blood formed under her gurney. Doctors and nurses emerged from behind the curtain to run for more supplies, their scrubs covered in blood. There was too much shouting, too many people.

Three nurses rushed in to help, leaving the curtain partially open. Anna turned her head in Sophie's direction. Anna's legs were splayed open; her right arm hung lifeless over the rail of the gurney. She looked so pale and scared, not making a sound.

Sophie smiled and raised a hand to her. Anna closed her eyes.

"No. Anna, hang on. Listen to Carol and stay with her. Come on, Anna!" Sophie begged.

Carol yelled out orders: "Send off a blood gas now! What's her blood pressure? Give her more fluid—just leave the IV wide open." Nurses rushed around Anna. "She's hemorrhaging. Get four units of O-negative ready to transfuse. We need Dr. Wagner over here right now."

Sophie couldn't pull her eyes away from the drama. Anna's bra and underpants had been cut off and thrown on the floor. IV bags and tubing, medication vials, countless surgical pads, and bloody sheets and towels were strewn everywhere. Anna looked unconscious.

"Be ready to intubate. She's going into shock!"

A woman clad in blue scrubs put a tube down Anna's throat.

"She's still hemorrhaging. She needs that blood now! And get the blood bank to send up two units of FFP."

Two nurses squeezed the transfusion bags full of viscous dark blood into Anna's veins. Sophie heard the wet slap of feet stepping through the puddles of blood.

Dr. Wagner forced his way through the crowd. "We have to section her, now. There's no time to get her to the operating room. We're doing the C-section here—stat!"

The nurses rushed to put together a makeshift sterile section of triage with portable curtain dividers and blue drapes thrown together to make a barrier. Again, Sophie lost sight of Anna. She heard more than she saw—the clamor of multiple alarms ringing, people yelling over each other, Dr. Wagner shouting out orders, the clanging of metal surgical instruments, bloody towels thrown on the floor. The nurses behind the curtain talked louder and faster. Thirty more seconds of this, then the weak whimper of a baby. Sophie breathed a sigh of relief.

An eerie hush fell. Slowly, the blue drapes were taken down. Sophie saw two nurses standing over Anna's lifeless body. They pulled their surgical masks down, shocked looks on their faces. Sophie heard the low flatline monotone coming from the monitor before Carol turned it off, leaving a deathly silence.

Anna's blood slowed to a trickle, dripping slowly onto the floor, where it had started to congeal. The metallic smell cut through any hint of disinfectant. Dr. Wagner stood next to Anna's gurney, gazing at the floor and absently rubbing his forehead. As one nurse pulled the sheet up over Anna's face, another nurse bundled the baby, put her in a transporter, and rushed her away.

CHAPTER 4

The nurses prepared to transfer Sophie upstairs to her postpartum room. Triage needed her bed right away for the next laboring mother. She had her belongings tucked in around her on the gurney—the clothes she had worn into triage, her boots, her jacket, her pocketbook, and the Kong.

Carol walked toward her, closely tailed by Adam. Once he saw Sophie, he ran to her. He pulled her to him in a strong hug.

"Oh my God, Soph. What happened? I'm so sorry I wasn't here. What happened?"

One of the nurses pushed Sophie's gurney out the door and toward the elevator, apologizing for the rush. Adam kept up as he held on to the gurney side rail. They rode the elevator to the fourth floor. Sophie told him everything that had happened.

"Adam, I'm so sorry. I don't know what happened. I keep trying to figure it out." She picked at her thumbnail. "I have no idea what I did!"

"Soph, relax. You didn't do anything. I'm just glad you and Danny are both okay."

"Sorry," she muttered.

"Shh! None of this is your fault."

They arrived at Sophie's assigned room, where Adam and the nurse helped her off the gurney and into bed.

"So where is he? Where's Danny now?" Adam asked.

"He's in the neonatal intensive care unit," the nurse replied.

"Can we go see him?" Sophie asked.

"It'll be a couple of hours before they have him settled. They'll be running a lot of tests on him, starting IVs, doing X-rays—and a whole lot more." The nurse was putting Sophie's few belongings away in the closet. "They don't let parents in until they have the baby stabilized and they're done admitting him. He may be little, but there's a lot that goes into saving babies like Danny."

Sophie and Adam squeezed each other's hands.

"I really need to see him," Sophie said.

"It'll have to be a quick five minutes. Tomorrow you'll have more time to be with him."

Adam pushed Sophie in her wheelchair and followed the nurse down the hall. She led them through the automatic doors and into the NICU. Stopping at a sink, the nurse showed them how to scrub their hands. They proceeded through the unit, Sophie rolling in her wheelchair, Adam pushing her from behind. Monitor lights displayed over each baby's incubator. The nurses' voices were low and the lights dim, casting a comfortable calm around the babies. They got to Danny's incubator. Taped to the outside of it was a blue card with his name, Sophie's name, and his date of birth written on it. By the incubator's small soft light, Sophie and Adam finally saw their son. He lay still and quiet, making an occasional reflexive twitch with his feet. He was tiny.

Sophie smiled as tears filled her eyes. "He's beautiful."

The nurse told them to go ahead, put their hands into the incubator and touch Danny, that he'd like to know his parents were there. Adam and Sophie followed her direction. They caressed the inside of his arms and watched him respond by clenching his fist. His eyes remained closed.

"Wow," Adam said. "This is our family."

After their allotted five minutes, they left the NICU and returned to Sophie's room. Adam called a neighbor and asked him to let Blu out, adding that he'd be home in the morning to feed him. Adam squeezed onto the hospital bed next to Sophie.

He spooned her as she nestled herself into him. They drifted off for a few hours of sleep.

The next morning, Adam woke Sophie with an armful of flowers, her favorite mocha latte, and a blue balloon that read CONGRATULATIONS! He had gone home, fed Blu, and changed his clothes. He wore his typical skinny black jeans, button-down shirt, blue high-tops, and NY Knicks athletic jacket. He'd skipped shaving, and his dark hair had gone uncombed, giving him the casual Sunday-morning look that Sophie so adored.

She thanked Adam for the coffee, then struggled to an upright sitting position.

He propped a pillow behind her and pulled a chair next to her bed.

"Soph, I love you so much. We're going to be the greatest parents this side of the Hudson." He moved to sit next to her on the bed and wrapped his arms around her.

She laid her head on his chest, content as he stroked her hair. *Everything's going to be okay*, she thought to herself.

They talked about Danny as Sophie ate her breakfast.

"The nurses said he weighs barely two pounds. He looks too small to even be alive," Sophie said. "I can't even believe it." They were new parents—fourteen weeks ahead of plan. Now what?

The nurse came in and helped Sophie into the bathroom. When she was done, Adam turned to look at her as she gingerly walked over to him. Her loose dark curls hung down almost to her waist. Her fair skin accentuated her naturally pink lips.

"God, you're gorgeous."

He leaned in and kissed her.

Sophie answered, "I sure don't feel gorgeous."

"You're already glowing in the radiance of motherhood."

"Oh please." She rolled her eyes but allowed herself a modest smile.

She felt a dull ache between her legs and reached out for Adam's arm. He slowly walked her to the wheelchair.

There was a knock at the door, and Dr. Wagner poked his head in. "Okay if I come in?"

"Sure," Sophie called out. "Adam, this is Dr. Wagner, the doctor who delivered Danny."

Sophie sized up the man who had delivered her son. He had an engaging smile. His dark hair was slicked back, and his brown eyes peered from behind frameless eyeglasses. He wore a well-groomed mustache and beard and was dressed in fresh scrubs covered by his long white lab coat.

"Hello, Mr. and Mrs. Young. Allow me to introduce myself to you, Mr. Young. I'm Dr. Mitchell Wagner." He pulled his hands from his pockets and shook Adam's hand. "And allow me to reintroduce myself to you, Mrs. Young, in a better manner than how we met yesterday." He chuckled, as if there was something funny about yesterday's fiasco. "I'm the chief of high-risk obstetrics here at Metro."

He pulled up a chair and got comfortable.

"First off, let me tell you I'm sorry that you delivered your baby so early. We tried to keep it from happening, but some things we have no control over."

Sophie and Adam glanced at each other.

"You are in one of the greatest maternity hospitals with the best NICU in the city. You can be assured your son will get the very best of care." He spent time explaining prematurity and what Danny's twenty-six-week gestational age meant in terms of length of time in the NICU and what they could expect in the weeks to come. As he spoke, Dr. Wagner fidgeted with something in his right pocket. The clicking sound reminded Sophie of marbles that she and her sister used to play with when they were kids.

He patiently answered all their questions and didn't rush out the door like so many doctors did. Sophie took a deep breath, relaxing into his reassurances.

Adam stood as Dr. Wagner got up to leave. They shook hands again.

"Thank you, Doctor, for everything you've done for my wife and child."

"Yes, thank you, Dr. Wagner. We feel so lucky to be here—if this had to happen, we're glad it happened here," added Sophie. "But I do have one more question. Why do you think I went into preterm labor? Everything had been going along perfectly for almost six months. It doesn't make sense."

"Your premature labor was what we call idiopathic," he explained.

Adam and Sophie looked at him with puzzled expressions.

"It was just something that happened, something that was out of your control. I know you're in shock right now, but that'll pass. You're okay, your baby is okay, and now you need to focus your attention on him. Soon, you'll all be home together as a family."

Sophie looked at him, willing herself to believe him.

CHAPTER 5

Adam wheeled Sophie down the hall to the NICU, cautiously avoiding bumps over thresholds and slowly maneuvering the wheelchair around corners.

"It's okay, Adam, I won't break," Sophie teased. "You can go a little faster."

Outside the NICU, the electronic doors were closed with no door handles and no apparent way to get in.

"I wonder how we're supposed to get i—"

Before Adam finished, the doors swung open, startling them both.

A nurse came through the door. "Hi. Can I help you?" she said, walking over to check the ID band on Sophie's wrist. "Oh, you're the Youngs! So nice to meet you," she said in a cheery voice, extending her hand. "I'm Kim." She wore silver-and-turquoise earrings that dangled low, below her earlobes. Subtle streaks of blue ran through her long dark hair. "I'm Danny's primary nurse. I'll be taking care of him until he goes home."

Sophie smiled back, liking her instantly.

Wheeling through the NICU, Sophie took in the expansiveness of the unit. It was filled with babies in incubators. There were machines and pieces of equipment that Sophie couldn't even guess what they were for. Staff dressed in scrubs buzzed around like worker bees. The sound of so many alarms going off at once and the racket of staff and parents and secretaries all talking at once overloaded Sophie's senses. The noises merged to create one loud, dissonant din. Her head ached, her stomach hurt, and she cupped a shaking hand to her mouth to keep the burning bile from erupting.

Overwhelm swept over her as the world turned surreal. She felt disconnected from her body, like she was watching a movie of herself. Everything around her moved in slow motion as Adam wheeled her through the unit. She watched the doctors and nurses walk by her in an exaggerated slow manner, their mouths moving, but she couldn't hear their voices. The cacophony of noises melded into one dull, distant roar. She looked up at Adam. His lips were moving, but she couldn't understand him. He sounded like a vinyl record meant to be played at forty-five slowed down to thirty-three—long, drawn-out sentences. The twenty seconds it took to wheel through the NICU felt like an hour.

She snapped back to reality when Kim leaned over to tell her that it wasn't always like this. The beginning of the day shift was always the busiest and loudest.

As Sophie worked to get over her initial shock, she noticed more. Most of the babies were tiny, fit-in-the-palm-of-your-hand-sized infants in incubators. They all were attached to machines with wires and tubes, blinking lights, and high-pitched electronic beeps. Four people dressed in scrubs rushed past her and Adam as the intercom boomed, "Delivery team to room ten for a thirty-two-weeker, stat!" Everything felt like an emergency.

Sophie closed her eyes, trying to block out the clamor. But the worst was the high-pitched blare of the heart monitor alarms. The sudden ear-splitting sound was enough to make her nerves scream.

Kim led them through the NICU and into Pod C, where the volume of noise was lower, but the place was still busy. She explained that the unit was divided up into pods, with each pod holding four babies and four sets of parents. Each set of parents had a small chest of drawers for personal belongings and a reclining chair next to their baby's incubator. The recliner doubled as a place to sleep if needed. There was also a parents' lounge with cots and couches if a parent wanted to stay overnight.

Sophie held tight to Adam's hand as she stood up out of the wheelchair, still dressed in her johnny and nonskid hospital slippers. They walked together over to Danny's incubator. She felt like she'd been whisked away to a foreign land, an over-the-rainbow feeling. But this place was no Oz. There, in the middle of the chaos of the NICU, she saw not a wizard but her precious little two-pound baby boy. He was lying in an incubator, just as he'd been the night before. But now, with all the lights on, she could see how scrawny and vulnerable he looked. Monitor wires were stuck to his tiny chest, and a tube protruded from his mouth and attached to a machine that was breathing for him. He had an IV in each hand, and a third came out of his umbilical cord and fed into a pump. The pump clicked every few seconds as it slowly pumped fluid into the IV tubing. Her little baby didn't move; he didn't cry. He just lay there, attached to all these contraptions. The whole scene terrified her.

"Adam, he looks like a little baby bird who fell out of its nest."

"Yeah, he does." He placed a hand over hers and squeezed.

In the next moment, Sophie felt a rush of love for this beautiful little life, and awe that he was here at all. She was blown away by how quickly her world had turned upside down. She looked up at Adam, who had tears in his eyes.

"He's so small I'm afraid to touch him. I'm afraid I'll hurt him," said Adam.

"I know. Me too," Sophie replied.

Kim stood beside them and explained all the pieces of equipment. "The tube in his mouth is to help him breathe. It's attached to that machine there, the ventilator. My guess is he'll be off the vent in a day or two."

She pointed to the monitor that displayed his heart rate,

blood pressure, respiratory rate, and oxygenation levels. There were IV pumps that calibrated the amount of IV fluid he received and other pumps for delivering neonatal doses of medications. Kim encouraged them to touch him and talk to him.

"He's still too little and fragile for you to hold. But you can still let him know you're here. He'll recognize your voices."

Sophie and Adam put their hands in the incubator and felt the warm air circulating around inside. They marveled at their son, this little being they had created together. Sophie blocked out everything around her as she focused only on Danny—his tiny hands, his soft little lips, his cap of fine silky hair. He had a doll-size diaper on and nothing else.

Then that blare of monitor alarms sounding off at once jarred her raw nerves, making her entire body tense.

She took Adam's arm. "Adam, what are we doing here?" She looked upward. "God, what have I done?"

"You didn't do anything, babe. Danny just wanted to be born early." He wrapped his arm around her waist and held her close. Sophie wasn't sure if it was a miracle or a curse that they were here in the NICU.

The alarms stopped as suddenly as they had started, and Sophie's tension began to ease. She felt the heavy discomfort from standing for too long and sat back down in the wheelchair. Kim was busying herself with another baby in the incubator next to Danny.

"How many babies are in the whole NICU?" Sophie asked Kim.

"Our average number is forty babies, give or take."

"Wow, I would never have thought that there could be that many premature babies in one NICU." Sophie watched Kim working, then turned to gaze at Danny. Her attention bounced back and forth between the two. Adam still had his hand inside the incubator, touching one of Danny's feet.

"Kim, what does *idiopathic* mean?"

"It means that doctors don't know the answer, without saying that they don't know. Anything they can't explain is called idiopathic."

"Dr. Wagner said my preterm delivery was idiopathic." His baritone voice still echoed in Sophie's head. "They don't know why it happened?"

"If you didn't have any medical reason to go into labor so early, like hypertension or an infection, then, yes, it would be called idiopathic."

CHAPTER 6

A group of doctors gathered outside Pod C, waiting to begin rounds. Kim came over to tell Sophie and Adam they had to step out of the pod for a few minutes. Morning rounds were starting, and for the sake of privacy, parents had to leave until they were done.

Adam pushed Sophie and the wheelchair out of the NICU and down to the lobby. They maneuvered over to the fish tank that stood in the middle of the lobby and was surrounded by kids. Dressed in hospital pajamas, with some on crutches and others in wheelchairs, they laughed and pointed at the colorful lionfish and clownfish swimming back and forth. Sophie stood and stepped away from the tank to call her sister. Kate lived four hours away in Boston. The last time they had talked, they were planning Sophie's baby shower, still weeks away.

Kate answered, "Hey, Soph. What's up?"

Sophie told her.

"Are you serious? What happened? How's he doing?"

"He's doing okay. He's on a respirator to help him breathe, but hopefully, he won't need it too much longer. This hospital has an excellent NICU, and I really like Kim, Danny's nurse. It's all so much, Kate. He's so small we can't even hold him. He's tiny, Kate."

"How much does he weigh?"

"Two pounds."

"What? Oh my God!"

"I know, and they say he's going to lose weight before he gains it again. I can't even imagine that. A lot is going on, and so much I don't understand yet. Twenty-six weeks and two pounds, Kate. You have to see it to believe it."

"That's my plan, sis. I'll be on a train down this weekend. I can't wait to see you! Do you need anything?"

"Nope, just bring yourself. I'll be so happy to have you here, you have no idea."

Back in Danny's pod, Sophie noticed another mother sitting next to her baby's incubator. Adam left to return the wheelchair, no longer needed, to Sophie's room. The mother looked up at Sophie with a warm, friendly smile. Her skin was a soft brown, her eyes the color of tidal pools. When she stood to introduce herself, Sophie marveled at her toned figure. She had just delivered a baby, and she looked like a million bucks.

"Hi, I'm Rihanna." She spoke with an accent that Sophie couldn't place.

"Nice to meet you, Rihanna. I'm Sophie. Mind if I sit?"

Rihanna gestured for her to pull up a chair.

"You don't sound like you're from New York," Sophie said. "Can I ask, where are you from?"

"De Bahamas."

"Oh, that's the accent I hear."

"And you?"

"I'm a New Yorker, through and through."

In less than an hour, they were chatting as if they'd known each other for years. Sophie was intrigued by this woman who was so calm despite being stuck in the same situation as Sophie. She asked what life in the Bahamas was like. Rihanna asked what life as a native New Yorker was like. They compared delivery stories. Rihanna's baby girl, Isabelle, was born eight weeks early.

"How come you delivered so early?"

"Preeclampsia," she answered in her Bahamian cadence. "My

blood pressure was getting dangerously high. The doctor gave me a dose of steroids to help the baby's lungs, then induced me. Good thing. By the time she was born, my blood pressure was off the charts. As soon as she came out, it came down. I love my obstetrician. He's so good."

They talked for over an hour. As staff walked by, Sophie noticed how they looked twice at Rihanna, no doubt because of her striking beauty.

One of the doctors came over to talk to Rihanna, interrupting their conversation. Sophie went back to sit by Danny's incubator. She watched Rihanna and the doctor together. They were at ease with each other in a way that only intimate partners could be. They murmured softly, their heads together, cooing to the baby. The doctor was preparing to leave when Rihanna called Sophie over to introduce them.

"Sophie, this is Sheldon. I mean Dr. Vandewater."

"Nice to meet you, Dr. Vandewater," replied Sophie.

"You as well, Sophie, but please, call me Dr. Sheldon. It's a lot easier." He smiled. "I'll be back in a few," he said to Rihanna before leaving the pod.

Sophie desperately wanted to hold Danny. Kim was out on break, and there was another nurse covering for her. Sophie called out to her and asked for some help when she had a minute. When the nurse came over, Sophie said, "I'd like to hold my baby. How do I get him out of his incubator?"

"Whoa there, mommy tiger," the nurse said with a smile. "He's not ready to be held yet. That tube down his throat is keeping him alive. See that machine attached to the other end of it?"

Sophie felt the sting of tears tickling her nose as she nodded.

"It's going to be a while before he's ready to be held. Didn't anybody explain that to you?" asked the nurse.

"I don't know, probably. I just don't remember." Sophie wiped at her tears.

"I'm sorry, but you have to wait until he's bigger." The nurse walked away.

Sophie's foot bounced as she chewed her thumbnail and the tears rolled down her cheeks. She hated this feeling of losing control. She was always waiting for the other shoe to drop. Now, finding herself in the NICU and forbidden from holding her own baby, the shoe had finally dropped.

CHAPTER 7

Later that afternoon, Dr. Vandewater came back into the pod, this time to talk with Sophie and Adam. He introduced himself to them as one of the NICU attending neonatologists.

"Hello, Dr. Vande . . . Vande . . . Geez, Doctor, I'm sorry." Adam looked to Sophie for help. He extended his hand in greeting.

Dr. Vandewater laughed as he shook Adam's hand. "Yeah, I know. It's not your run-of-the-mill last name." He laughed. "As I told your wife earlier, call me Dr. Sheldon—it's easier."

Dr. Sheldon was on the short side, coming up only to Adam's forehead. He wore thin wire-rimmed glasses that kept sliding down, stopping to rest in a permanent line on the bridge of his nose. His curly dirty-blond hair had a bedhead look to it. His Oxford shirt was one size too big, with a gaping space between his neck and the collar. He wore a loosely knotted, wrinkled tie and scuffed-up shoes. His shirttail hung untucked outside his pants. The overall impression was of an absent-minded professor. When he smiled, his whole face lit up. Sophie found him attractive in an endearing way.

Dr. Sheldon listened as Sophie and Adam recounted Danny's unexpected arrival.

"You know, Dr. Sheldon, I came here with a little minor cramping, never expecting to deliver. The poor woman who came in at the same time ended up *dying*. It's been a very strange, not to mention upsetting, twenty-four hours. I just can't understand why I went into such early labor, especially since my pregnancy had been going so well."

Looking directly at Sophie, then at Adam, he said, "I am truly sorry for all you've been through. It's such an unpredictable business we're in." His calm voice helped to soften Sophie's anxiety. "I wish I could give you better answers."

He picked up the preemie-sized stethoscope attached to the incubator and examined Danny. When he was done, he closed the incubator portholes and turned back to the couple.

"Congratulations to you both. You have one fine young boy."

That clinched it for Sophie; she loved this doctor. Nobody yet had called Danny a fine young boy.

After they'd finished the conversation with Dr. Sheldon, he stood up to excuse himself and let them know he looked forward to getting to know them and Danny better over the next several weeks. On the way out of the pod, he slipped over to Rihanna's baby, stroked her head, and quietly talked to her. After a few minutes, Rihanna still hadn't appeared, and Dr. Sheldon left the pod.

Soon after Dr. Sheldon walked out, Rihanna rounded the corner of their pod and went over to Isabelle. Sophie joined her. They started chatting again, picking right back up on their earlier conversation. Then Sophie asked about Dr. Sheldon.

"Rihanna, I couldn't help but notice you and Dr. Sheldon look like pretty close friends."

She smiled. "Yeah, there's a story there."

Sophie raised an eyebrow, waiting for more.

Rihanna explained that after taking care of her ailing mother in the Bahamas for five years before she finally passed, she came to New York for a visit. She met Sheldon one Sunday while ice-skating in Central Park. They fell in love, and not long after, she got pregnant. She decided to stay in New York and have the baby.

"Sheldon is a different kind of guy. I think I fell in love because he's got a little bit of a bad-boy streak in him. Have you ever been attracted to the bad-boy type, Sophie?"

"Ah, no, can't say I have."

"He was raised by a single mom. In fact, he and Dr. Wagner are half brothers. They have the same mother. I don't know how many people know that, so maybe don't say anything."

Sophie drew her thumb and finger across her lips, vowing silence.

"But Sheldon, he's laid-back. He doesn't take life too seriously, which I like—it reminds me of the Bahamians. And he's a good doctor." Rihanna paused, resting her hand on Isabelle's stomach. "He was kicked out of prep school, which is a little bit of the bad boy, but still graduated from med school. Life has always come easy to Sheldon. He was married briefly, but that didn't last; it complicated his life."

Rihanna paused, thinking. "He's one of the best men I've met. He's smart, he's a ton of fun, and he has a heart of gold." A smile broke out across her face. "We didn't mean to fall in love and get pregnant. It just happened."

"Bad boy meets Bahamian beauty—I love it."

"Yeah, we have a good time together." Her smile faded. "I don't know, though. Now, with Isabelle, I'll have to see how much fun he thinks having a baby is."

Later that afternoon, Adam and Sophie sat close to Danny's incubator, curtains closed around them, trying to keep the NICU world at bay. They had a nice quiet cocoon, just the three of them. Sophie and Adam explored every inch of their baby, studying his tiny toes, his downy hair, and his minuscule fingernails. His chest rose and fell with the rhythm of the ventilator.

"Remember that song called Particle Man?" Adam started humming the tune. "He looks like a little particle man."

"He does kind of, doesn't he?" Sophie gazed at Danny. "Our little particle guy."

Then that horrific screeching alarm sounded, demanding immediate attention to a baby's slowing heart rate. Over the intercom boomed a voice calling for help to Pod B, stat.

Sophie peeked out from around their curtain, anxious to know what was happening, worried about the baby whose monitor wouldn't stop alarming. Watching through the plate-glass windows, she saw the sides of the baby's incubator drop, giving full access to the baby. One nurse covered his face with a rubber mask and squeezed it repeatedly, breathing for the baby, and another nurse started pushing on the baby's chest. One of the residents stepped up and put a breathing tube down his throat. Doctors called out orders, and a portable X-ray machine was wheeled in. The alarms continued to blare.

Sophie closed her eyes, praying that the baby would be okay. She and Adam squeezed each other's hands tightly, each feeling the tension in the other. Kim came in and tried to distract them by talking about how well Danny was doing, but Sophie couldn't help listening to what was happening across the way and hoping for the voices to calm down. She waited for the alarm to stop.

Eventually the alarm quieted, and the heart monitor returned to its reassuring regular rhythm. Without missing a beat, the staff quickly returned to what they had been doing before this hiccup in their routine, almost as if nothing had happened.

Irritated, Sophie turned to Adam. "This place is crazy."

"You'll get used to the alarms and all the activity," Kim told them. She pulled her stethoscope from her pocket and hung it around her neck. "Usually, helping a baby to recover from a low heart rate isn't so involved. Almost all preemies have these apneic episodes where they stop breathing. It's all part of being premature, and it's usually not a big deal. This one was a little more serious. But it's all good now—another baby saved in the trenches of the NICU." She smiled sympathetically at Sophie and Adam.

After the commotion settled down, Sophie saw Dr. Wagner in the periphery, pacing, scowling, and glancing up every few minutes to watch what was happening. When it became apparent that the baby was going to be okay, he turned on his heel and left. Sophie turned to Kim.

"Why does Dr. Wagner hang around the NICU? Isn't he an OB?"

"He is," she said, busying herself with cleaning her stethoscope.

"Maybe he's just following up on the babies he delivered so he can talk with the mothers with up-to-date information?"

"Yeah, maybe," Kim replied.

CHAPTER 8

"Hey, you two. Do you have a minute?" Dr. Sheldon peeked around the curtain of Danny's incubator space. Adam and Sophie invited him to pull up a chair.

"As you just saw, apnea is a problem in premature babies. It's called apnea of prematurity. You've probably heard of some adults using a CPAP machine at night?"

They both nodded.

"That's because they have sleep apnea. In preemies, apnea happens because their immature brain forgets to breathe. If the apnea continues for more than twenty seconds, then the heart rate starts to drop. That's why you hear a lot of alarms going off—usually it's because a baby has become apneic and they need a little stimulation, something as simple as a pat on the back to remind them to breathe. Danny has had a couple of these episodes, but nothing bad, because the ventilator is there to breathe for him if he forgets."

He paused and distractedly rolled and unrolled the bottom of his tie, adding a few more wrinkles to the already crumpled mess.

"We treat apnea of prematurity with caffeine citrate. It stimulates their brain, reminding them to breathe. Once they're older and more mature, usually around thirty-four weeks, they can usually come off the caffeine."

Sophie waited for Dr. Sheldon to get to the point.

"I'm doing a research study on caffeine citrate under the trademark name BrainHealth. I'm looking at how we can use caffeine in a different way. We think that, if caffeine is given early and long enough, it can also help preemie brains to develop better. Even without being in the study, Danny will likely be started on caffeine because of his extreme prematurity. My study involves tracking the caffeine through the body as it gets metabolized. I also monitor brain activity in response to the caffeine. Are you with me so far?"

Sophie and Adam nodded.

"Good. It's important that you know, even if you decline to enroll Danny in the study, his care will remain the same. He'll receive caffeine like any other preemie who needs it."

"What will you be doing to him?"

"I'll be running blood tests on him, which will coincide with his daily blood tests. Every couple of weeks, I'll be injecting his caffeine dose with an isotope solution into his IV. When he's bigger, I'll do a series of three brain scans."

"Is it safe? I mean, we wouldn't want to sign on to anything that could possibly hurt him."

"Of course. Like I said, he will in all likelihood be getting the medication anyway. If you enroll in my study, it will just mean a few extra tests that are paid for by the hospital."

Sophie and Adam looked at each other, trying to read what the other was thinking.

"I'll tell you what," Dr. Sheldon added. "How about I leave you with some printed material to look at, and I'll check back with you later."

"That sounds fine," Adam said. "We need to talk about it together."

"Absolutely. We believe that the study will show that with proper dosing and prolonged treatment, a preemie's development and later performance in school will be better."

"Wait, what is this isotope you're talking about?" Adam asked. "It sounds a little sci-fi to me. Aren't those dangerous?"

"You're thinking of radioactive isotopes. We don't use those; we use stable isotopes. The isotopes are like little tracers that attach to the caffeine molecules so that I can track them through Danny's body. I can assure you they're completely harmless."

He handed them a piece of paper with *Informed Consent* printed at the top. "Read through this. I'll come back later and answer any questions you have." Dr. Sheldon stood to leave. "Whatever you decide is fine."

Sophie looked down at the consent form with *BrainHealth* written on the first line. At the bottom, she read, *Not approved by the FDA*.

"Ah, Dr. Sheldon." Sophie cleared her throat. "What is this? Not approved?"

"That just means that the FDA hasn't approved it for anything other than treating apnea of prematurity. If you read the fine print, it says the BrainHealth patent is pending and that, for now, using caffeine citrate to help with brain development is only experimental. That's why I'm doing this study. To get it FDA approved for this new purpose. But the drug is perfectly safe. We've been using it for years."

Rihanna had been listening to the conversation. When Sophie turned to her, Rihanna looked away.

CHAPTER 9

In the parents' lounge, Sophie introduced herself to a circle of mothers seated in rocking chairs. They welcomed her in and made space for her to pull up a rocker. Sophie listened as the mothers exchanged delivery stories. A mother sitting next to Sophie was in tears as she recounted the delivery of her baby who was so premature she was told he may not survive. Sophie couldn't believe that there were babies younger and smaller than Danny. Her heart went out to this mother.

Another mother excitedly recounted her delivery in detail, including how her husband passed out and collapsed into a chair. "The nurse had to give him smelling salts for him to watch our baby being born." She chuckled as she told the story. "Luckily he was okay—the baby, that is." A couple of the mothers gasped. "No, I'm kidding. My husband's fine too." The group of moms laughed.

As they spoke, Sophie flashed back to her own delivery. She remembered she had brushed Dr. Wagner's hand away as he got ready for the delivery. She had tried a second time to get his hands off her. She knew why that baritone voice of his that echoed in her head made her feel so anxious. She was back in college—a blind date that had ended in rape. That nightmare had come rushing back when she felt Dr. Wagner's hands in places that were all wrong. Or was it just her imagination? Was she blending her delivery with the memories of her date rape?

She shook her head, trying to make the thoughts go away,

but the memory stuck. Over the years, she had buried it, forcing it down so that it could never resurface. But it had returned with disturbing clarity. She felt her heart in her chest and blood pounding in her ears as those feelings of shame and then anger flooded over her. She sat on her hands to keep them from shaking and worked to focus on what the other women were saying.

"And you know, I'm embarrassed to even say it, but Dr. Wagner was touching me in a creepy way while he was getting ready to do my delivery," said one mother. "Like, his hands were in places they didn't belong for catching my baby." She blushed as she looked around to the other mothers, then lowered her head.

Sophie nodded. She wasn't blending. Dr. Wagner had touched her and this other mother in ways that weren't okay.

Once the circle broke up and the women had dispersed, Sophie introduced herself to the woman who had sat next to her.

"I think you and I had similar experiences with Dr. Wagner."

"I am so glad to hear you say that," the woman said. She grabbed Sophie's arm, embarrassed. "I'm sorry, I didn't mean to say it that way. I'm not glad that it happened to you, but glad that you know what I'm talking about. I keep going over my delivery in my head and keep coming back to Dr. Wagner's hands."

"I don't think it was your imagination," Sophie said. "Are you going to say anything?"

The mother shrugged and looked at Sophie with the same uncertainty that Sophie felt.

Later Adam caught up with Sophie in the cafeteria. The lunch crowd was just thinning out. The window next to them looked out over an expansive open space revealing a snow-covered lawn. Ice hung heavily from the tree branches, weighing them down until they nearly touched the ground. Sophie told Adam about her recall of Dr. Wagner delivering Danny.

"Adam, I'm going to administration. Just because he's the chief doesn't mean it's okay for him to touch his patients inappropriately."

"I totally agree."

"And it wasn't just me. I talked with another mother who had the same thing happen when Dr. Wagner delivered her baby."

"Want me to go with you?"

"No. I should do this alone." As they got up to leave, Sophie paused. She looked again out the window. "This place must be beautiful in the spring."

"Yeah, I bet it is," Adam agreed. "I just hope we're not still here to see it."

CHAPTER 10

Sophie returned to her room to grab some makeup. Surprised to see Dr. Wagner standing in her room with his back to the door, she noticed him scrolling through the nurse's computer. She cleared her throat to let him know she was there. He spun around and quickly closed the laptop.

"Hi, Dr. Wagner."

"Sophie, hello. You surprised me. I was just reviewing your records and getting ready to discharge you."

"Great."

Sophie's nurse walked in, flipping through the stack of papers she had in her hands. "Sophie, Dr. Wagner is discharging you." When she looked up from her papers, she saw Dr. Wagner at her computer. "Oh, hi, Dr. Wagner. I saw your order from earlier, and I was just getting ready to discharge her now." She turned back to Sophie. "Congratulations, you're free to leave," she said as she cut her hospital ID band from her wrist. "I'm leaving the second band on. You'll need it to get in and out of the NICU, so keep it on until Danny goes home."

"Thanks. Yeah, I'm not going very far. Anyone looking for me will find me in the NICU."

Picking up the laptop, the nurse asked, "Is there anything else you need, Dr. Wagner?"

"No." He pulled the front of his lab coat closed and excused himself.

Sophie listened to the nurse's discharge instructions and signed the paperwork, thanking the nurse for her care. She changed out of her hospital johnny into the jeans and sweater that Adam had brought earlier, then headed down the hall to the NICU. She went into Pod C and unloaded her toothpaste and toothbrush, hairbrush, lipstick, and phone charger into the drawer of the small table next to Danny's incubator. She'd bring some more clothes from home tomorrow. She planned to be here for as long as Danny was in the NICU.

She peered in at him, kissed her finger, and touched it to his lips. Then she closed the portholes and left to go downstairs and wait for Kate.

CHAPTER 11

Dr. Mitch Wagner stood in the middle of the triage unit, doing what he loved best—orchestrating the activity of triage. It was early evening, and the unit was bustling with activity. Nurses were busy admitting and evaluating mothers. Some were in labor, others complained of terrible nausea and vomiting, and there were those with vague complaints of abdominal pain. This was why Mitch got up every morning, to play master of his universe—master of maternity triage.

Mitch reflected on how his life had brought him to where he was now. His father had been a well-respected orthopedic surgeon in Manhattan. During those early years, his father wasn't home much. In addition to being busy with office hours and surgeries, he also presented at conferences. But when he was home, he spent time with Mitch. He paid attention to him, showing interest in his friends and his life at school.

After his parents divorced, he stayed in close touch with his father. They saw each other during the week when his father had the time. Always before the end of the visits, his father spoke about plans for medical school, even while Mitch was still in grade school.

Mitch was smart, and school was easy for him. He attended private school on the Upper West Side. Once Mitch had started school, his father didn't just encourage him to go into medicine; he expected it. Clearly, there was no option for Mitch to consider another path. His mother offered no opposing ideas either. "Do what your father tells you. It's best." In high school, he impressed his teachers when he memorized the periodic table of elements before the end of the first week of ninth-grade chemistry class. He was a straight-A student and captain of the freshman track team. He was a son any parent would be proud of.

Mitch wanted to be a doctor, but he didn't want to go into orthopedics like his father. Orthopedics was for jocks, guys who had spent many afternoons getting their broken bones and dislocated joints put back together. To be an orthopedic doctor, you had to be good with tools—drills, saws, screws, and metal plates. He was a track runner, not a jock or a tool guy.

Nope, he was drawn to obstetrics and gynecology. It was the one area of medicine where he could practice both medicine and surgery. Once, when Mitch was in tenth grade, his father found him looking at one of his gynecology textbooks and knocked him hard on the top of his head.

"What the hell is the matter with you? You don't want to be an obstetrician." His father said that ob-gyn was not a manly area of medicine, like orthopedics was. "And think about the crazy hours you'd be working, the outrageous malpractice insurance, and you're looking at women's crotches all day. Trust me, after two days, it gets old." His father scoffed. "It's sissy medicine."

Senior year in college was when Mitch told his father about his final decision to specialize in ob-gyn. His father made no attempt to hide his disappointment. His derogatory remarks caused a deep crack in their relationship.

His father's disapproval weighed heavily on Mitch, causing him to frequently doubt himself and his decision. He lived under that cloud that he would never be a good enough doctor in his father's eyes. However, when he was in triage and delivering babies, he was in his element. He was good at what he did, and the mothers needed him. That felt important and powerful—something he never felt around his father. He persisted, even in the dark times of serious self-doubt. He was determined to show his father that he could succeed and that his work mattered, even while his father's voice played over in his head, "Sissy medicine."

He snapped out of his reverie when he heard Amanda call his name. Amanda was his right-hand nurse. So smart and competent, she worked by his side whenever they were on duty together. While evaluating a patient, she called over to Suzanne, another experienced nurse, to give her a hand. Suzanne had recently started working at Metro, having moved from Georgia, where she had worked at Vanderbilt University Hospital. A laboring mother whom Mitch recognized from prior triage visits was struggling with her pain.

"It's likely back labor," Mitch said, looking over Suzanne's shoulder. "Just get her positioned right to relieve the pressure that the baby is putting on her sacrum."

Amanda helped Suzanne as they tried to get her more comfortable. Nothing worked. The patient was crying, in so much pain that she couldn't sit still.

"Amanda," Mitch said from behind her. "Let's just get the baby out. She can't go on like this."

Amanda handed Suzanne a vial and told her to give it. It would help with the pain.

Suzanne looked at Mitch. "Dr. Wagner?"

He nodded.

Suzanne injected the medication. Two minutes later, the mother was writhing, screaming in pain, and clawing at her belly, trying to escape the building contractions that just wouldn't abate. She was sweating, pulling at her johnny, legs spread wide, yelling for Dr. Wagner to get the goddamn fucking baby out of her *now!*

Mitch stood over the patient. He gave her a small dose from one of the vials on the cart next to the patient, then positioned himself between the mother's legs, ready to deliver the baby. An uneasy feeling started to build in him, a vague sense of impending doom. His brow furrowed, and a small bead of sweat ran down the back of his neck. He yelled for Amanda to get over and help him, unaware that Amanda was right behind him. He showed Amanda his reason for concern. The baby was breech. Why hadn't anyone known this? Didn't anybody check the baby's position? This delivery was going all wrong. A breech delivery is trouble, and double trouble when nobody is prepared for it.

Suzanne slapped a mask over the patient's face and turned up the oxygen that blended with a sweet-tasting gas. The patient instantly relaxed and soon fell asleep. With the baby already descending out the birth canal, bottom first, there was no time for a C-section. It had been a while since he'd done a breech delivery. He'd learned from the seasoned doctors who had experience and knew what they were doing, but it was tricky. Mitch reached up inside, grabbed the baby's shoulders, and pulled hard. Suzanne put all her weight into pushing on the mother's abdomen, forcing the baby down and out. Finally, the butt appeared, along with a set of testicles, followed quickly by the body. The head was not so quick to follow. It was stuck. The mother, waking up despite the anesthetic gas, screamed again. The baby's body hung by its neck from the mother's vagina. His legs were blue and motionless with his head still stuck inside. Mitch gave another half a dose, hoping one more good contraction would push the head out. Instead, the contracting uterus tightened the cervix around the baby's neck.

"Oh, shit, this isn't good," said Suzanne.

Mitch commanded, "Amanda, get her back to sleep."

Amanda covered the patient's face again with the gas mask. Instantly, the patient fell asleep, relaxing her muscles. Amanda and Suzanne both put all their strength into pushing on the mother's belly from above while Mitch pulled from below. A minute later, the baby boy was born. He was limp, blue, and lifeless, with an Apgar score of 0 at one minute.

"Shit," Amanda said under her breath, then yelled, "I need help over here! Full resuscitation!"

Doctors and nurses scrambled to intubate the baby, quickly inserted an umbilical line, and pushed medications to get his heart rate going. Apgar score was 2 at five minutes. Mitch was tending to the mother, stitching up her episiotomy, while another physician called out orders for more meds for the baby and to keep giving chest compressions and ventilations. By ten minutes, the baby's Apgar score was 5. Not terribly optimistic for his future, but one never knew for sure.

Two nurses and a respiratory therapist took the baby to the NICU while the mom went to recovery. Standard blood work was sent on the mom, including toxicology. Drugs needed to be ruled out as the reason for preterm labor.

Thirty minutes later, the tox screen results came as a surprise. There was a dangerously high level of Pitocin in her blood. Suzanne showed the results to Amanda, who brought the results to Mitch. After a pause, he gave reassurance to Suzanne and Amanda that it made sense. He had given the mother some extra Pitocin at the end to get the baby out faster.

"But, Dr. Wagner, that much?" Suzanne questioned.

He shrugged. The results must be a mistake. He'd double-check it with the lab. Several minutes later, while Suzanne was writing her notes, she started talking out loud to herself about meds, breech babies, low Apgar scores, and poor outcomes. She exclaimed, "Oh my God! What have we done?"

Mitch grabbed her arm and hushed her. In a loud whisper, he replied, "*We* haven't done anything. The baby would have died in utero if we hadn't delivered him. You saw the monitor. He was compressing the umbilical cord, cutting off oxygen to his brain. We had no choice. We all did a fine job in saving this baby's life. And you, Suzanne, should be congratulated for your help."

In shock, Suzanne walked out of triage and away from Mitch.

"Where is she going?" Mitch asked Amanda. "Go get her. Stop her!"

CHAPTER 12

Sophie waited outside the hospital entrance for Kate. She had on her Ugg boots and her winter jacket that she could now fully zip up. The wind funneled up the hospital driveway, blowing cold air that froze her nostrils and made her eyes water. A taxi pulled up to the roundabout, and Kate jumped out of the cab, pulling the collar of her winter jacket tighter to her neck.

The two of them hugged.

Sophie buried her face in Kate's scarf. Muffled, she said, "Oh God, Kate, I am so happy to see you. It's been a crazy few days."

Kate stood back to look at Sophie. "Well, little sis, you look good, even with all you've been through. Where's Adam?"

"Upstairs. Come on."

They hooked arms and entered the hospital. They walked down the hallway past the sign to the maternity triage unit. Two physicians joined them in the elevator. They rode in silence until Kate and Sophie got off on the fourth floor.

Sophie swiped her parent ID, and the doors to the NICU swung open. Sophie showed Kate how to scrub her hands. When they got to Danny's incubator, Adam was already there.

"Hey, Kate." Adam gave her a hug.

Sophie walked Kate closer to the incubator. "Meet your nephew."

Standing between Sophie and Adam, Kate gasped and grabbed both of their hands. "Oh my God, you guys, he's so tiny!"

After a few minutes of oohs and aahs, Adam turned to Sophie.

"Soph, since Kate's here, I'm going to head home and get some work done. I'll see you guys later." Adam gave Sophie a kiss.

The sisters talked as they looked through the plexiglass at Danny. "Tell me what happened, Sophie. Why was he born so early?"

"That's the worst of it, I just don't know. It started with a little cramping around noon the other day . . ." Her voice drifted off. She lowered her head and held her hand against her forehead. "Gosh, I've lost all track of time. Anyhow, whenever it was, I came here, then everything went downhill." She told Kate everything that had gone on since Danny was born. "The bottom line is there's no explanation for my early delivery. They tell me it's idiopathic, but I don't think they're telling me everything."

Kate looked at her in surprise.

"But I'm not sure. I really don't know what to think."

Kate brought her chair closer, so their knees touched. She leaned over and hugged Sophie. Sophie hung on tightly to her sister.

"Kate, I'm terrified. I'm scared of being responsible for this tiny little baby. What am I supposed to do with him?"

They hugged a while longer until Sophie felt ready to lift her head and wipe a few tears away. She took a deep breath and released her hold on Kate.

"Thanks for that." Sophie managed a smile. "They say that he should be ready to come home around his due date."

"I'm here for you, Soph. You can count on me for whatever you need. Remember how much you helped me with Elizabeth's stillbirth? I was all alone. Rick was away on business. That was the worst experience any mother could go through. But you saved me. I couldn't have done it without you."

Sophie answered, "I don't know about that. I think you're exaggerating."

"No, I mean it. You were there for me when I needed it most."

Kate put her hands through the portholes into the incubator and gently held Danny's foot. She put her face close so Danny could hear her, and cooed softly. Sophie smiled, happy to have her sister here with her. The cooing stopped. Sophie looked at Kate.

"Is that Dr. Wagner?" Kate asked.

Dr. Wagner was in the next pod, over at the incubator of the latest admission. He was talking with one of the nurses. He had one hand on her shoulder and gestured with the other hand, as if explaining something. The blonde nurse nodded while watching the baby and its monitors.

"Yeah," Sophie answered. "He delivered Danny. He's the chief of obstetrics. Why? Do you know him?"

"He delivered Elizabeth."

"He did? Weren't you in a different hospital?" Sophie asked.

"Yes, but it was Dr. Wagner who delivered Elizabeth. I'll never forget. I think he was moonlighting at the hospital downtown." A moment later, Kate brightened. "But that was then. Moving to Boston has been such a good thing for Rick and me. I love my job, and he's moving up the corporate ladder. And . . . we're trying to get pregnant again!"

"Oh, Kate, that's great!" Sophie hugged her again. "I'll keep my fingers crossed for you. I'd love for Danny to have a cousin his age."

Kate and Sophie spent the next two hours catching up on each other's lives. It was a nice distraction for Sophie. She watched as Kate's eyes followed Dr. Wagner out of the unit.

CHAPTER 13

Sophie convinced Kate to move out of her hotel and stay at her and Adam's house.

"I'm never there, and Adam could use the company. So could Blu," she pleaded with her sister.

"But where are you sleeping? Aren't you going home at night?"

"No, I can't do that yet. I need to be here, in case anything happens to Danny. I either sleep in the pull-out chair next to him or in the parents' lounge. It would be good for Adam to have some company."

"Okay, sounds good to me."

Kate checked out of the hotel, and they took a cab to Sophie's house. Seated in the back of the cab, Sophie glanced at the Boston newspaper in Kate's pocketbook. *Dead Fetus Discovered in Freezer of South Boston Apartment*, read the headline.

Sophie grabbed the newspaper. "What is this?"

"Oh shoot, sorry. I didn't mean for you to see this. Kind of sick, right?" Kate stuffed the paper and its headline deeper into her pocketbook.

They had turned onto Sophie's street. Looking out the window, she was so excited to be heading home she forgot the newspaper.

Sophie scrambled out of the taxi, thrilled to be home. She ran inside to an excited Blu, who greeted her by jumping up and licking her face. Laughing, Sophie tried to push him off, telling him to sit. Blu wouldn't have it. He kept jumping up and licking her face. Sophie laughed with delight.

"I haven't heard that laugh in forever," Adam said, smiling as he walked around the corner of the kitchen. He had coffee brewing and some fresh pastries he had picked up at the corner bakery.

"Man, you're the best." Kate gave him a sisterly peck on the cheek, then went upstairs to unpack.

"Hey, I'm heading to school," Adam said to Sophie. "I've got some catching up to do for next week's classes."

He kissed Sophie on the lips, then yelled up the stairs to Kate, "See ya later, Kate."

Sophie sat at the kitchen table with her sister next to her and Blu under her chair. She allowed herself to enjoy the moment of normalcy.

"You know," she said to Kate, "I really liked Dr. Wagner initially. But I've been talking with other mothers and thinking back to my own delivery. His booming voice echoes in my head, and I remember him touching me in a creepy way."

"What do you mean?"

"I was getting flashbacks from that night at college."

Alarmed, Kate said, "Sophie, what do you mean?"

"The flashback lasted only a few seconds, but it scared me." Sophie paused and looked at Kate. "It's like he was touching me in a sexual way. I know that sounds sick." Sophie reached down to pet Blu.

"Whoa, that's serious stuff, Soph. Maybe it was accidental, or at least wasn't what he meant to do."

"Except that there are other mothers who have similar stories. I met another mom. She and I talked, and we both agree what he did was wrong."

Neither spoke. The only sound was of Blu scratching his ears.

"Are you going to say anything?"

"Well, I haven't seen a complaint board or suggestion box anywhere," Sophie joked. "But, yeah, I talked with Adam, and he agreed I need to tell someone. I talked to Kim, Danny's nurse, about it a little. Just to see if she had any advice for me."

"And did she?"

"She was reluctant to say much. I think she didn't want to be too unprofessional by talking about one of the doctors, but she did tell me to tread carefully. Dr. Wagner is highly respected in the hospital. She also said that there's another side to him, a side that most people don't see. She alluded to something about a vengeful side of him, but she wouldn't go into details. I think she was saying that if I accuse him of inappropriate touching, I'd better be able to back it up."

"How are you going to do that? You don't have any proof."

"I know. That could be a problem."

CHAPTER 14

That night, Sophie tried to get comfortable in the recliner next to Danny's incubator. Unable to fall asleep, she left the NICU in search of a late-night snack. She found some vending machines in an otherwise empty corridor. The hallway was dimly lit with a few flickering fluorescent lights. The red exit signs marked each end of the hallway. Studying one of the vending machines and trying to decide what she felt like eating, she heard footsteps and the wheels of a crib rolling down the hall. The sound of the wheels stopped. She looked down the hall. It was too dark for her to see anything clearly. Who was up at this hour? She stood against the wall, making sure she was hidden in the shadows.

When the crib started moving again, she peeked around the corner. A man, dressed in a lab coat, was wheeling the crib into an office. She watched him swipe the lock of the door with his hospital ID.

When the door opened, the light from inside lit up the man's head. It was Dr. Sheldon.

What is Dr. Sheldon doing at two in the morning with someone's baby? Why is there no mother or nurse with the baby?

CHAPTER 15

The next morning, Sophie made an appointment with Mr. Charles Buckley, in administration. His secretary said he could squeeze her in at eleven o'clock, briefly. He had an extremely busy day.

Mr. Buckley came out to greet Sophie and motioned for her to follow him into his office. On the way down the hall, Sophie noticed an office that ran the full length of the hall. The shades were pulled down. On the door was a sign: WMI - WESTCHESTER MEDICAL INDUSTRIES.

Once they were both seated, he asked, "What can I do for you, Mrs. Young?"

"Mr. Buckley, I'd like to talk to you about a complaint I have. It's about Dr. Wagner."

He frowned and raised an eyebrow, then invited her to explain.

"During my delivery, which, by the way, was fourteen weeks early, Dr. Wagner touched me in an inappropriate way."

"What do you mean by inappropriate?"

"He was touching me in areas that were not part of the birth canal." Sophie felt her face turning red. "And he touched me in a creepy way. My regular doctor never did that."

"Explain 'creepy,' please, Mrs. Young." He was twirling a pen in his hand.

"Well . . ." she started, embarrassed to say this out loud to a man she didn't even know. "He had his fingers up high, in all the wrong places, which, if you know your female anatomy, is not where the baby comes out."

"Go on," Mr. Buckley said, jiggling his pen up and down.

"His hands . . ." She thought back to the time of her labor. "It brought back some difficult memories, and I found it terribly awkward and just plain wrong."

"Mrs. Young, you were delivering a baby. Of course he's going to be down in that area. He was probably doing what he needed in order to open your birth canal to help the baby out."

Bastard, thought Sophie. *He's patronizing me.*

"My baby weighed two pounds. I was working to keep him inside and *not* coming out. My birth canal didn't need any help."

"I'm sorry to hear this, Mrs. Young. Your hormones must be wreaking havoc with you." *Oh please.*

"But I assure you, I take every complaint seriously, and I will certainly look into it right away. Usually, complaints are simply a matter of miscommunication."

He tossed the pen on his desk as he looked at his watch and stood up. "I'll work on this and get back to you in a day or two. Again, I'm sorry for your experience and that you felt the need to report Dr. Wagner. But I understand you have to do what you feel is right."

Sophie forced a smile as she stood and shook Mr. Buckley's hand. "Thank you, Mr. Buckley."

She left his office, trying not to slam the door in frustration. She leaned against the hallway wall and sighed heavily. *Hormones? Really?* She knew her complaint would go nowhere. She could tell Mr. Buckley didn't believe her and that her word against Dr. Wagner's was like David fighting Goliath. *What is it with these men? They're supposed to be responsible physicians in charge of women's health. Instead, they're arrogant, condescending asses with a penis between their legs.* She smiled at her snarky description.

Turning to find the elevator, she saw a group of men dressed in suits walking out of the WMI office. Leading the group was Dr. Wagner. She ducked behind a corner and counted to ten. When she stepped out from behind the corner, Dr. Wagner was looking directly at her. She lowered her head and walked down the hall in the opposite direction.

CHAPTER 16

The following day, Sophie was busy changing Danny's diaper. Kim came in and gave Sophie a happy good morning, then got started taking care of a baby at the other end of the pod. All the other mothers were out of the NICU, either showering or getting breakfast.

"Mrs. Young."

Startled, Sophie turned around. Dr. Wagner stood right behind her. Her heart started to race. She saw a look of anger flash across his eyes. Quickly, his expression softened.

"I understand you were upstairs talking to Mr. Buckley about some dissatisfaction you have with my bedside manner." That voice so unnerved her.

"Yes, I—"

"Mrs. Young, I apologize if my bedside manner made you uncomfortable. I certainly didn't mean to offend you. I'd like to think I'm good at delivering babies. I had no idea I made you or any of my patients feel uncomfortable. Please accept my humble apology."

Caught off guard, Sophie answered, "Well, okay. Thank you."

He nodded his head slightly, then turned and walked away, leaving Sophie to digest his apology.

CHAPTER 17

Mitch headed to the elevator to go up to the suite of administrative offices. The nurses called it the tower of terror, an apt description in Mitch's opinion. He had a meeting with the powers that be, followed by a meeting with Charlie Buckley. The meeting with Charlie had nothing to do with Sophie Young's complaint. It was a different issue altogether. Mitch knew it meant one of two things: either he was keeping the chief officers of WMI happy and getting his promised bonus, or they expected more from him. Either way, he was fucked. He was committed to the project, and he had no choice but to answer to Charlie. He didn't come up here much. In fact, he hated this place. He didn't particularly care for Charlie either, except Charlie was responsible for getting Mitch to where he was now—chief of high-risk obstetrics. Mitch's ten years of success had directly impacted the rise and financial success of Metro Hospital, which was no small accomplishment.

As he waited for Charlie, he stood in the middle of the suite of offices. The floor-to-ceiling windows looked out over the city. The noise of the city was muted by the thick plate glass. Here in the tower, he was removed from it all. Life eight floors below played out like a silent movie.

An ambulance pulled up to the emergency entrance. EMTs pulled the stretcher out of the back of the ambulance, carrying a bloody, unconscious, very pregnant woman—probably a car accident, thought Mitch. A taxi pulled up and dropped off a man with a big bouquet of flowers. Mitch watched two people argue over one parking space. A group of four surgeons ran back from the corner Starbucks with large cups of coffee, still wearing their surgical caps and booties, bracing themselves against the cold.

Charlie's secretary touched Mitch's elbow, interrupting his thoughts, and escorted him into Charlie's office. A group of doctors, several administrators, and their secretaries were seated around a large conference table. Mitch was surprised to see Josh and Amanda there. Josh was the representative from Kindred Pharmaceuticals. Metro Hospital was Kindred's biggest account.

The president of the hospital called the meeting to order. One of the administrators loaded his PowerPoint and projected it onto a blank wall. He went on to discuss the quarterly financials of the hospital. Two doctors stood to present their ideas about how to cut costs and bring in more business with more advertising outside of the city, by extending into the boroughs and onto Long Island. The meeting droned on for forty-five minutes.

Finally, the group stood to leave. Jabbering among themselves, they filtered out of the office. Charlie, Mitch, Amanda, and Josh remained behind. Mitch turned to see Rita, Charlie's associate, walk in. She was the numbers person. She knew the NICU numbers—how they changed throughout a shift, a day, a year—and she kept up with every admission into the NICU and every discharge or transfer out.

"Sorry I missed the meeting," Rita said, "but it wasn't anything I needed to be there for." She took a seat at the table.

"Mitch," Charlie said, "we want Amanda more involved. She spends more time in triage than you."

Mitch knew Amanda was the best nurse in triage. She always knew his next move and next decision almost before he did. She knew her maternity triage business better than any nurse he'd met. But crossing into his territory of what he did in triage? *Uh-uh.*

"No way," he shot back.

Rita jumped in. "Mitch, calm down. Nobody is usurping your power. Amanda is in a perfect position to help."

Mitch couldn't deny that. He looked down and examined his fingernails. They did work well together, and there was no denying a physical attraction—mutual, he was sure. He waited a few moments, then looked up at Charlie. "On second thought, I think it's a great idea."

"Good," Charlie answered, "because you're not getting the job done fast enough, Mitchell. You need to ramp up your work. They're watching our numbers, and right now, they're not too happy with what they see. You've got to do more."

He felt like he was twelve years old again, back in the living room with his father. Mitch reached into his lab coat pocket stuffed with small squares of scratch notepaper and found a paperclip. As Charlie talked, Mitch cleaned his cuticles, looking up every so often to let Charlie know he was listening, even if he wasn't fully paying attention.

"Look, Mitchell. We need you. You're a fine doctor, and you have the respect of all your colleagues. But if you want to play, you've got to pay. I don't know what you're going to do to make it happen, and I don't want to know." He poked his finger on Mitch's chest as he said, "Pay to play. Got it?" He turned to Josh. "And you've got to keep those medication carts fully stocked. I don't want Mitch or Amanda having to scramble to find the meds they need. Understood?"

"Understood, boss."

When the meeting ended, Mitch was the first one out the door. Josh caught up with him as he waited for the elevator to go back down to triage.

"Yo, Mitch, no hard feelings. We're all feeling the pressure here. We're cool. It's all good. You'll see."

Mitch waved him off. "Yeah, okay, whatever."

Josh disappeared through the door to the stairwell.

Amanda was the last to leave the office. She ambled up next to Mitch, where they stood together waiting for the elevator. Mitch took a step back to admire the way Amanda's scrubs hugged her hips, something he'd never noticed before. He decided that, yes, this meeting had gone just fine. He would be quite happy to work more closely with Amanda. There could be some benefits in it for him.

Later that evening, Mitch and Amanda were leaving triage at the same time. The halls and elevators were less crowded than during the day. They got on the empty elevator together, and Amanda started talking over the details of their last delivery.

Once the doors closed, Mitch took a step toward her. Her face was plain with pale green eyes and thin dirty-blonde hair that hung limply to her shoulders. He moved closer, close enough to feel her breath. She didn't pull back. He put his hands on the back of her neck, feeling her ponytail brush his hands. He gently pulled her to him and kissed her.

Amanda yielded and opened her mouth. *I knew it*, thought Mitch. He forced his knee between her legs and leaned into her harder.

Thirty seconds later, the elevator bounced to a stop. They stepped apart. Mitch slicked his hair back, straightened his jacket, and strode off the elevator. He could feel her eyes on him as he walked away. *Christ, I'm almost old enough to be her father.*

CHAPTER 18

Morning medical rounds began on time, with doctors, nurses, social workers, and pharmacists standing in a tight circle. Kim explained to Sophie that the team moved from pod to pod to discuss the condition of each baby, any changes over the past twenty-four hours, the latest lab results, and the plan for the day. Rounds could take anywhere from one hour to all morning, depending on the census of the unit and the acuity of the babies—the sicker the babies, the more there was to discuss.

Sophie watched as rounds were interrupted by a stout woman dressed in a hideous pantsuit marching into the pod. Her heels clicked on the linoleum floor, and her hair was pulled back in a tight, efficient bun. Nobody's shoes clicked in this unit. The woman walked over and started talking to Kim. She glanced up when she felt all eyes on her.

"Please, don't let me interrupt," the woman cheerfully said to the gathering of people.

Kim and the woman stepped back from the crowd and shuffled through some papers. They spent a minute more together, then the woman left and moved on to the next pod. Sophie casually asked who the woman was.

"That's Rita. We jokingly call her 'lovely Rita, the meter maid.' She's the utilization review coordinator. She keeps track of the daily NICU census—how many babies are here each shift, every day. She uses the numbers for planning staff numbers and reports the census to her boss. She also considers how critical each baby's condition is. The sicker the baby, the more of a nurse's time they will take, which means more nurses need to be staffed. It's a constant work in progress, having enough staff scheduled so that nobody is forced to do overtime. If there are too few babies, then a nurse has to take the shift off. We're unionized, so there's a system in place. But the hospital would prefer to have higher numbers of babies in the unit and pay for overtime than to not have enough babies. Rita keeps track of all these moving parts and numbers that change daily, even hourly sometimes."

"You said this unit holds forty babies?"

Kim nodded. "Sometimes there are fewer, sometimes there are more, all depending on how many preterm babies are delivered on any given day. Full moons? Forget about it—it's crazy busy," she added.

A nurse from Pod D came over to Kim and Sophie.

"Sorry to interrupt," she said, "but, Kim, I need your help with a dopamine drip. Can you double-check my math on this?"

"Sure." Kim introduced Sophie to Christy.

Sophie smiled and gave a little wave.

"Nice to meet you, Sophie. You're the lucky mother of this cute little guy?"

Sophie smiled even more.

"Looks right to me," said Kim. She handed back the paper with Christy's calculations.

"Cool, thanks. Lunch today?"

"Sounds good. Anyhow"—Kim turned back to Sophie—"there was a time when the NICU census was way too high, and we were working our butts off—twelve-, sixteen-, sometimes eighteen-hour shifts, including our days off—to keep this place running. At the end of that stretch, which went on for close to six months, management came and told us what a good job we had done. Their way of thanking us was by having catered meals brought in for each shift. Catered meals were sandwich platters from a local deli. Pretty pathetic. We were all so burned out it wasn't worth it. And food certainly wasn't the answer we were looking for. After that, the union got involved and has made sure we don't get taken advantage of like that again."

"So that's why Rita is here going over patient numbers with you."

"You got it." Kim smiled at Sophie.

"I don't see Dr. Wagner on rounds." Sophie shifted the conversation.

"No, these are medical rounds for the NICU only—the docs and staff that are caring for these babies. Dr. Wagner isn't caring for any of these babies. His job was done once they were delivered."

CHAPTER 19

Rounds moved on. Dr. Wagner strode into the NICU, stopping to talk to one of the pediatricians who was listening to Dr. Sheldon discuss one of the babies. Dr. Wagner put a hand on his shoulder in a friendly gesture, and the doctor looked up and smiled broadly at him. The two doctors looked in Sophie's direction.

"Looks like Dr. Wagner is going to introduce you to Dr. Patel. He's one of the best pediatricians in the city. All the parents love him. You will too, you'll see," Kim said.

Dr. Wagner and Dr. Patel made their way over to Danny's incubator.

"Sophie, I'd like you to meet Dr. Patel, a dear friend and one of the very finest pediatricians around," Dr. Wagner said. "Am I right, Kim?"

"Absolutely."

Dr. Patel smiled graciously and shook hands with Sophie. He held her hands in both of his for several moments, his deep brown eyes connecting with hers.

In an Indian accent, Dr. Patel said, "It is truly my pleasure to meet you, Mrs. Young."

He let go of Sophie's hand and looked into the incubator. He opened the portholes, slowly reached in, and caressed Danny's head. He spoke softly to Danny, then withdrew his hands.

"I will be happy to be Danny's pediatrician," he said with a smile. "It would be my honor."

Then with a slight bow, he excused himself and slipped out of the pod to rejoin rounds. Dr. Wagner explained to Sophie that Dr. Patel's father and his father were the best of friends through medical school and after. Naturally, Dr. Wagner and Dr. Patel became friends as well. Now, on Dr. Wagner's request, Dr. Patel had agreed to accept Danny into his otherwise closed practice—that is, if Sophie would like. Kim vigorously nodded her head at Sophie, giving her a thumbs-up. Sophie gladly accepted and thanked Dr. Wagner. *Maybe he really doesn't know that he makes women uncomfortable during labor.*

Dr. Wagner's pager went off, and he left the unit.

Kim looked at her computer screen. "Hey, Sophie, good news! Dr. Sheldon has written an order for Danny to be extubated. He can come off the ventilator."

Suddenly there was a commotion outside of the pod. A man with a parent ID clipped to his jacket was stumbling around the unit, wielding a knife. Eyes glazed, and unsteady on his feet, he yelled loudly that he was there to take his son home.

Sophie panicked. She instantly knew the threat this man posed even before she saw the weapon. She'd seen this same crazy look in her father's eyes when he came home drunk and looking for a fight. Something had set this guy off just like something always set her father off. It never made sense but could bring out the worst, most violent behavior. Sophie and Kate had learned early to either hide or run away.

"They can't keep him! He needs to come home with me. The doctors don't know what they're doing!" slurred the man.

The charge nurse, who had been on the phone, hung up and turned to the man, trying to talk him down.

"Get away from me!" yelled the man, raising his weapon.

Then came the overhead, hospital-wide announcement: "Security alert: armed intruder, fourth floor, NICU." The charge nurse tried again, talking to him in a calm voice. Rounds had ended abruptly, everybody scattering to take cover behind doors and chairs.

The charge nurse told him that she had called security and they were on their way. Could he please put the knife down?

"There's no need to scare everybody—we can work this out. Think about what security will do if they see you with this weapon. Just put it away so we can talk."

Sophie trembled as she watched the scene unfold. The security alert boomed over the intercom again. "Repeat, armed intruder, fourth floor, NICU."

Sophie texted Adam: *There's a guy with a knife. Don't come in. Keep Kate away. Security's coming.* She grabbed Rihanna and pulled her behind a portable X-ray machine.

Dr. Sheldon stepped between the charge nurse and the man. Rihanna gasped. Sophie put her hand over Rihanna's mouth to quiet her.

The man turned toward Dr. Sheldon with the knife raised over his head. "Stay away!" His eyes darted around the staff beginning to crowd around the escalating scene.

Dr. Sheldon continued to talk to the man, drawing the man's attention back to him with his stream of conversation. Dr. Wagner came back into the NICU. He and Dr. Sheldon made brief eye contact, and Dr. Wagner came around to face the man. He towered over him and began to talk.

"Give me the knife, sir. Give it to me, and we'll get your son home to you. But we can't get him ready to go with everybody cowering from you and your weapon." Dr. Wagner continued talking, slowly circling him.

The man frantically looked around, disoriented. The hand holding the knife began to shake.

"Hey, focus here. Look at me," Dr. Wagner said, putting two fingers up to his own eyes.

The man looked at Dr. Wagner.

"Good. Now, just drop the knife, and we'll get your baby ready to go home with you." Dr. Wagner continued distracting him as they waited for security to show up.

Four security guards ran in and forced the father to drop his knife. They dragged him out of the unit, the man yelling threats and obscenities as they pulled him into the elevator.

Everybody started talking at once.

"How did he get up here with a knife?"

"This was a first for me," Kim exclaimed.

"Is everybody okay?"

Sophie collapsed into a chair.

That afternoon, after things had settled down, Sophie texted Adam to tell him the doctors were going to extubate Danny soon. He immediately texted back that he and Kate were on their way in.

"We're coming in the triage entrance. Come down and meet us there."

She went down to the lobby and left through the main entrance. As she rounded the corner and headed toward the triage entrance, she nearly bumped into them. Adam was sweaty, dressed in his running gear. Kate walked beside him, bundled up against the cold.

"You're running in this weather?"

"Yeah. You know me, Soph. I run best when stressed."

"Makes sense to me," Kate, who was also a runner, said.

Adam led Sophie and Kate through the maternity triage entrance.

"Why are we going this way?"

"I always come this way. It's closer to where I park the car." He waved to the nurse on duty at the triage desk.

She smiled and gave him a wave back. "Hey, Mr. Young. How's Danny doing?"

"You know the staff down here already?" Sophie whispered after they walked by the desk.

"Kind of. I've been in and out of here so much in the past couple of days."

Kate and Sophie snickered at Adam's blushing face.

CHAPTER 20

The next night, Sophie went back to the vending machine corridor. She watched from the shadows. The elevator across from Dr. Sheldon's office hummed, then stopped. Dr. Sheldon wheeled a crib off the elevator and into his office. Sophie snuck down the hall and stood around the corner next to his office. The door swung open, and a young guy—practically a kid, Sophie thought—came out. He didn't see Sophie as he headed toward the vending machines. When he came back and opened the door to go back in, Sophie caught a glimpse of the inside of the office.

This was no rinky-dink office. It was a huge laboratory space. In the back, there were two people in white lab coats. They were talking in hushed voices. Bright overhead lights reflected off the stainless-steel countertops that held metal instruments. The counters ran the length of the lab. Among the disorganized lab equipment and notebooks, she saw microscopes, a pile of surgical towels, gauze pads in sterile packages, specimen cups with different colored labels, and racks of test tubes.

Sophie's head snapped back when the door closed in her face. *What is going on?* Unseen, she made her way back to the NICU.

Over breakfast, Sophie told Adam and Kate about seeing Dr. Sheldon and his office. She had no idea what Sheldon was doing, but she intended to find out. She was going back.

Kate said, "Sophie, are you sure? It sounds kind of spooky. Experiments happening in the middle of the night?"

"I know, but I need to see what he's doing."

Just after midnight, Sophie waited in the vending machine hallway. She had her hair pulled back in a ponytail and was wearing the sweats that she slept in. She looked like any other NICU mom, unable to sleep, who wanted a midnight snack. Waiting, she scrolled through her phone. She heard footsteps. She put her phone away and stood perfectly still, waiting and listening. They were coming closer. She barely breathed. Then the footsteps turned and moved away. Sophie exhaled, and for the next half hour, all was quiet. After an hour, with still no sign of Dr. Sheldon, she went back to her pod.

Sophie didn't get it. She knew what she had seen the night before. Was the stress of the past few days getting to her? Maybe she was imagining things. She could barely keep track of what day it was. Maybe her mind was playing tricks on her. *Don't be ridiculous*, she told herself. *You know what you saw.*

Sophie returned to the hallway the following night and the next night, and the one after that. Waiting for Dr. Sheldon to appear, she patiently stood in the corridor shadows, only to be disappointed when there was no sign of life at Sheldon's office door. She started to doubt that she'd ever seen anything.

Each morning, she met up with Kate and reported what had happened the night before—nothing.

"Soph, what's your plan anyway? Are you waiting for a midnight invitation? Have you even thought this out?"

In truth, she'd only partly thought it out. She had seen the kid in the white jacket use his hospital ID to get in, probably with a fob on the back of it. Her NICU parent ID wouldn't work on this door, but maybe Danny's night nurse's ID would. Most of the NICU nurses wore their hospital IDs clipped to their scrubs jackets. For much of the night, Danny's night nurse left her jacket hanging over the back of a chair.

She began to formulate a plan.

CHAPTER 21

Sophie and Adam went to Dr. Sheldon's office the next morning. They knocked. There was no answer. They knocked again. Suddenly the door flew open.

Though surprised to see the two of them at his door, Dr. Sheldon quickly recovered. He invited them in and asked how he could help.

"We have a question about your study that Danny's in."

"Sure, what's on your mind?"

Sophie looked around. Nothing from the other night was there. No signs of a lab or of any experiments going on. It looked like any ordinary office with books and papers and a few items scattered on countertops.

Adam asked, "We're just wondering how Danny is doing. Like is he helping? Are you getting the results from him that you want?"

Dr. Sheldon cocked his head, confused. "It's too soon to say. Why do you ask?"

"Oh, right, of course it's too soon," Adam said. "We were just wondering."

Sophie took a business card from Sheldon's desk and slid it into her pocket. She glanced at Adam. She had seen enough to know this was just a regular office and they wouldn't find anything that would answer their questions about what she had seen the other night.

"Thanks, Dr. Sheldon. Sorry to bother you," Sophie said, and they left.

Later in the afternoon, Sophie casually asked Rihanna if she knew anything about Dr. Sheldon's research work.

"I thought I saw him with a baby in a crib going into his office in the middle of the night. Do you have any idea what he might be up to?"

Rihanna did not.

"Really? You have a child with a man who is chief of this unit, and you have no idea what he's doing in the middle of the night?" Sophie pressed. "Are you sure?"

Annoyed, Rihanna answered, "Sheldon made it clear from the beginning that our life together, and now with Isabelle, is separate from his work life. Very separate. Even though Isabelle is a patient in the NICU, we don't talk about his work. And I don't ask. He was probably working on his research. You know the consent form that you and Adam signed, giving him permission to use Danny as a guinea pig for his BrainHealth study?"

"Didn't you sign Isabelle up to be part of his study?"

"No way. I love the man, but no way is anybody going to experiment on my daughter."

"Huh," Sophie muttered. *Guinea pig? Is that what I agreed to for my son? For someone to experiment on him?* "But he said Danny would be given caffeine anyway, whether or not we agreed to the study. Sounded pretty straightforward to me."

Rihanna shrugged. "Probably you're right. It's just not for me."

That night, after the eleven o'clock change of shift, Sophie returned to the hallway equipped with an ID with a fob. When Danny's nurse was busy, Sophie had unclipped the ID and slipped it into her pocket. Sophie wouldn't be long, and she knew the nurses' routines by now. Danny's nurse wouldn't need her jacket or ID until three, when she'd go on break and leave the unit. She would be busy for the next few hours—doing hourly assessments, checking labs, adjusting ventilators, and suctioning breathing tubes. The NICU nurse's job was never done, not until the next shift showed up to take over.

Sophie's patience paid off. From the vending machines, she heard the elevator door open. She watched Dr. Sheldon wheel a crib into his office, letting the door swing shut behind him. Sophie slipped down the hallway and paused outside the door. When she thought enough time had gone by, she quietly swiped the fob to unlock the door. Her sweaty hand slid off the door handle. She swiped again and gripped the handle tighter, turning it slowly. The latch clicked open. She held her breath. She half expected Dr. Sheldon to be right there, in her face, asking her what the hell she thought she was doing.

But when she poked her head around the door, Dr. Sheldon was on the far side of the lab with the two other white coats. Sophie tiptoed in and gently closed the door. She held the handle down, hoping that when she let go, the click wouldn't be heard across the lab. She hid behind a portable curtain about twenty feet from the baby and the white coats. Her heart raced, and she hoped she couldn't be seen. The flimsy curtain did the job of hiding her—all except her slippered feet.

Dr. Sheldon and his assistants were deep in conversation when they suddenly burst into laughter. Startled, Sophie nearly knocked the curtain over. She heard the clattering of metal instruments. She risked a quick peek around the curtain, holding tight to its edge to make sure the wheels didn't move and give her away. She watched as one of the white coats dipped a pacifier in a bottle of 5 percent dextrose, sugar water, then picked the baby up out of the crib. The baby, a robust full-term infant, happily sucked on his pacifier. The white coat placed the baby on a mini operating table, where he pulled the large operating room–style light over to shine directly on the baby's diaper. Dr. Sheldon came over and pulled down the diaper to expose him—his little penis popped out, and his testicles hung down. One of the assistants gently held the baby's arms still while another held his legs. Both took turns holding the pacifier in his mouth.

Sophie watched and tried to make sense of what she was seeing. She held her hand tightly over her mouth to keep from uttering a sound. The baby whimpered and was immediately quieted by one of the assistants securing the pacifier tighter in his mouth. Sophie's cell phone chirped. She muted it, closed her eyes, and prayed nobody had heard it.

Dr. Sheldon and the assistant next to him stopped what they were doing and turned around. Sophie stood perfectly still.

After a few moments, they turned their attention back to the baby.

When she looked around the curtain for a better view, Sophie felt a tap on her shoulder. She spun around, her heart in her throat.

CHAPTER 22

Dr. Wagner's dark, menacing eyes bore into her. This time, there was no softening of his eyes or words of apology for her.

He grabbed her by the elbow and roughly pulled her over to the operating arena.

Dr. Sheldon turned around, a look of surprise on his face. "What . . . ?"

"It's okay, Sheldon, I got this." Dr. Wagner ordered Sophie forward. "Since you're so determined to see what goes on in here, you're going to watch."

Sophie pulled back, trying to twist out of his grasp so she could run the other way. Dr. Wagner squeezed her arm harder and pulled her over to stand next to him. He placed each of his hands on either side of her head and held it like a vise, forcing her to face the baby, the doctors, and the scene that played out before her.

Blue drapes covered the baby. The men in white coats wore surgical masks and gowns. With a small clamp, one of the assistants held up the baby's dried umbilical cord. Another assistant moved to his right, blocking Sophie's view, but not before she caught a glimpse of a small stainless-steel probe in his hand. After a minute of low conversation between Dr. Sheldon and the assistants, she heard a clicking sound and saw a waft of smoke rise into the air. One of the white coats carried a clamp to the counter and placed what was held in the clamp under the microscope.

Sophie's eyes remained fixed on the scene in front of her, but her attention was interrupted.

"Mitch, I don't think Mrs. Young should stay. She's already seen too much."

Sophie felt sick. "Dr. Sheldon, what are you doing to these poor little babies? Why are you letting him make you do this?"

Dr. Wagner grabbed her arm and pulled her toward the door. She felt like she was part of some nightmarish sci-fi movie.

"How can you get away with this?" she growled at Dr. Wagner. Over her shoulder, she called back to Dr. Sheldon, "Does that baby's mother know what you're doing?"

"It's just a circumcision," one of the white coat assistants yelled back.

She tried to run out the door, but Dr. Wagner held her tight.

Once they were in the hallway, he loosened his grip. "Look, Sophie," he said in a calm tone. "I've been playing nice. I've gotten your son into the best pediatric practice on the Upper East Side. I've apologized for what was misconstrued as inappropriate bedside behavior during delivery. Whatever you're thinking, just forget it. Sheldon is working on something that will save the lives of many children, young boys like Danny. But he can't announce it yet because he's not ready. It's not ready."

Sophie glared at him. "So he's not just doing a circumcision" was more a statement than a question.

Ignoring what she said, Dr. Wagner continued. "I can see the wheels turning." He lightly tapped her on the forehead. "I know you're planning on telling Adam, or Kim, or anybody who will listen to you. But I strongly advise against that. For one thing, it will be your word against Sheldon's and mine. Trust me, you don't want to go sticking your nose where it doesn't belong."

Sophie started to say something.

He put his finger on her lips. "Shhh. Nobody will believe you. If you try to bring anybody here, there will be nothing here to back up your story. You'll sound like a crazy woman with post-partum psychosis," he said with a wolfish smile.

Her guard started to weaken.

"What happens in Sheldon's lab stays in Sheldon's lab until we're ready to release the results." With his hands on both her shoulders, he looked directly at her. She couldn't read what was going on behind those piercing brown eyes. "And, Sophie," Mitch went on, "if that's not enough to convince you, just remember that Danny is in *our* NICU. Okay?"

She felt deflated, no longer wanting to fight.

Sophie turned and started to walk away from Dr. Wagner. Once she was out of his reach, she broke into a run and fled back to the NICU, wiping away tears. Outside the NICU, she paused and took some deep breaths to collect herself.

She walked into the pod, where all was quiet. It was 3 a.m. She had to hurry. Danny's nurse was walking toward the chair where her jacket hung.

Sophie called out. "Excuse me, do you have some Tylenol? I'm having the hardest time falling asleep."

"I'm not really supposed to give parents any medicine." The nurse moved closer to her jacket, then stopped in front of the chair and turned to Sophie. "But you know what might help?"

Sophie looked quickly from the nurse to her scrubs jacket, where the ID should have been. "What?" she nearly shouted with nervousness.

"Some warm milk. I'll go heat up a mug in the microwave."

Sophie breathed a sigh of relief. Then, with alarm, she wondered if that meant the nurse would have to leave the unit and take her ID with her. "Oh, no, that's okay."

"It's no bother. There's a mini fridge and a microwave behind the nurses' station. I'll be right back."

Danny's nurse called into the next pod, asking for someone to keep an ear out and telling them she'd be right back. Before any alarms could go off, Sophie returned the ID to its rightful place on the jacket.

Later, Sophie tossed and turned. She had to tell Adam and Kate about what she had witnessed. Then she remembered Dr. Wagner's menacing voice and that look in his eyes, silently threatening her to not even think about saying anything. She wanted to let Rihanna know what her lover boy was up to. But that wasn't going to happen. At least not yet.

She pulled out the business card that she had taken from Dr. Sheldon's desk earlier. Clasping the card, Sophie drifted off to sleep, the warm milk finally taking effect.

CHAPTER 23

Mitch and Sheldon headed up to the doctors' lounge. Most of the doctors were either asleep or handling middle-of-the-night emergencies. They got comfortable, free to talk in the empty lounge.

"Sheldon, what is up, bro? Mrs. Young sneaking into your office in the middle of the night? What's that all about?"

"I have no idea how Sophie ended up in there."

"Me neither. Is it possible she knew what you were doing?"

"No way."

"Fill me in. Are you working with that insurance company?"

"Yeah, I accepted their offer."

"Why didn't you tell me?"

"Mitch, you've been so busy with your own stuff."

"Okay, well, now you can tell me. All I know is that Mrs. Young didn't belong in there, so I got rid of her and hopefully scared her quiet. But fill me in."

"A couple of months ago, the president of HHI—you know, Helping Hands Insurance?"

Mitch nodded.

"Well, he took me to lunch, wined and dined me to get on board with this idea of how to cut costs for the company."

Mitch smirked, eyeing his disheveled appearance. "Did you at least iron your tie for the occasion?"

"Yeah." Sheldon grinned. "With a little research, I learned HHI is investigating new ways to curb the incidence of certain X-linked diseases. They're focusing on muscular dystrophy and hemophilia A. They already know how to screen for kids that carry the genetic mutation, but they have yet to identify which kids will actually get sick with the disease. Since they're X-linked diseases, the majority of those who get sick with the diseases are boys."

"Yeah, Sheldon, I went to med school too. Go on."

"Sorry. Anyhow, I met with the president of the company, and he asked for my help. They want to take the screening a step further and know for certain which kids will develop the disease. There's a little more to it, but that's basically it."

"Huh." Mitch paused. "And you're involved in this? I don't believe it. You're supposed to be the ethical one of us."

"You're right, I wasn't sure I wanted to get involved. But as he described what they were doing, I have to admit I was curious." Sheldon explained the details of the project to Mitch.

"And you're able to get consent for this?"

"It's included in the lengthy circumcision consent form that parents have to sign if they want their son circumcised."

"And what about those boys who don't get circumcised?"

"We tell them that since their child is a carrier, we need to run some more blood tests on them, and give them a consent form to sign, again with the experimental consent within the document."

"I still can't believe you're doing this."

"Like I said, you've been busy, and these guys wanted help. All I'm doing is running more tests on the babies, that's it. What you saw me doing is as far as I'll go with this project."

Mitch stroked his beard. "Maybe I should take over where you leave off."

"That's up to you, but after the testing, I'm done." Sheldon pulled out the card with the HHI logo on one side and the WMI insignia on the back and handed it to Mitch.

"Thanks, I think I'll give him a call."

CHAPTER 24

The next morning, Dr. Sheldon pulled up a chair next to Sophie, who was sitting by Danny's incubator. Kate was chatting with Kim, admiring her earrings—authentic eagle feathers from Arizona.

Sophie's internal antennae were buzzing. "What are you *doing*, Dr. Sheldon?" she said in a loud whisper.

Dr. Sheldon sat quietly and looked at Sophie. "I can imagine what you must be thinking, after sneaking into my office last night and seeing what you saw."

"I saw a baby with his diaper off, a probe, and a waft of smoke. What am I supposed to think?"

"What do you think I was doing?"

"A circumcision, I guess, but how should I know? I've never seen one done."

"All the babies brought into my office are there to get circumcised because their parents requested it."

"Then why did Dr. Wagner threaten me not to tell anyone?"

"He's protecting me." Dr. Sheldon took off his glasses and cleaned them with his tie. "We're half brothers. Did you know that? Yeah, of course you did. Rihanna would have told you." He put his glasses back on, still smudged. "We've been hired by HHI, a health insurance company, to help boys and men who are sick with certain illnesses. We're working on how to eradicate these diseases." He offered a disarming smile. "Doesn't that sound like worthy work?"

Sophie searched his face, then answered, "Yeah, I guess."

"Dr. Wagner is a brilliant doctor," continued Dr. Sheldon, "and he has some good ideas for this insurance company. I assure you, we are doing nothing to harm the babies. You saw that one. Was he crying? Was he in distress?"

"No. But it just felt weird. And why in the middle of the night?"

"Because I need the office space during the day for my regular work. Night is the only time we have." Then he smiled and added, "And, Sophie, Dr. Wagner's bark is worse than his bite. Usually."

He rose to leave. "Hey, I need to go find my lovely Isabelle and her mother." He patted her hand. "Thanks, Sophie."

"Thanks for what?"

"For being such a good friend to Rihanna. Any friend of Rihanna's is a friend of mine."

He pushed his glasses up and walked out of the pod.

Sophie sought out the hospital chapel, anxious for a place to sit quietly by herself. The chapel was an oasis in the middle of the busy hospital. It was a nondenominational sanctuary. Stained-glass windows were all that suggested it was a chapel. She considered it a place for anyone to sit and pray or meditate, or just be alone. Twenty minutes was all she needed to reset and reboot, to prepare herself for whatever she would have to face tomorrow.

Her mother had taught her to trust three things in life: her sister, Kate; the church; and the doctors who took care of her mother during those years of abuse with her deranged father. Their threesome—Kate, Sophie, and their mother—was quite the force when her father got out of hand. It was when he stopped taking his medications, combined with drinking, that he became unpredictable. Her mother, ever the protector of Sophie and

Kate, bore the brunt of her father's violence. But when he took his meds and didn't drink, their family was happy. Those were the good days. As Sophie got older, though, they were fewer and farther between. The doctors helped her mother through those times when she needed medical attention. But her broken arm was the final straw. The cops came and took her father away. He fought hard against them, but his punches never landed—he was too drunk. He shrieked and ranted like a lunatic. That was the last time Sophie ever saw her father.

Now she was a parent, and it was her responsibility to protect her child. No matter what.

CHAPTER 25

Sophie and Adam waited at the nurses' station for the charge nurse. She was determined to get an answer to why their son was lying in the NICU, fighting for his life. She would start by reviewing her medical records. If anyone wanted to challenge her request, she was prepared to fight.

When the charge nurse finally arrived, she gave them a pleasant hello and asked how she could help.

Sophie said, "I'd like to see my labor and delivery records."

"Sure, I can help you with that."

"Oh good," Sophie answered, relaxing her tensed muscles. "Thank you so much."

"You'll just need to have someone from medical records sit with you as you go through your record. Hospital policy." She picked up the phone and spoke with someone in medical records. When she hung up, she said, "Now's a good time to go. Take the elevator to the ground floor, and you'll see the signs."

"Perfect, thanks." Sophie smiled at the nurse.

They knocked on the locked door of medical records. A woman let them in and, after hearing what the couple was there for, asked if they wanted to see Sophie's records in paper or electronic form. At the back of the room were shelves that ran the full length of the wall, stacked with folders. There must have been thousands of folders holding numbered medical records, organized in a color-coded system. There were conference rooms off to the side and one large conference table in the middle of the main room.

"Paper, please."

The woman walked to a shelf full of files and retrieved a thin folder with Sophie's name on it. She led them to an empty table and handed Sophie the folder. "If you have any questions, don't hesitate to ask." She went back to her desk.

Sophie and Adam sat at the table. Sophie opened the folder and took a deep breath. Her eyes scanned the pages, looking for clues.

When she got to the end of the chart, she looked at Adam. "I don't see it."

She went back to the beginning of the chart and read more slowly, her finger going over the pages line by line. She slid the chart over to Adam. "See if you can find anything."

Time of admission, time of onset of labor, time of delivery, vital signs, a list of medications administered—Ativan and progesterone—and the type of IV fluid. The pathology report of her placenta revealed a completely healthy placenta. Her blood work was normal. Sophie looked at Adam. They looked through the chart two more times.

"There's nothing there. I don't get it. A normal labor and delivery according to this. Twenty-six weeks is on the admitting note, but otherwise, you'd never know anything was wrong."

Adam closed the chart. "Sophie, go through your delivery again. Close your eyes and tell me everything that happened in triage."

Sophie went through the entire afternoon, from her lunch break to her delivery, to Anna's death, to the minute Adam walked into her hospital room.

"Maybe it was the guy you nearly bumped into at the stoplight?"

"No. Once Carol gave me meds to stop the cramping, I was fine. I was ready to go back to work." Sophie held her head in her hands, eyes closed, concentrating, remembering. "There's something about the sound of marbles coming from Dr. Wagner's pocket. And his voice."

Sophie raised her head and looked at Adam, trying to connect the details. "I've heard the same clinking in Kim's pocket when she gives Danny his medications. She pulls the vials out of her pocket, draws them up in separate syringes, then puts the vials back in her pocket while she injects the medications into his IV. Carol did the same thing with me."

She was trying to make sense of all the sounds and images whirling around in her head.

"What are you thinking, Soph?"

"Danny has a little plastic container of supplies at his cribside. It's got all his medications, along with the syringes and needles. Narcotics are locked away and not at the cribside. But everything else, the medications they commonly use, like the ones that Danny receives two or three times a day, are there. I've noticed Kim—in fact, every nurse—has a routine. They pull the vials they need from the container, put them in their pockets, then do whatever they need to do for the baby—taking vital signs, checking IVs, doing a quick exam, and last, giving the medications. Then they either throw the empty vial away in the red sharps container, or they put the vials back in their pockets. They finish up by charting everything on the computer.

"These aren't medications that need to be kept under lock and key. The nurses probably don't have time to be running back and forth every time they need a medication. These babies are on so many it makes more sense to just carry what they need with them." Thinking out loud, she said, "Yeah, I bet that's right." She paused before continuing. "I wonder if that's what happens in triage too. Do they keep their meds with them? That place can get so busy I bet they do."

They closed Sophie's chart and handed it back to the records lady.

"Thanks."

CHAPTER 26

Dr. Wagner came around the corner of the pod.

"Good morning, Mrs. Young. Kim, if you wouldn't mind . . ." He handed Kim his half-empty cardboard coffee cup. "I'll be quick so I can leave you to your work." He put the infant-sized stethoscope in his ears and listened to Danny's chest and abdomen. He gently poked his belly and felt around the top of his head and down his spine. He checked his reflexes.

When he unfastened the tape holding his diaper on, Sophie stood up. "What are you doing? He has plenty of doctors examining him every day." She nudged him aside as she put her hands into the incubator and refastened his diaper.

"I like to check on the moms and babies I deliver. I feel personally responsible for Danny, almost like his life is my responsibility."

She narrowed her eyes at him.

"After all, I am the chief of—"

"Yes, I know. Obstetrics. Not the NICU."

He placed the stethoscope back inside the incubator and closed the portholes. Sophie watched him warily.

He leaned down, picked up Danny's blue name card off the floor, and stuck it back on the incubator, pressing hard to make sure it stayed.

He stood up, extending to his full six-foot, two-inch height.

"Sophie, I'm on your side. I consider myself part of Danny's team. Even though I don't directly manage his care, I remain interested and concerned. I have your and your son's best interests at heart. Try to remember that."

"And a mother's love for her son is an unrivaled force of nature. With all due respect, Dr. Wagner, *you* should remember *that*." She walked away from Dr. Wagner. *Wow, that was bold. Where'd that come from?*

CHAPTER 27

Kate and Adam showed up that afternoon, carrying two large platters of fresh fruit—pineapple, kiwi, firm and juicy grapes, cantaloupe that was actually ripe, and the best part, strawberries dipped in chocolate. They laid the platters on the front desk of the nurses' station. Those who weren't busy with patients flocked around, oohing and aahing at the colorful presentation. The smell of fresh pineapple was mouthwatering.

"Finally, someone thought to bring us something other than doughnuts."

Everyone laughed. One of the nurses called for Kim to come to the front; there was something here for her. Curious, she walked to the desk and saw Kate, Adam, and Sophie standing next to the desk with the fruit.

"Oh my God!" Kim gave all three a hug. "Thank you so much! You have no idea how much we all appreciate something other than doughnuts." She popped a strawberry in her mouth and licked her lips. "Yum."

The crowd of staff around the desk broke up, each taking a small plate of fruit with them back to their pods. Sophie, Adam, and Kate walked to Pod C.

Christy from the next pod over popped her head in, said, "Thank you guys for the fruit!" and then ducked back out, retreating to her pod.

A doctor carrying a big black case, with a contraption on his head that made him look like a coal miner, walked in behind Kim.

"The ophthalmologist is here for Danny's eye exam. Sophie, you all can wait in the parents' lounge until he's done."

Sophie and Adam had been told early on, by one of the neonatologists, that all preemies got routine eye exams. Just like every other organ in their bodies, their eyes were still immature. Danny would need regular eye exams to be sure that his vision would be okay.

"No, I need to stay with him," Sophie said.

"That's not a good idea. Believe me, you really don't want to watch."

"Why?"

"I've dilated Danny's eyes with drops so that the doctor can look into his pupils. That way he can see all the way into the back of his eyeball to evaluate his optic nerve and retina. But he needs Danny to keep his eyes open for the exam. He uses a mini retractor to hold his eyelids open. It's not pretty. But don't worry," she reassured Sophie with a pat on her shoulder, "I'll be with him the whole time."

"Come on, Sophie," Kate said. "Let's go wait somewhere else."

They took the elevator down. Sophie googled eye exams on preemies. "Yeah, I think Kim was right. I don't need to see that. I just want to know the results."

The cafeteria line was long, as doctors, nurses, and visitors waited for food. The trio took up their places at the back of the line. A group of young men and women walked by, chatting and joking together. INTERN was printed in big letters across their hospital IDs.

Sophie's stomach lurched. She tugged on Adam's sleeve. "Hey, those are the guys that were in Dr. Sheldon's lab."

Adam turned to see where she was pointing, but by the time he looked, they were lost in a sea of blue and green scrubs.

They found an empty table in a corner of the cafeteria. On the wall was a poster of an adorable chubby baby face with shining blue eyes looking at the camera. The caption below read: *BrainHealth—Good for Your Baby, Good for You.*

Sophie glanced at it, then turned to Kate and Adam.

"Sophie, are you going to say anything about what you saw in Dr. Sheldon's office? Have you even mentioned it to Rihanna?" Kate asked.

"No, for now, I'm not saying a word to anyone. I may mention it to Rihanna eventually, but she's got enough on her plate right now."

"But why aren't you reporting what you saw?"

"Because, for one thing, I'm not even sure what was going on in there. I can't prove anything. It could have just been a circumcision, I don't know. And for another thing, Dr. Wagner made it perfectly clear that I should mind my own business. I don't want to test him."

"So that's it? Case closed. Pretend you didn't see anything?" Kate blew on her steaming coffee.

"For now, that's the way I'm playing it," Sophie answered firmly.

"Adam, what do you think?"

"I'm with Sophie one hundred percent. I don't want to risk anything happening to Danny. I don't know what Dr. Wagner thinks he can do, but I don't want to find out. And as Sophie said, what would she say? 'I saw them put a probe into a baby'? Who's going to buy that? Especially when, during the day, his lab is a plain old office."

"You know, Kate," Sophie turned to her sister and said in an edgy voice, "what would you do? What would you do if your critically ill baby was at the mercy of some doctors—doctors who you saw doing something you weren't sure about but had the feeling wasn't right? I can't report something I'm not able to prove. Tell me, what would you do?" Sophie's voice rose. "Risk your baby's life? Go to someone you don't know and trust them to hopefully do something about it?" Glaring at her sister, she shouted, "Well? What would you do?"

Nurses at the next table turned and looked.

Kate was stunned. Sophie took a deep breath, trying to calm her trembling nerves, as Adam put his arm around her.

Sophie lowered her voice. "I'm sorry, Kate. I didn't mean to yell. But I don't know what the fuck to do!" She looked helplessly at Adam as he tried to hide his surprise at her outburst.

"It's okay, babe. We'll figure it out."

Kate added, "Sophie, I can't even imagine what you're feeling. I'm the one who should apologize for pushing like that."

"No, it's okay. Anyhow, Adam and I are focused more on Dr. Wagner. He's the one responsible. We need to nail him, not only for what he's done to our lives but for the other mothers too."

As she calmed down, Sophie continued, "Kim has warned me about Dr. Wagner. She knows Adam and I are suspicious of him causing Danny's early delivery. She said if I'm thinking of messing with him, I better know what I'm doing. She told me about a time he screwed over one of the charge nurses. He took two doses of morphine from the narcotics box, which threw off the narcotics count. It's a big deal if any doses are missing, and it's ultimately the charge nurse's responsibility. Everybody knew it was Mitch who took the two doses, but they weren't sure whether he was playing a joke or getting revenge. If she had done something to piss him off, that was his way of getting back at her. It got to the point that she got fired for his prank."

Kate's eyes opened wide. "Are you serious?"

"Yup. And he didn't do a damn thing to help her."

Thirty minutes later, they were back in the NICU, waiting to hear what the ophthalmologist had to say.

"To be honest, I'm a little concerned. Your son will need

close follow-up. I'll plan to do another exam next week. Kim, could you be sure he's dilated? Same time."

"What do you mean 'concerned'?" Sophie interrupted.

"It means that his eyes aren't developing as they should. His vision will probably be affected, but that could change. I'll be back next week." He packed up his equipment and left without another word. *Mr. Personality*, Sophie thought to herself.

Kate headed out to do some shopping, and Adam went back to school to teach his last class of the day. Sophie went down to the chapel. She noticed a man sitting in the back row with his head bowed. He wore a large winter overcoat and glasses tinted a dark shade, even though he was inside. He had a long, unkempt mustache that had turned mostly gray.

She eyed him as she walked to her usual seat up front. She prayed for Danny's eyes to be okay. She tried to keep her sniffling quiet so she wouldn't disturb the man. When it was time for her to leave, the man turned to watch her as she walked by.

CHAPTER 28

When Sophie got back to the NICU, she walked past Pod E and stopped short. Rihanna stood outside the pod looking in. Sophie noticed a mother with a tearstained face clutching a baby blanket. She stood alone on the periphery of the group of doctors and nurses that surrounded her baby. Hers was the only baby in the pod that normally held four. The others had been moved out because of all the equipment this one baby required. Sophie had quickly learned that the more equipment there was attached to a baby, the sicker the baby.

Most surprising to Sophie was that this was no small premature baby; she was the size of a robust full-term infant. But there was nothing robust about her. She lay perfectly still, eyes closed, seemingly asleep in the center of all the frenetic activity around her. Next to her was a machine the size of a mini sports car. Coming out of this machine were two large tubes that looked like small garden hoses. With a closer look, Sophie was surprised to see that these tubes went into the side of the baby's neck.

Sophie went over to Rihanna, who was talking with Dr. Sheldon.

"What is wrong with this baby?" Sophie asked.

"Shh," Rihanna whispered. "This poor babe inhaled her own poop before she was born."

Dr. Sheldon left them to consult with one of the doctors reviewing the baby's lab work.

"That huge thing is called an ECMO machine, according to

Sheldon, and it works like a heart-lung bypass. It keeps the baby alive while her lungs recover from inhaling her poop."

"Why are we whispering?" Sophie whispered.

"She needs to stay calm. They don't want her stressed or agitated the slightest little bit."

"She's so still. She looks like a normal full-term baby, except she's not moving, not crying. Is she even alive?" Sophie asked.

"Of course she's alive, you dolt."

Sophie looked at Rihanna in surprise. "Did you just call me a dolt?"

"Sorry." Rihanna smiled. "I only know this medical stuff because Sheldon tells me. The baby is paralyzed so she can't move and heavily sedated so she doesn't feel anything. That's why she looks like that. See those two huge tubes in her neck?"

Sophie nodded. "Yeah, kind of hard to miss."

"Those are her lifelines. If anything happens to those, if they get moved the smallest bit, she'll die."

Sophie stared at the baby. "Are you for real?"

"It's true," Rihanna continued. "Sheldon said they can't risk anything disturbing those lines. That's why they keep her paralyzed and sedated."

"My God. How horrible." Sophie turned to the mother and offered a look that she hoped expressed her sympathy. She watched the intensity of all the activity swirling around the baby. There was a constant stream of nurses, speaking in hushed voices, running blood samples back and forth to the lab. Pharmacists delivered medications to the nurses. Doctors huddled to carry on quiet discussions and then wrote orders, which were immediately carried out. The ECMO technicians focused all their attention on the machine and the numbers on the monitors. As soon as an alarm went off, all heads turned to the monitor. This spurred more urgent whispering, then someone adjusting the machine.

An ultrasound tech scanned the baby's brain. Blood samples were drawn and rushed to the lab. Sophie thought it looked like a three-ring circus working in astounding synchronicity. The number of people and the complexity of the machinery surrounding this seven-pound baby was what Sophie found so incredible. To think of all the technology and knowledge collected in that one pod. The nurses spoke in hushed voices.

"Sheldon or Dr. Morrison will stay here in the pod for as long as the baby is on ECMO," Rihanna said.

They continued to watch the doctors and nurses coming and going. It was exhausting to see the intensity of the staff caring for this baby. There were frequent urgent discussions about the baby, nurses vigilantly studying the monitors and reacting to every alarm, and doctors reviewing the chart with tired eyes and doing whatever it took to keep this baby alive. Twenty-four hours a day.

"I just hope she'll be okay," Rihanna said.

"I can't even imagine," answered Sophie. "I'll say a prayer for her next time I'm in the chapel." Now she understood the look she'd seen on the mother's face. It was a look of desperate hope.

CHAPTER 29

Mitch and Amanda were taking their dinner break at Evening Rounds, the local bar near the hospital. A plate of nachos sat between them.

"Dig in," Mitch said. The bar was crowded with doctors and nurses coming off shift and stopping in for a drink before going home. To Mitch, it felt like a buffer zone between work and home, before leaving the city and driving home to face his wife and two teenage kids. He had prep school bills, upcoming college tuitions, and a high-maintenance wife, who was likely going to divorce him once the kids were gone.

Mitch munched on the nachos and took a drink of his O'Doul's. "Amanda, tell me a little about yourself. Where are you from? Do you have family here in the city?"

Amanda wiped salsa off her mouth. "No. My family still lives in the woods of northern New Hampshire." She bit into a guacamole-loaded chip. "Once I graduated high school, I left as fast as I could. A nursing scholarship was the fastest way out of there." She licked her fingers. "And I've never looked back. Good riddance to that hick life."

"Do you ever go home?"

She peered at him with a look that told him he was getting too close. "Nope again. I haven't seen them since I left eight years ago, and I don't expect I'll see them in the next eight years either. Or the next eighty-eight years, for that matter."

THE VERY BEST OF CARE

Mitch stopped pressing for information. He turned to see Adam Young making his way toward them through the crowd.

"Hey, Dr. Wagner! Is this seat available?" Adam asked, pulling out a barstool.

Mitch waved his hand over the stool, indicating it was free.

Adam climbed onto the stool, offering a smile and a handshake. "Budweiser, please," he said to the bartender.

Mitch watched him carefully. Had Sophie said anything to him?

Adam turned to Mitch. "Can I buy you two a drink?"

"No drinking while on call," Dr. Wagner said, showing Adam the label on his alcohol-free beer. Amanda shook her head no.

Adam nodded as he removed his hat and put it on the bar.

When the conversation turned to basketball, Amanda took her cue. "Sorry," she said to Mitch. "I have to get back." She said goodbye to Adam and left the bar.

"A Knicks fan?" Dr. Wagner asked, looking at Adam's baseball cap.

"You bet. Best team in the league."

Mitch guessed that either Sophie hadn't said anything about Sheldon's office or Adam had also agreed to keep quiet. *Good*, thought Mitch.

They chatted more about basketball, then moved on to running track.

"You'd never know it," Mitch said, "but I was a track star in high school."

"No kidding! Just a few years ago I'm sure," Adam joked.

Mitch laughed. "Thanks for the compliment, but it was a little longer than that. I still love to run, but it's tough to find the time anymore."

"Hey, maybe I'll see you out running one of these days once the ice melts. Central Park maybe?"

Mitch smiled. "Yeah, you just might."

Adam ordered himself another beer and added a shot. He held up his beer to Mitch. "You sure?"

"Yeah, no thanks. But don't let me stop you."

"Thanks, I won't. I'm not on call." Adam grinned.

Mitch stood to leave. "You take care and say hi to your wife."

"Thanks, Doc."

Mitch stepped out onto the sidewalk and texted Sheldon: *Don't worry, we're good.*

CHAPTER 30

Sophie took advantage of the lull in Kim's busy day. Kim was stocking Danny's incubator with his mini little preemie diapers.

"Kim, I just want to tell you how much Adam and I appreciate the care you give to Danny. There is nothing more a mother could ask than for her child to be cared for as kindly and lovingly as you do. Thank you so much."

"Oh gosh, Sophie, you don't need to thank me!" Kim put an arm around Sophie. "We are in this together. It's my *privilege* to protect and care for all these munchkins." Then she lowered her voice. "And to be totally honest, Danny's my favorite. Probably because you and Adam are such amazing parents."

Sophie rested her hands on Danny's incubator and looked in at her son. "Thanks, we're trying." After a minute, she remembered what she wanted to talk to Kim about. "Hey, Kim, can I ask you something?"

"Sure. Shoot."

"Do you carry Danny's medication vials in your pocket all day? Or do you put them back in the medication room once you've given him what he needs?"

"That's a strange question."

"This is a strange place," Sophie joked.

Kim laughed. "It depends on the med. Some meds need to be refrigerated, so those I don't keep with me. Others need to be locked up, and obviously I don't keep those either. But a lot of the drugs we use for preemies, we give in their IV, and you're right. They come in little single-dose vials that we can carry with us. It would be a huge waste of time to always be going back and forth to the med room to grab a dose of, say, Lasix or caffeine. A lot of babies are on those meds, so yeah, to answer your question, we carry around some meds, or we leave them at the cribside in the medication container. At the end of the shift, we put back what we don't use."

"Do you think the doctors and nurses in triage do the same thing?"

"What is this, the Spanish Inquisition? I've got to get back to work. But, yes, I know that Suzanne carries around the common meds she uses in triage, the same way we do here. It's just more efficient that way."

Sophie sat next to Danny, texting one of her friends from work. Then that screeching alarm went off. She looked up to see where it was coming from, which baby needed help to bring their heart rate back up. With horror, she realized that the alarm was coming from Danny. Sophie shot out of her chair to look inside his incubator. She watched the color in his face change from pale pink to pale to a mottled blue. She screamed.

"Help! Kim! Somebody come over here!" she yelled. "There's something wrong with Danny!"

Sophie watched her son turn a darker shade of blue as he struggled to breathe. His heart rate dropped to eighty, to sixty, to thirty in a matter of seconds.

"Danny!" she yelled, giving him a firm pat on the back. "Danny! Wake up!" The sound of his heart monitor beat agonizingly slow. The alarm wouldn't shut up.

Two nurses ran over—one hit the red code button on the wall and yelled into the intercom, "Dr. Morrison to C bay, stat!" The second nurse put the preemie-sized resuscitation bag and mask over Danny's face and gave him slow, deep breaths.

Sophie followed the rhythm of the rise and fall of his chest with each manual breath the nurse pumped into his lungs. When she looked up, a doctor, a third nurse, and two respiratory therapists were busy working to stabilize Danny.

Sophie was squeezed out of the way and had to stand on her tiptoes to see her son. She desperately wanted to touch him, to let him know his mommy was here for him. That she would keep him safe. She watched from what seemed like the end of a tunnel. It was that slow, drawn-out passing of time that she'd experienced before, like everything was happening to someone else. Sophie didn't understand all the medical jargon. She just knew that she was terrified for her little Danny.

In under three minutes, Danny was intubated and back on a ventilator. Almost immediately, his heart rate rose to a more stable rate of 150. In five minutes, blood tests were drawn and sent to the lab, and an IV had been placed in his right hand.

Fifteen minutes later, Danny was settled. Color had returned to his face, and his heart rate and blood pressure were back to normal. The ventilator was breathing for him. If it hadn't been so frightening, Sophie would have called what she'd just seen a well-choreographed dance. She called Adam, hanging up before his voicemail kicked in.

The team of lifesavers dispersed to return to their own NICU patients. One of the doctors came over to reassure Sophie. She introduced herself as Dr. Morrison, one of the neonatologists, and explained that Danny had just gotten tired. He needed a break from working so hard to stay alive.

"Eating and breathing are tough work for these little guys." She put her arm around Sophie's slumped shoulders. "We're going to help him out, take the effort out of breathing, and give him a break from eating. He'll get his nutrition through his IV for the next few days. We're running some tests to make sure there wasn't something else we might be missing, like a problem with his heart or an infection."

Sophie looked up at her. "An infection? What kind of infection? How could he get an infection in here?"

"Don't worry. He's on antibiotics just in case. I really think Danny will be back on the mend in just a day or two."

Sophie broke down crying, from the stress of watching what had just happened and from the relief now that it was over. She was so grateful to Danny's team. He couldn't survive without them.

Then that nagging feeling surfaced again: *Maybe he would still be inside of me if something hadn't gone wrong in triage.* She shut that thought right down, telling herself now was not the time to go there.

She thanked Dr. Morrison, sat down next to Danny's incubator, and pulled out her cell phone. She called Adam again. He wasn't picking up. Where the hell was he?

CHAPTER 31

Adam got to the NICU after all the commotion had settled. Sophie looked up and glared at him.

"Where have you been? Danny nearly died, for God's sake! I've been trying to call you."

Adam gently pulled her up out of her chair and wrapped his arms around her. She softened and buried her head in Adam's chest. He pulled her close. She tried to tell him everything that had just happened, but it came out in garbled, sniveling half sentences.

"They said it was just a setback," she muttered. She pushed herself away and looked up at him. "Where the hell have you been anyway?" It was easier for her to feel angry at Adam than sad and helpless about Danny. With her nose up near his face, she sniffed. "Have you been drinking? Jesus, Adam, this is not the time to be getting drunk."

Adam sat down hard. "I'm not drunk." Then he meekly added, "But you're right, Soph. I'm sorry I wasn't here."

She turned away and busied herself with folding Danny's little T-shirts. She sniffled softly and wiped her nose on the back of her hand. She couldn't hide the fact that she was upset. This scenario wasn't unfamiliar to her. Whenever Adam used to return home drunk, she'd get mad, and he'd be quiet, allowing her to vent. Then they'd go to bed, her still angry and him feeling guilty.

But that hadn't happened for a while—at least since Sophie found out she was pregnant. They'd made a pact: if she couldn't drink because she was pregnant, then he wasn't going to drink either. Maybe he thought the rules had changed. If she was no longer pregnant, then he could drink again.

Adam put his hand gently on her shoulder, which she brusquely shook off.

"I can see I'm not helping here." Adam paused. When Sophie didn't respond, he added, "So I'm going home to bed. I'll be back tomorrow morning on my way to work." He gave her a little peck on the cheek. "I'm sorry," he said, and left.

The next morning Sophie was sitting on a stool next to Danny, one arm draped over the side of the incubator, the other arm in the incubator, her finger caressing his little head. She was lost in thought as she murmured to him, urging him to get better so he could get stronger and big enough to go home.

Adam came into the pod, as promised, on his way to work. He had brought her favorite latte, and they sat and drank their coffees together.

"Nothing's changed with him," Sophie said in a flat tone that matched her mood.

Adam stayed long enough to finish his coffee, then stood to leave. "I have to get to work." He kissed his finger and put it through the incubator portholes, landing it on Danny's nose. He turned to Sophie and kissed her on the lips. "Are we okay?" he asked.

She shrugged and turned away. "I am. What about you?"

"I was thinking. Maybe I, or we, should talk to a social worker. I know this is taking its toll on me. I can only imagine what it's doing to you."

Sophie looked at him and almost smiled. "You know, I think that's a really good idea."

CHAPTER 32

Sophie sat next to Danny, talking softly to him through his incubator portholes. He still had the breathing tube in but was doing much better. She knew he was listening to her voice. Rihanna sat with Isabelle, who had graduated out of an incubator and into an open crib.

Dr. Sheldon came in and went over to Rihanna. Rihanna stopped singing and looked up at Sheldon. They spoke in sharp whispers. There was a pause in the conversation, and Dr. Sheldon gently stroked Isabelle's head. He turned, said something more to Rihanna, then abruptly left the pod.

Sophie gave it a minute, then went over to Rihanna. "Hey, Ri. Is everything okay?"

Rihanna wiped a tear and looked at Sophie with her beautiful smile. "Yeah, everything's okay."

"Do you want to talk about it?"

"I knew this was going to happen. Something's changed with him." Rubbing her baby's back, she said, "Isabelle is what's keeping him around. He's too busy for me these days. He's always got something else to do. His work is definitely coming between us, but I think there's something more."

"Oh, Ri, I'm so sorry." Sophie wasn't sure what else to say. "Maybe it'll get better once you and Isabelle go home?"

"The truth of it is, I need Sheldon. I need him to help me get my US citizenship. Isabelle is all set because she was born here. But if I want to stay here with her, I need to be a citizen."

"Ooh, that's a big one."

"Yeah, and he's my ticket."

"Wow, that's a little harsh."

"I didn't mean it like that. We really were in love, and we both love our baby, and I think we can be a family . . . if he wants to. Anyhow, things are a little rough now. But I think it'll all work out."

"Yeah, I'm sure it will. You two make a good couple."

Sophie went back to Danny's incubator. A couple of minutes later, when they were the only two in their section of the pod, she called over to Rihanna. "Ri? I'm curious. Did you ever ask Sheldon what's going on in his office?"

"No."

"Did you tell him I saw him outside his office door in the middle of the night?"

"Nope."

That evening, Sophie and Rihanna were together again in their pod. Nurses came in for change of shift, melted snow dripping off their hats and jackets.

"Damn, it's nasty out there!"

"I can't believe more snow!"

"It better be gone by the end of shift, that's all I can say. I'm *not* staying here for the night."

Sophie turned to Rihanna and laughed. "Do you realize there's not one window in our pod that looks outside? There could be a tornado happening out there, and we'd have no idea."

"It's like a time and weather warp in here," replied Rihanna. "Too bad, I love watching the snow fla—"

Suddenly all the lights went out, plunging the NICU into darkness. All the ventilators and monitors started alarming simultaneously. The only light in the unit came from a few dim emergency lights and the red emergency exit signs over the doors.

"Hey! What's going on?" someone yelled.

Every piece of lifesaving machinery in the forty-bed NICU was sounding off. Computer screens flickered, then went black.

"Someone turn on some lights!"

"Hey, what the hell?"

"Turn on the lights!"

Parents started talking and then yelling at once. Nurses ran around, flashlights in hand, shouting out to each other.

Sophie yelled, "Hey! I need some help over here. Someone, please help me! My baby's ventilator isn't working."

Other mothers were crying out for the same help. Nurses and respiratory therapists rushed to plug ventilators into emergency outlets. They waited, expecting the hospital generators to kick in. Alarms continued to blare. The dying ventilators whined and groaned as their energy supply died out. The oxygen wall outlets whistled, then the sound faded away.

Sophie began to panic. "Kim!" she yelled out again.

By the dim light of the emergency exit sign, she grabbed Danny's resuscitation breathing bag and attached it to his breathing tube. She squeezed it, as she had seen Kim do many times. Even without electricity, the ventilator still blared its alarm. *Big help the alarms are. There's no electricity to fix what they're alarming about.*

The alarms continued like warning bells, announcing that electricity needed to resume soon.

"Kim!" Sophie screamed in desperation.

Beads of sweat broke out on the back of her neck as Sophie tried to focus on keeping her baby alive. It was all on her right now.

She continued to bag oxygen into Danny's breathing tube, willing the generators to start running and get the ventilators working. She prayed she was doing it right. She couldn't see his color in the dark, but his chest was moving up and down with the rhythm of the breaths she was giving him. When she put her hand lightly on his chest, she could feel the steady beat of his heart. *Okay, that's good.*

The piercing NICU alarms continued to sound off. *Why isn't someone fixing this?*

The chief respiratory therapist announced over the hospital-wide intercom system, "All available respiratory therapists to the NICU, stat!" There was a lot of frantic yelling about what to do next.

Respiratory therapists flooded into the NICU, with flashlights lighting their way into the pods. They spread out to first help babies on ventilators, then moved on to any baby who required oxygen.

"There's power in the rest of the hospital. Why is the NICU the only place without power?"

The electronic doors were propped open. Hospital staff filled the hallway to catch a glimpse of the bedlam unraveling in the NICU.

Seven long minutes. Then, as suddenly as the electricity had gone out, it came back on.

Frantic voices began to calm.

"What was that all about?"

"Why just the NICU?"

"Must be the weather."

"But why not the whole hospital?"

As the urgency of the moment subsided and activity returned to normal, people chattered on, relieving the stress of the past several minutes that had felt longer. The electronic doors resumed working. Sophie looked up to see the doors closing and caught a glimpse of the chapel guy standing in the hallway.

CHAPTER 33

A few days after the power outage, Danny had weaned off the ventilator and now was attached to a CPAP machine with little oxygen prongs going up his nose. The CPAP helped to keep his oxygen levels up and prevented him from having apneic spells. Checking the monitor frequently, Sophie saw that all his numbers were good. He had resumed tube feeds of Sophie's pumped breast milk. Just as Dr. Morrison had predicted, he was on the mend. The world had righted itself, and Sophie was able to relax and breathe.

Today, Kim wasn't her usual upbeat self. She was short-tempered and impatient. It took a couple of tries for Sophie to get her attention.

"Hey, Kim, how's your day going?"

"Oh hey, Sophie, my day's going just fine. It's tonight that I'm kind of worried about," Kim replied while slamming a drawer that held alcohol wipes and small gauze bandages.

"Why? What's up this evening?"

"We have a 'mandatory,'" she said, making air quotes, "staff meeting at Mezza Luna, that new restaurant, up the block. It's supposed to be super nice and have great martinis and food."

"And what's so bad about that?"

"Because it's mandatory! My boss tells me I have to go. It's being paid for by Kindred Pharmaceuticals. They supply us with everything—our meds, our preemie formula, needles, syringes, IV fluids, even preemie diapers. They're just one of our supply companies, but they get the most business from Metro Hospital." She slammed another drawer, this time catching her finger in it. "Damn it!" she exclaimed as she stuck her finger in her mouth. "Sorry."

She continued. "We shouldn't be made to sit and listen to a sales pitch from a drug rep. They're bribing us with food and drinks. People complain about how expensive health care is. This is why. Big Pharma is buying our business, and it's all wrong."

"Huh," Sophie said thoughtfully.

"I'm sorry, I shouldn't be taking this out on you. You've got more than enough to think about." Kim sat down next to Sophie.

"That's okay. You feel pretty strongly about it, huh?" said Sophie.

"Yeah, I do."

Rihanna snickered. Kim and Sophie looked over at her.

"Rihanna, what do you think? You know Dr. Sheldon. Should the pharmaceutical companies be paying for extravagant dinners for the nurses every month?" Kim asked.

"You ladies don't know the half of it. Last year, a group of docs took a golf trip to Hawaii. It was an all-expenses-paid trip with an unwritten agreement that the doctors would prescribe their latest asthma medication."

Kim added, "And the doctors and nurses have administration's ear and can influence which company they order from. It's shady and it's crooked."

There was a pause.

"But don't mind me," Kim said, lightening the conversation. "That's just my humble opinion. Please don't repeat." She stood up and gave Sophie's knee a pat.

Later in the day when Kim was sitting alone, charting her notes for the shift, Sophie watched a guy wearing an official-looking ID talking with her. Kim was nodding and smiling as she listened to him. He left some papers on the table next to her before he left.

Sophie went over to her.

"Hey, Sophie, what's up? I'm just wrapping up here and getting ready to sign off to the evening shift."

"Yeah, and getting ready for your Mezza Luna meeting," Sophie teased.

Kim cringed. "Thanks for reminding me."

Sophie picked up the pile of papers the man had left next to Kim. They were brochures with *Kindred Pharmaceuticals* stamped on the back. She leafed through them.

"Oh, those," Kim said. "Josh just dropped those off. He's the rep who's running tonight's meeting. I guess he expects me to brush up on the drugs he'll be talking about. That's not gonna happen." She tossed the brochures in the trash and glanced at Sophie. "You didn't just see that."

Sophie pretended to cover her eyes, and they both laughed. "I'm sure your meeting will be fine. Hey, can I ask you something?"

"Sure, ask away."

In a more serious tone, Sophie said, "You remember Anna? The mother who hemorrhaged and died in triage the same day I was there?"

"Oh, that was horrible."

"Supposedly her baby came to the NICU. Do you know what happened to her?" asked Sophie.

"I don't remember seeing that baby up here." Kim put her charts down, trying to recall what had happened to that baby. "I suppose she could have gone to another NICU in the city." She thought for another moment. "Yeah, maybe she was transferred in the middle of the night, though I don't know why they would do that." She paused. "Huh. That's all I can tell you."

"I was just wondering."

CHAPTER 34

Sophie and Adam found the social work department and the door with Jody Carter's name on it. They knocked and were greeted by a smiling thirtysomething woman.

"Hi, I'm Jody. And you must be the Youngs." Dressed in designer jeans and a casual silk button-down blouse, she invited them in. Sophie and Adam sat next to each other on the couch, while Jody pulled a chair from behind her desk and sat.

"How are things going?" Jody adjusted the clip that held her long dark hair swept up on top of her head. "I heard that Danny is doing better now after a little setback."

They both started to talk at once, then stopped with a nervous laugh.

"You go first," Adam said to Sophie.

Sophie looked at Jody. "Yes, Danny is doing better, thanks. But it's actually *us* that we want to talk about."

"Okay," answered Jody.

"I guess I'll dive right in. I'm stressed, I feel guilty, I'm worried about the future, and I wish this had never happened," Sophie blurted out. "Some days I feel so lost and depressed I don't know what I'm doing. I don't know how I'm supposed to act, what I'm supposed to say to people, how I'm supposed to fill my time when all I can think about is Danny."

Jody pulled a tissue out of the box sitting on her desk and handed it to Sophie. "These are totally normal feelings, Sophie. Believe me, you're not alone in this."

THE VERY BEST OF CARE

"Adam and I desperately wanted a family. We worked so hard to get pregnant. But this? This is the last thing we expected. This was so far off our radar of all the things we planned for."

Silence. Then Jody asked, "Adam? How about you?"

"I'm stressed but not quite the same way as Sophie. All I can think about are the bills, which have already started to come in. How are we possibly going to pay for this? I have no idea how much my teacher's insurance will cover. Statements show up that claim 'this is not a bill' but show the numbers of what the bill *will* be. Our dining room table is cluttered with statements that come in five different languages." Adam held his head in his hands. "I just don't see how we're going to be able to pay for all this." He paused. "And once he comes home, what other expenses will we have as he gets older? What if he has brain damage, or is blind, or any other horrible thing that can go wrong?" He looked at Jody.

"Hold on there," said Jody. "You are worrying about things that you have no idea will happen. Go easy on yourself. Try not to conjure up the worst-case scenarios."

He sighed heavily. "You're right, but sometimes my imagination gets the best of me, especially in the middle of the night."

"I can help you with navigating the insurance and costs of Danny's hospitalization. There are resources available to help families like yours. It's not perfect, but there is help for you. Neither of you should feel like you're going this road alone."

Adam nodded in appreciation. "Another reason we wanted to come see you is to talk about an issue that came up recently." He looked at Sophie, who nodded. "A little while ago, I stopped and had a few beers at Evening Rounds. It happened to be during that time that Danny took a turn for the worse and needed to go back on the ventilator. Sophie was pissed, to say the least."

Sophie explained, "We'd had an agreement that while I was pregnant, I wouldn't drink, and neither would he. And he broke it. He changed the rules of our agreement without telling me."

Jody crossed her legs, waiting for Sophie to go on.

"My father was a drunk. When he was sober, he was a great father, but when he was drunk, he was a mean son of a bitch. Adam knows that. We both enjoy a couple of beers together, no big deal. But that other night coming into the hospital so buzzed? That was not okay. I guess it's because things are different now. We're parents."

"You're right, Soph. I get it and I'm sorry." He looked at Sophie. "It won't happen again. I promise. And I can also promise I'm not going to turn into your father."

Sophie nodded and pulled Adam's hand into hers.

"What else? Adam, you look like you have more you want to say," Jody said.

"I've got so many things going through my head," Adam said, leaning forward with one elbow on his knees, his other hand still in Sophie's. "I love Danny so much, more than I ever thought possible. But sometimes when I look at how small and fragile he is, I feel sad . . . and a little disappointed."

Adam took a deep breath, then continued. "He's not the robust baby boy I was expecting. Then I get mad at myself for thinking that way, but I can't help it. I'm sorry, Soph. I had dreamed of a son who would be like me—tall, athletic, great on the basketball court. But, instead, he's going to be small, probably asthmatic, and need glasses."

"Adam, he can't help it!" Sophie said. "It's not his fault he's like this. If anything, it's my fault." Sophie took her hand back from Adam and clasped both her hands in her lap.

"Hey, babe, I'm not blaming anyone, least of all you. Of course he can't help the way he is. It's just that it's hard for me to watch." He looked at Jody and added, "Then on top of it all, I'm worried about Sophie. I know this is taking a toll on her."

Jody looked to Sophie.

Sophie nodded and said, "I get sad sometimes too. I worry a lot of the time, but most of all I'm scared."

"Scared?"

"Yeah. Of something bad happening to Danny. I have nightmares of someone giving him the wrong medication or doing something to him that was meant for another baby, and he dies. I don't know, I'm just afraid of something going wrong. That's why I won't leave the NICU. I'm there all the time. I pretty much live there."

"Do you want to talk more about that?"

"No, it's okay. I have people who I can talk to—my sister and my NICU friend Rihanna."

"Do you have many friends outside of the hospital?"

"I have some girlfriends from work, but they wouldn't understand. A couple of them have babies, but what would we talk about? Our experiences as new moms are so different." Sophie stared at the floor again, fiddling with her wedding band. "It's okay. I'm fine."

"Sophie, going back to what you said earlier," Jody said, "why do you feel this is all your fault? You said something about feeling guilty. Most mothers do, but is there any particular reason you feel guilty?"

She took a deep breath. "Because, back in college, I had an abortion after . . . never mind that. I had an abortion, and later, my ob-gyn told me that it may cause a problem if I ever decided I wanted to get pregnant." She blew out the breath she'd been holding in. "I am so embarrassed about it."

Adam moved closer to Sophie and put his arm around her. "Sophie, you can't keep blaming yourself. None of this is your fault. We both agreed to put those parts of our pasts behind us." He pulled her to him.

"I know. My abortion *was* behind me. That whole date thing, I thought I was over it. Until now." She wiped a tear away.

Silence followed, each person lost in thought.

Then Jody asked, "What else?"

Sophie said softly, "I wish there was a magic pill that I could take, one that would take us back two months so I could erase ever walking into Metro triage, skip this whole horrible episode of our lives, and fast-forward to delivering Danny on my due date."

"I know, babe, me too," said Adam.

They talked a few more minutes about Adam's job, Sophie's plans to return to work—or not—and about her sister, Kate.

Jody wrapped the meeting up. "If there's nothing more, we'll end now. But if you ever want to talk again, don't hesitate to call. Having a baby in the NICU is traumatic. Some marriages don't survive such an ordeal, but I think you guys will do well. You both seem committed to each other and to Danny. I'd like to help you in any way I can, so please call me if you need me. Oh, and Adam, let's plan to meet to go over your financials sometime in the next couple of weeks."

Sophie and Adam said their thank-yous and left the office.

CHAPTER 35

"We've got more to talk about that doesn't need to be a part of our conversation with Jody." Adam held the elevator door open. On the way down, he said, "Hey, I know! How 'bout a date night tonight?"

"Yeah." Sophie smiled. "I like that idea. Kate's busy tonight meeting up with some old friends. Let's do it."

They got back to their house, where Sophie showered, changed her clothes, and put on some makeup. She almost felt like her old self. Together they drove to Mezza Luna for dinner.

Adam took a sip of his beer. "I hope you're not mad about the things I said to Jody. I'm just trying to figure out how to handle all this stress. And all these huge changes in my—I mean, *our* lives."

Sophie lifted her wineglass to toast Adam. "Here's to our new life." She gave him her best attempt at a smile, took a sip, and looked in the direction from where she felt cold air was coming. The restaurant door closed behind a man who walked over to the bar. She nearly spat out her wine.

Adam turned to see what made her react like that. "Who's that?"

"That's the chapel guy. At least that's what I call him. I see him sometimes in the hospital chapel."

Adam looked at her. "And?"

"There's something about him. I wonder what relative he has in the hospital to bring him to the chapel that much." Sophie watched as the chapel guy joined a table of eight already engaged in lively conversation. "Well, isn't that interesting?"

"What?" asked Adam.

"Our pediatrician, Dr. Patel, is sitting at the same table."

"What are you saying, Soph?"

"What's the connection between Dr. Patel and the chapel guy? And who are all those other people at the table?"

"They're probably from the hospital."

"Hmmm, I wonder." Sophie twirled her wineglass between her fingers.

"Anyhow, back to what we were talking about—answers." Adam pulled Sophie's attention back. "Your premature delivery didn't just happen for no reason, but according to your medical records, it did."

They talked through dinner. The conversation wandered from the mystery of her delivery to how the school basketball team was doing without Adam coaching, then ended up on what to plant in their garden come spring. By dessert, they were back to talking about Danny.

They paid the bill and put on their coats to leave. On the way to the door, Sophie walked past the table of eight and smiled hello to Dr. Patel. He returned her smile and offered a wave before turning back to his conversation with the woman beside him.

When they stepped outside, the wind was blowing, and sleet pelted their faces like little shards of glass. They hurried to Adam's car.

Adam stopped short a few steps from his car. "What the hell is this?" Two of his tires were slashed. He walked around his car, then looked up and down the street.

"Who would do this?" asked Sophie.

"I don't know," answered Adam, yanking off his gloves to dial his cell. He called a twenty-four-hour tow truck service, then called a taxi.

When they pulled up to the front entrance of the hospital,

Sophie said, "One of these nights, I'll come home. I'm just not ready to leave Danny for that long."

They kissed a warm, lingering kiss goodnight.

"See you tomorrow."

Sophie settled in for the night next to Danny. A small crowd of doctors and nurses wheeled in an incubator. Earlier, Kim had prepared a space in their pod for this new admission. A night nurse and Dr. Sheldon waited in the pod, ready to accept the baby for admission and to get the report on the baby. The obstetrician told them this was a thirty-two-week baby girl.

"Mom came into triage with premature rupture of membranes. She was group B strep positive, and even though we started antibiotics, she still had some significant fetal decels. So we gave mom a dose of steroids, then sectioned her. All good now," the satisfied obstetrician said.

"Nice job," said Dr. Sheldon, patting the obstetrician on the shoulder. Leaving the pod, he looked over in the direction of Danny's incubator space. He saw Sophie and gave her a wave.

"Good night," called out Sophie as she closed the curtain around her and Danny.

Barely five minutes into her sleep, Sophie was awakened by a code alarm, alerting all doctors and nurses on the code team to Pod B stat. She got up to see what was going on in the next pod over, where a baby had been admitted earlier in the night. The code was not for the baby. It was for the mother.

CHAPTER 36

Nurses rushed into the pod. Sophie could see the mother was struggling to breathe. Then she went limp and fell to the floor. Sophie cringed at the sound of her head hitting the floor. Her eyes rolled back in her head. Her arms jerked up and down, and her back arched. Sophie watched in horror as the woman had a full epileptic seizure.

An adult code was called, bringing with it extra confusion. Sophie wondered how long it had been since these baby specialists had taken care of a seizing adult. The adult code team from Metro General next door rushed in. They stopped the seizure, stabilized the mother, then wheeled her away on a stretcher. Later, Sophie heard from the NICU nurses that she'd had a stroke, causing her to seize.

The next day, the father sat by the baby's incubator, his eyes red and swollen. Probably from crying, as well as from exhaustion, thought Sophie. Her heart went out to the poor man. His wife was stroked out in the adult ICU, and his baby was here in the NICU. How could one person survive so much sadness? Why was life so unfair?

Dr. Wagner entered the NICU. He spoke with Dr. Morrison while glancing in the direction of Pod B. They walked together past Pod C on their way to the baby's bedside. As their conversation grew more animated, Sophie heard the anger in Dr. Morrison's voice. Her hands were on her hips. Dr. Wagner kept shaking his head. After Dr. Morrison left the pod, Dr. Wagner sat with the father for several minutes, then stood up to leave. He gave the father's shoulder a squeeze, then left.

Sophie pulled out a slip of paper and wrote down the mother's name and the baby's date of birth. She was starting a file. She planned to gather information on all the babies who were in the NICU for prematurity. Those delivered by Dr. Wagner would go in one file and those delivered by other obstetricians in another. She couldn't prove anything with only names and gestational ages, but she could at least start keeping track of preterm admissions. Today was the beginning of the end for Dr. Wagner.

CHAPTER 37

The NICU was overcrowded. For every baby, there was equipment that took up twice the space of the baby. The smaller the baby, the more equipment there was. There were ventilators, monitors, IV pumps, rolling tables that held multiple pumps designed to deliver microdoses of medications, special phototherapy lights, supply bins that held different sizes of syringes and needles, and a crash cart for each pod—equipped with everything needed to resuscitate a baby. The single-sized recliners took whatever little space remained. Sometimes, those recliners were removed to make space for the nurses to work. Most parents either opted to go home to sleep or slept on the couches in the parents' lounge.

Once the NICU reached official full capacity, the nurses had to find a way to squeeze a fifth baby into a pod. This was possible, Sophie noticed, with babies who were less critical, usually closer to full maturity and who didn't require as much equipment or intensive nursing care. Sometimes, even a sixth baby would be allowed into a pod for a short while, doubling the assignment for nurses. This was the tipping point when the census went well over the max of forty. Eventually the numbers would climb into the fifties.

The overcrowding put everybody in an irritable mood. Nurses snapped at each other. Doctors barked their orders. There was always tension in the air. Kim did her best by staying upbeat and pleasant with the parents as she stepped around overflowing garbage cans or skirted around another IV pole standing in the middle of the pod. But even Kim lost her patience sometimes. There just wasn't enough space—no room to have a private conversation, no room to be alone with your baby. There was barely enough room for nurses to do their work.

Sophie considered the crowded unit. She hadn't seen much of Rita, the lovely meter maid. It was no wonder. There was hardly enough room for her to walk through the place without tripping over something. Maybe she was getting the numbers she needed for staffing from the head nurse. Sophie thought that the overcrowding must compromise the care of the babies. Certainly, it took its toll on the mental health of the parents, and it pushed the nurses' stress levels to the limits. Why didn't they transfer babies to other hospitals, ones with empty beds? How could there be anything good about all these preterm babies crowding the NICU?

CHAPTER 38

Sophie needed some air. She called Kate and asked her if she had time to join her for a walk. Kate promised to be there as soon as she could break away from her Skype meeting.

Forty-five minutes later, Sophie met Kate in the lobby. Sophie wanted to explore the whole hospital, or at least the first floor. The entire complex ran the length of five city blocks.

"Like we did when we were kids. Remember playing Harriet the Spy and running reconnaissance of the neighborhood?" The sisters laughed together.

They began in the lobby of the Metro Women's and Children's Hospital, the northernmost building. Turning in a southward direction, they walked down a long hallway that opened into a large, ornate, older lobby. It was filled with people hurrying about—hospital staff, visitors, patients, pizza delivery men, flower deliveries. It was like a small city within the hospital.

"Looks like this is the main Metro General Hospital." They stopped to read the directory, which listed fifteen floors of inpatient units and medical offices.

They continued through another hallway that led them to a large atrium-type building with an auditorium and an extensive medical library attached.

The hallway that stretched in front of them led to another building farther to the south. Looking down the crowded hallway, Sophie thought she saw Dr. Sheldon. Before she got a good look at him, he disappeared through a doorway with an emergency exit sign overhead.

"Was that Dr. Sheldon?" Kate asked.

"I think it was. I guess the NICU isn't the only place he spends his time. I'm sure he's got other responsibilities in the hospital."

"Really? Like where? He's the chief of the NICU, Soph."

Sophie shrugged.

Kate added, "I wonder what the cute doctor is up to over here by family planning."

They kept walking and finally reached the last building, five blocks away from where they had started. It was a four-story building that held the family planning clinic on the main floor and offices on the three floors above. All the buildings were connected by the interior hallways that Kate and Sophie had just walked, and by outside walkways that people used in nice weather.

The two sisters went outside to return by way of the street.

"Hey, let's grab a bite. I'm not ready to go back yet," Sophie said.

They crossed the street to a small sandwich shop. After they ordered, they sat down with their coffees. Waiting for their food, Sophie and Kate watched the people walking by—some rushing at a fast clip, dodging the people in their way, others casually stopping to window-shop. Across the street she saw Dr. Wagner.

"Kate, look!"

Kate turned. "Looks like the good Dr. Wagner to me. He's probably out getting some lunch too." She turned back.

"No, look closer."

Kate turned again. They watched Dr. Wagner pull out some keys and unlock a door to the family planning clinic building.

"What's he doing in the family planning building?" Kate said.

Sophie kept her eyes on that side of the street. A minute later, she said, "What the heck?"

"What is it?"

"There's the chapel guy. Back a little way behind Dr. Wagner."

Kate looked. "Who's the chapel guy?"

"He's a guy I've seen in the hospital chapel a couple of times. And other random places too."

"Funny, isn't it? How, on this busy street, we see Dr. Wagner and the chapel guy practically at the same time. Who's next, Dr. Morrison?" Kate joked.

"Actually, here's Adam." Sophie laughed. "I texted him we were here, in case he had time for lunch."

Adam joined them and guzzled a Red Bull.

"Is that your lunch?"

"Yeah, today it is. What are you guys up to? Sisterly shenanigans?"

"Hardly," said Sophie. "I needed a break from the unit. We just walked the length of the whole hospital, all four buildings and five blocks of it."

Kate spoke up. "Speaking of sisterly shenanigans, Sophie, I'm going to have to get back to Boston soon."

Sophie put her coffee down. "I knew this was coming."

"Sorry, sis." Kate put her coffee down too. "But hey, I'm not leaving yet. I'm still here for another few days."

"Okay, good." Sophie laid her hand on top of Kate's.

CHAPTER 39

Now that Danny was finally starting to gain weight, Sophie was allowed to hold him, wrapped in warm blankets, for short periods. She liked to hold him close to her chest, sometimes attempting to nurse him. Those attempts were largely in vain, and he tended to fall asleep nestled between her boobs. *Oh well, at least it feels good to us both.* Today, she held him in her lap, trying to feed him with a bottle. It was like getting a baby seal to suck on a bottle—adorable, but more milk landed on Sophie's lap than in Danny's mouth.

Kate sat next to Sophie, laughing at the show. Seeing Sophie's frustration, Kate urged her to relax. She leaned over and tried to help Danny get a better seal on the bottle, only to wind up with Sophie's pumped breast milk all over her hands and arms.

"Eew, gross! No offense." Kate grabbed a blanket to wipe her hands.

Sophie kept trying. She and Kate overheard Kim on the phone asking Amanda to come up to her pod and check in on her latest admission.

"She's a mom who also happens to be a nurse with a twenty-five-weeker. Her baby isn't doing well," Kim explained. "You were at her delivery, and now the mom is looking for answers."

Sophie made a mental note to add this baby's name to her growing file.

Kim continued talking into the phone. "I tried him. Dr.

Wagner isn't available right now. I've given her all the hope and reassurance that I can about her baby, but Amanda, she's looking for answers that I can't give her. Can you come talk to her?"

Kate left to use the ladies' room.

Amanda came into the pod and sat down next to the mother. Sophie studied Amanda. Her skin was pale, more than just winter pallor. She had some old acne scars on her cheeks and along her jawline. Her dirty-blonde hair was pulled back in a thin shoulder-length ponytail. Sophie thought that if she washed her hair a little more often and put on a touch of mascara, she might be pretty, in a simple way.

Amanda spoke matter-of-factly, offering no physical contact of comfort to the mother. Sophie hoped she was at least trying to be compassionate. Kim busied herself with the baby, listening to the conversation. The mother wanted to know what medications she had put into her IV.

Amanda pulled out a vial. "This is what I gave you—progesterone to stop your contractions. And it worked. For a little bit."

"Until it didn't!" exclaimed the mother. "Are you sure you didn't accidentally give me something other than progesterone?"

"Oh no, that's not possible. I've been doing this too long to mix up medications."

Sophie looked closely at what Amanda held in her hands. All she could see was that it was a white-capped vial. She couldn't read the writing. Kim asked Amanda to stand up a minute so she could move her chair to make more room.

"Such tight quarters in here sometimes," Kim mumbled. She moved the two chairs and the table on wheels, shuffling them around to make more room for reaching the baby. When Amanda stood to move her chair, Kim bumped her hip.

"What are you doing?" Amanda asked.

"I'm just making more room," answered Kim. "There, now there's more space."

Amanda looked suspiciously at Kim as she patted her pockets. "I had some meds with me. Where'd they go?"

She searched her pockets, pulling out papers, pens, and hemostats but no vials.

"I don't know what you're talking about." Kim pulled out her own preemie-specific meds to show Amanda.

"Huh," Amanda muttered to herself, "maybe I left them in triage."

Amanda wrapped up the conversation with the mother, explaining that they did everything they could to stop her labor but the drugs didn't work. "Sorry" was all Amanda had to offer. She left in a hurry, still patting down her pockets.

After Amanda left, Kim joined Sophie to look at the vials that Kim had slipped from Amanda's pocket. There was a white-capped progesterone vial. There was also a pink-capped vial with the name *Ativan* on it.

"What's she doing walking around with this?" Kim asked in disgust. "This stuff isn't supposed to leave triage."

The third vial was capped with a tan-colored top with a Pitocin label.

"Do you think she made a mistake?" asked Sophie.

"I don't know. Why would she give a mom only twenty-five weeks pregnant Pitocin? It doesn't make any sense. She must have drawn from the wrong vial."

Later, Sophie told Adam and Kate what she had seen with Amanda and the vials in her pockets.

Kate said, "Soph, that doesn't prove anything other than that they carry these vials around."

"What about the mothers I've talked to whose early labors

were idiopathic? It had to have been the meds. They must have been given the wrong medications." Sophie considered the implications of what she was thinking. "Or," she said out loud, "they got the intended medication."

CHAPTER 40

Amanda was back in the pod the next day. She looked around, smiled, and nodded a casual hello to Sophie. She then spotted Kim at the other end of the cluttered pod and started to make her way over to her. Medical equipment was stacked on carts. Pocketbooks were stuffed out of the way, and linens were laid on chairs, with nowhere else for them to go.

Kim was giving Amanda an earful, and Amanda clearly wasn't having it. She held her head up, jaw clenched and chin jutted forward. She glared at Kim. Amanda reached into her pocket, pulled out a piece of jewelry, and shoved it into Kim's hand.

Amanda's pager went off. "Gotta go." She scurried away, jumping over the clutter on the floor.

Sophie looked closer at Kim's hand—there was a gold necklace that she recognized as Rihanna's. That must be why she had seen Amanda slinking out of the pod the other day.

CHAPTER 41

The next morning, Sophie walked into Pod C, where Rihanna was sorting through Isabelle's T-shirts and onesies.

"I can't believe you're leaving already. What am I going to do without you?"

"You'll be fine. I'll miss you terribly, but I'm so happy to be leaving here."

"Let me help you pack your stuff up. When do you leave?"

"Tomorrow morning," Rihanna said as she crossed herself. "God willing."

Kim brought over some empty boxes for the two women to start filling with baby supplies—formula, diapers, and T-shirts. Kim handed Rihanna a supply of BrainHealth.

"The first one's free," said Kim. "After that, for the next two years, it's on you."

Sophie whispered in Rihanna's ear, "That's what the drug dealers say—the first one's always free."

Rihanna looked at Sophie, and they burst out laughing.

Sophie turned to Kim. "On the back of our information pamphlet for Dr. Sheldon's study, it says 'not approved by the FDA.' What's up with that? When I googled it, there's nothing on any medication called BrainHealth."

Kim explained, "That's because they're using it off-label. It's just caffeine citrate—the same caffeine all these babies who have apnea get. That's what Dr. Sheldon's research is all about—to get the FDA to approve it for brain development."

"That's exactly what he said," answered Sophie.

"Good, that means I've got the party line right." Kim laughed. "Just kidding."

Sophie gave a short laugh.

"Hey," Sophie said to Rihanna. "Do you feel like doing some sleuthing on your last day here?"

"What's sleuthing?"

"Spying, snooping."

"Okay. Where? What are we sleuthing for?" Rihanna asked.

"The doctors' lounge. We're looking for more on Brain-Health, or about Dr. Wagner. I don't know. Let's just go look. I feel like being nosy."

Rihanna followed Sophie out of the NICU, down the hall to the doctors' lounge. "Sheldon doesn't let me go in there with him. 'It's just for doctors'"—she mocked Sheldon's voice—"which of course just makes me more curious." She giggled. They looked for Sheldon in his empty office. "Must be at lunch." Rihanna took one of his spare fobs, and they snuck into the doctors' lounge.

"Nice digs," Sophie whispered, even though they were alone in the lounge. Several on-call rooms, equipped with beds, computers, and televisions, branched off the hallway that led to the lounge. There was a kitchenette, cushy couches, and several tables, one with a backgammon inlay. The tidy lounge, topped with the smell of lemon-scented furniture polish, told Sophie the cleaning lady had just been through. On one of the tables lay a neatly stacked pile of glossy postcards with the WMI logo on the front. She read:

Westchester Medical Industries—All Things Medical and More
- *Parent Company to New York's Leading Hospitals*
- *Kindred Pharmaceuticals*
- *Gene Therapy*

- Health Insurance - Helping Hands Insurance (HHI)
- Staffing Services: Home Health, Blood Donor Drives, Lab Technicians
- Reproductive Services and Family Planning
- Internal Medicine
- Women's Health

"Whoa. WMI seems to have cornered the medical service market."

Sophie put one of the cards in her back pocket. She noticed the corner of a letter sticking out from under a stack of medical journals. It bore the WMI logo.

Sophie pulled it out and started to read, "Dear Dr. Hennessy. It is with great pleasure th—"

The lounge door opened, loud voices startling Sophie and Rihanna. The talking and laughing got louder as they walked down the hallway toward the two. Sophie shoved the letter in her front pocket as she grabbed Rihanna's hand and they scurried to the opposite side of the lounge, ducking around a corner. Relieved to find another exit, they slipped out. Rihanna returned Sheldon's fob to his desk.

Back in the NICU, Sophie pulled out the letter. Out loud, she read:

Dear Dr. Hennessy,

It is with great pleasure that I invite you to join our new team of Metro Hospital professionals working on an exciting new enterprise. Using innovative, state-of-the-art technology, we are helping couples who, until now, have been unable to have children. The project is in its infancy with promise of tremendous growth. The company and I hope that you will consider the offer and become the second physician on board.

If you'd like to learn more, please call the number provided below to arrange an appointment at the WMI corporate headquarters.

Sincerely yours,

The bottom of the letter was torn off.

"Dr. Hennessy must have taken the name and number with him." She put the letter back in her pocket.

Knowing this would likely be their last time together for a while, Sophie and Rihanna spent the rest of the afternoon together in the pod, chatting away as only good friends can. Other moms came and went. Kim left at the end of her shift, telling Rihanna and Sophie that she'd see them in the morning.

"I wonder what that letter was about." Sophie pulled the letter and brochure from her pockets. "Do you know anything about WMI? I know they own the hospital, but it looks like they do a whole lot more."

"I hear Sheldon on the phone with them every so often. I think they talk about research projects. But beyond that, I don't know."

Sophie flipped the brochure around in her hands, then put it and the letter back in her pockets. She sat back in the rocking chair and sighed. "Wow, Ri, home tomorrow. What a huge milestone for you. What about Sheldon—are you guys sticking together?"

"I dunno. He says he's got a new project that's taking up more time than he expected. I'm afraid we're cramping his style. So, really, the timing is perfect. I'm so happy to be taking Isabelle home."

"Did Kim give you back your gold necklace?"

"Yes. How did you know about that?"

"I saw Amanda hand it over to her."

Rihanna looked at Sophie in confusion, as if trying to put pieces of a puzzle together that wouldn't quite fit.

CHAPTER 42

The next evening, Sophie helped Rihanna load Isabelle and all her supplies into a cab. Trying to look cheery, she waved goodbye as they drove away.

She wasn't ready to go back upstairs. It would be too lonely without Rihanna there. Adam was staying late at school for a faculty meeting, leaving Sophie with time on her hands. She wandered over to Metro General's lobby. She sat and watched the bustle of people carrying on with their daily lives. She thought about how much she missed her old daily life. She wouldn't trade Danny for anything in the world, but this whole Metro NICU experience? She'd gladly trade it in for her old humdrum life.

She walked back to her wing of Metro and stood in front of the fish tank, watching the soothing movement of the fish. She must have been there for a while because when she turned to go back upstairs, the flow of visitors had slowed to a trickle, telling her it was getting late.

Sophie rode the elevator to the fourth floor. On the wall, there was another picture of a cute Asian baby, propped on her hands and knees. This caption read: *BrainHealth—Providing the Best for Your Baby's Brain*. Sophie pulled the WMI postcard from her pocket and studied it.

By the time Sophie returned to the NICU, it was close to 10 p.m. She walked by Pod D and saw the telltale signs of a new admission. Doctors, nurses, and respiratory therapists all worked to stabilize the baby. A different attending neonatologist was there supervising.

As Sophie slowed her steps, she peered through the small crowd at the open warmer where the baby lay. She stopped. The baby was fully exposed under the warming lights, making access to him easy for the nurses. The usual monitors, IVs, and ventilator that were familiar to Sophie were all there. She was surprised to see how extra tiny he was—smaller than Danny when he was born. His skin was translucent, and she could see the blue veins just below the surface. *Sheesh, how early can they save these babies?*

She went to sit with Danny for a little while, then said good night to him and left to go to the parents' lounge. When she walked back past Pod D, things had settled. Only two nurses remained with the baby, along with the rhythmic sounds of the ventilator breathing life into him.

Sophie met Kate for coffee the next morning. They walked by Pod D. The baby from the night before was gone.

"Huh," said Sophie. She turned to Kate. "There was a tiny little baby admitted last night—smaller even than Danny. But there were no parents with him. Normally, they always bring the moms up, either in a wheelchair or on a stretcher to see their baby. But not last night. And now he's gone. It's almost like the baby and family never existed."

"Maybe the baby died," Kate whispered.

I wonder.

The NICU census dropped as babies were discharged. Order was restored in Danny's pod, back down to four babies and four sets of parents. No more mothers had stroked out. The saddest recent event was the twenty-four-weeker who had been born a couple of weeks ago. Sophie had had a bad feeling about that baby from the beginning. The baby had held on for a week. Sophie spent days worrying, not only about Danny but also about that little girl. One day she would have a good day and seem to be doing well. The next day was filled with monitor alarms and emergency calls to her pod. The doctors and nurses worked tirelessly to keep her alive.

On the eighth day, there was no bringing her back. When she died, Sophie was shaken to the core. Her heart ached for the parents as she listened to them wailing over their baby's incubator. She could hardly imagine the depth of their grief. Even though Kim had told Sophie that babies born that early don't usually do well, even if they survive the NICU, it put Sophie in a funk for days. It was so unfair. She teared up just thinking about it.

"How do you do it?" she had asked Kim. "How can you stand to watch these babies die?"

"Because, Sophie, there are so many more who survive. There is so much good that comes out of this place, thousands of little lives that do well—they far outweigh the sad-but-fewer unfortunate outcomes. And one thing you can't take away from a person is hope. These parents hold tightly to their hope. Plus, look at Danny! He's going to be a huge success story." She gave Sophie a quick hug.

CHAPTER 43

Suzanne was one of the nurses who was experienced in both triage and NICU. Her warm Southern demeanor made her popular with the other nurses, as well as the male residents. On any given day, Suzanne could be assigned to work in the NICU or in triage—it all depended on staffing numbers. Today, she was assigned to the NICU, and Sophie heard her happily chatting with Kim as they worked together in Pod C, restocking the crash cart and the IV shelves with supplies. Between her singsong Southern accent and her blonde hair and blue eyes, Sophie wondered how it was that she was still single. The two nurses talked loud enough so that Sophie and Kate could hear their conversation.

"You guys, listen to this," Kim called out to Sophie and Kate. "Suzanne has the best triage stories."

"Yeah, I've got a good one," Suzanne drawled. "The other day, one of our frequent fliers came in. Single, about thirty-two weeks pregnant, she comes in at least once a week with various complaints. Last night, she was in because she had been having headaches and was afraid her blood pressure was high. So I'm there checking her blood pressure, doing a full preeclampsia assessment to make sure her blood pressure isn't causing more problems than just her headache."

Suzanne paused, a smile beginning to crack on her face. "In comes another patient, ready to deliver, and she's with her husband. The first lady with hypertension freaks out and starts pointing and yelling. The lady with the husband starts screaming back at her, then screaming at her husband. We were all like, what the heck? It was a catfight, and the guy was the dog caught in the middle. It turns out, he was not only the father of his wife's baby but the father of the hypertensive patient's baby too. She was his girlfriend! You should have seen the look on his face! He looked at his girlfriend totally pissed off, like he wanted to kill her, as if it was her fault he'd been caught. Then he turned to his wife with the guilty look of a puppy who ate the T-bone steak off the counter, asking for forgiveness. Then they both turned on him, and I swear, if they hadn't been attached to IVs, they would have scratched his eyes out. Screaming and yelling at each other, then at him, then back at each other. It was like a scene from women's MMA. Imagine, wife and girlfriend meeting each other face-to-face in maternity triage! It was hilarious, but kind of sad too, I guess. Security had to come and separate the three. The women kept yelling and throwing stuff at each other—hairbrushes, tubes of lipstick, mascara, whatever they could pull from their pocketbooks. Finally, the wife was taken upstairs to have her baby, and the girlfriend was sent home."

Sophie and Kate listened in amazement to Suzanne's story, laughing with her as she told it.

"Honestly, you can't make this stuff up. Next time, he should pick a girlfriend on the opposite side of the city."

"Or maybe a different city altogether!"

They all dissolved into more laughter.

CHAPTER 44

The day came for Kate to leave. Sophie and Kate said their goodbyes, promising to talk every day on the phone. Sophie watched the back of Kate's head as she and her Uber merged into the snarl of the city traffic. She went back inside and took the stairs up to the fourth floor. Reaching to open the NICU doors, Sophie caught sight of Dr. Wagner and Amanda as they stepped onto the elevator. They had their heads together, arms so close she wondered if they were holding hands. The elevator door closed.

Walking into the pod, Sophie immediately sensed it. Something wasn't right. It felt off. When she walked up to Danny's incubator, it was empty. His IV pole stood there with the tubing still connected to the bag of fluid, but the end that should have been attached to Danny's arm was dangling from the top of the pole.

"Kim!" Sophie yelled.

There was no answer.

"Kim!" she called again. "Kim! Where did Danny go?" She spun around, shrieking, "Where's my baby?"

She looked to the three other mothers and the cleaning lady wiping out a sink. "Did any of you see what happened to Danny?"

They looked at her, not knowing what she was shouting about.

"Kim went to the front desk for a minute. She'll be right back. What's wrong?"

When they saw the empty incubator and Sophie's hysteria, they started talking at once.

"What happened?"

"How can a baby just disappear?"

"What do we do . . . ?"

"Maybe—"

"I thought I saw—"

"Isn't there secur—"

"He can't have just disappeared!"

Sophie ran out of the pod. "Where is my baby?" she screamed. "Where's Danny?"

Kim came running and grabbed Sophie by the shoulders. "What is it, Sophie?"

"Someone took Danny! He's not in his incubator."

Kim rushed over to where Danny should have been. When she saw the empty crib, she left as quickly as she had come in. She called security, who announced a "Code Amber"—baby abduction—and ordered a lockdown of the unit, followed by a hospital lockdown. When Sophie heard the code over the loudspeaker, she started to shake.

Security came and questioned the other mothers—no, they hadn't seen anybody suspicious in the pod. As they recounted the past fifteen minutes, they realized that there had been a couple of minutes when only Kim was in the pod. She had been busy securing a baby's breathing tube and had had her head down. That must have been when Danny went missing.

Security had already shut down the hospital exits and was preparing to shut down the city block when Dr. Sheldon walked in. He was wheeling a transport crib with Danny inside, sound asleep.

Kim went nuts. Grabbing the crib away from Sheldon and wheeling it to Danny's bedspace, she demanded, "Sheldon, where in the world have you been? What were you thinking?"

Sophie collapsed in the chair. "Where did you take him? Why did you take him out of here?"

"Sheldon, why didn't you tell me?" Kim demanded.

"I did. You must not have heard me," he answered.

Sophie glared at him. "I can't believe what you just did. What were you doing with him?"

"Sophie, don't you remember? Today was a day for his isotope infusion. I had him down the hall in my office. Geez, I'm sorry to have set off a kidnapping scare."

Sophie was livid.

"I gotta go," Sheldon said, clearly feeling the heat from Sophie and Kim. He ducked out the door.

CHAPTER 45

Sophie missed her sister. She missed Rihanna too—two of her greatest supports had left. She went down to the lobby and returned to the fish tank. She watched the slow, graceful movements of the fish through the water. *They say fish tanks help lower blood pressure.* As she began to relax, she believed it.

After she called and talked to Kate for a bit, she called Rihanna and asked if she was up for a visit.

"Oh, absolutely, love! I've missed you."

Sophie stepped outside, looking forward to some fresh air and a brisk walk to Rihanna's Uptown apartment. The wind whipped around the city corners, forcing Sophie to walk with her head down and her hands in her jacket pockets. The frozen sidewalks made for slow walking, and her fifteen-minute walk turned into twenty-five minutes. She thought about Danny coming home. She realized she hadn't even thought about work since he had been born. When would she go back to work, or more importantly, *would* she go back to work? Work used to be such a big part of her life and her identity. Now her life was all Danny.

Looking up at the numbers on the buildings, Sophie found Rihanna's place. She pressed the buzzer to 705.

"Who is it?" Rihanna's voice crackled over the intercom.

"Hey, Ri, it's me," Sophie spoke into the speaker.

The door buzzed, and Sophie stepped inside. Riding the elevator up, she checked her phone. A missed call from Adam. She'd get back to him later. The elevator door opened on the seventh floor, and Sophie found her way to apartment 705. Rihanna opened the door and threw her arms around Sophie, holding her tight. Sophie hugged her back, and the two women laughed with delight at seeing each other again. They made their way into the living room, where Rihanna had coffee already laid out. Sophie admired the decor of Rihanna's apartment, all done in Bahamian colors—pinks, coral, aqua blues, and greens. The bouquet on the kitchen table gave off a fresh floral scent. Isabelle lay in her bassinet in the middle of the room, sound asleep. Sophie marveled at her long eyelashes and full pink lips.

"She's a beauty, Ri, just like you. The two of you look like life at home is a recipe for happiness."

"Thanks, Sophie. Yes, it's wonderful to be home. And it's so good to see you! Fill me in on what's happening in the NICU. How's Danny?"

Sophie told her of the latest goings-on in the NICU—the mother who had a seizure, how crowded it had gotten with too many preemies, and how Kate had gone back to Boston.

"Basically, it's pretty stressful these days. And I miss you," Sophie said. "But I'm trying to make the best of it. Adam and I are still looking for answers to my preterm delivery." Sophie lowered her voice. "Between you and me, we think that Dr. Wagner is somehow causing babies to be born prematurely."

Rihanna's eyes went wide.

"I know. It sounds far-fetched. But we're looking for answers. Plus, we're not the only ones. There are other mothers whose stories are similar to mine, all with the same common denominator—Dr. Wagner."

The doorbell went off. Rihanna went over to buzz the downstairs visitor in. A few minutes later, Sheldon appeared. He gave Rihanna a peck on the cheek and turned to look for Isabelle. When he saw Sophie, she watched the looks first of surprise, then suspicion, then finally friendliness flash across his face in a fraction of a second.

"Hey, Sophie, fancy meeting you here."

"I know. Who would have guessed?" she joked.

Sheldon walked over to the bassinet. "I won't stay long. I just wanted to see my little beauty."

Sophie glanced over at Rihanna, who had returned to the couch, where she remained seated, hands clasped in her lap.

"Okay if I pick her up?"

Rihanna nodded. Isabelle gave a little snort when she was disturbed, then quickly settled into Sheldon's arms.

Rihanna explained to Sheldon that Sophie had just told her how crowded the NICU had gotten.

"Why is he doing this, Sheldon?" asked Rihanna.

"Who, doing what?" Sheldon gently put Isabelle back in her bassinet.

"Mitch, delivering premature babies to fill the NICU."

Sophie looked at Rihanna, silently begging her to stop.

Sheldon hesitated. "Rihanna, are you implying that Mitch is *intentionally* causing babies to be born early?"

Rihanna held her eyes on him.

"Don't you think that's a bit of a stretch?" Sheldon, still wearing his coat, leaned up against the doorframe between the living room and the kitchen. "I mean, it's true, the NICU makes a lot of money for the hospital. It's the one department that almost always operates in the black. But the census, the number of babies in the NICU on any given day, is complete happenstance. When the NICU is busy, the hospital makes money. The bottom line for any business—which Metro is, by the way—is always profit. Even hospitals need to make a profit. It's just the nature of the beast."

"How much do you guess Danny's total hospital bill will be?" Sophie asked him.

Without hesitation, Sheldon replied, "Easily a million. Probably more."

Sophie struggled to wrap her head around that number. But, at the same time, she knew there was nothing too much or too expensive for Danny. She would go to the ends of the earth to keep him alive.

Sheldon shifted his weight. "The board of trustees loves the numbers of a high census month. But what you're suggesting, Rihanna? That's out of line. The truth is that modern medicine is advancing in ways that make it possible to save more babies at younger and younger gestational ages. And that's why neonatal medicine is growing so fast. It's becoming a billion-dollar industry."

Sophie shook her head. "It almost sounds like a joke: What do babies' lives and spreadsheets have in common? Except I don't know the punchline. It's all too disturbing to be a joke."

The three of them made small talk for a few minutes, then Sheldon stood up straight. "I'm sorry, I gotta go. Sophie, good to see you."

"Wait," Sophie said. "Before you go, what is WMI exactly? I know they're the parent company for Metro. But what else do they do?"

Sheldon leaned back against the doorframe again. "Why do you ask?"

"When I was upstairs in administration, I saw the WMI logo on the door of one of the offices. And I saw it on a letterhead in the doctors' lounge."

"What were you doing in the doctors' lounge? You can't go in there."

"Snooping. But back to my question, what is WMI?"

Sheldon hesitated. "Like you said, they own Metro Hospital. It stands for Westchester Medical Industries."

"Do they own anything else other than Metro?"

"They own other hospitals in the city. That's about all I know."

Sophie studied his face. "I don't believe you."

Dr. Sheldon looked surprised. Rihanna looked amused.

Sophie pulled out the WMI postcard flyer. "It says here they do a lot more than just own hospitals."

"Well, yeah. They provide a lot of services to health-care businesses. I thought you were referring only to them being a parent company to hospitals. Look, I really do have to get going." He leaned over to give sleeping Isabelle a kiss. "And, Sophie? If you're still snooping and think you have something on Dr. Wagner, leave it alone. Focus on getting Danny home." He reached out as if to shake Sophie's hand, then pulled her in for a gentle hug. "I promise, I'll do everything I can to help make that happen."

"Thanks, Dr. Sheldon. I appreciate it." She stepped back. "I know you and Dr. Wagner have a special bond, but I'm not going to stop digging until I find out why we ended up in the NICU. And if Dr. Wagner had anything to do with it . . ." She paused. "He should know not to screw with a mother and her child."

Rihanna smiled in agreement.

"You're right, Sophie. He should know that. Ri, I'll see you later."

Rihanna walked him to the door, where he gave her another peck on the cheek and left the apartment.

"I guess the honeymoon's over, huh?" asked Sophie.

"Just like I told you. He's distancing himself. But he loves Isabelle, and I have to believe he'll always take care of us, or at least her." Rihanna got up and tucked Isabelle's blankets around her, then turned to Sophie. "Do you think he could be having an affair?"

"Oh, Rihanna, I have no idea. I sure hope not."

"Why do you think Amanda had my necklace?"

"I think she stole it," Sophie answered.

Rihanna stared off into the distance.

"Ri, don't even go there. Sheldon's a good guy, and he's going to be a great dad. Did you see how she snuggled right into his arms?"

Rihanna smiled. "Yeah, she did, didn't she?" She got up and took their coffee cups to the sink.

Sophie thought back on what Dr. Sheldon had said. She spoke loud enough for Rihanna to hear her in the kitchen. "Dr. Wagner is making the hospital money by putting preemie babies in the NICU."

"I'm not sure that's what Sheldon was saying," Rihanna said, walking back into the living room. "In fact, I'm pretty sure he said that is not what's happening."

"Think about it, Ri. With a full NICU, administration is happy. Mitch gets paid kickback bonuses, the hospital makes money, everybody's happy . . . everybody except for the babies and parents."

Rihanna furrowed her brow. "But how would he do that?"

"I'm almost certain it has something to do with the vials in his pocket. There's something about that sound of them clinking together that . . ." Sophie's voice faded off.

"Earth to Sophie," Rihanna said. "Come in, Sophie."

Sophie smiled. "Sorry, I was just thinking."

"Yeah, I see that. But back to what you were saying, why would he do that? Why would he do such an evil thing? It can't be just for the money. There's too much risk involved."

Sophie shrugged. "Yeah, I think you're right. There's got to be something else motivating him to gamble with these pregnant mothers. There's that botched breech delivery. And the mother left half paralyzed. That's serious collateral damage." Sophie's mind was going a mile a minute.

Rihanna interrupted her thoughts. "Sophie, be careful messing with Dr. Wagner. He's powerful, and he's vengeful. Don't poke the bear."

Sophie laughed. "Hey, how'd you learn that saying? You're becoming more and more Americanized."

"Is that a good thing?" Rihanna half smiled, then grew serious again. "Sheldon has told me some stories."

"I know. Like the nurse who was fired for two narcotic doses missing on her shift. I heard Dr. Wagner's signature was all over that one. What an asshole."

Sophie got ready to leave. She and Rihanna hugged again.

Rihanna playfully tugged on Sophie's long ponytail. "Hey, let's do this again soon."

"Definitely," answered Sophie.

CHAPTER 46

Sophie left the apartment building and stepped outside. It was only midafternoon, and already the overcast sky shed a dark gloom over the city. The automatic streetlights were turning on. She pulled out her phone. Adam hadn't left a message. She texted, *What's up?* and put her phone away. She pulled her collar up tighter around her neck and headed back to the hospital.

Two minutes into her walk, she sensed it. She glanced back behind her. The crowd was going about their New York City business, talking on their phones, walking with their heads down and earbuds in, everybody in their own little world. There was nothing out of the ordinary. She turned north on Second Avenue, a direction that took her away from the hospital. When she looked behind her again, she noticed a hooded brown ski parka. She'd seen that hood when she left Rihanna's.

She next turned west on Fifty-Second Street, then north again on Lexington, then east on Fifty-Fourth, making her route back to the hospital a zigzag. She casually turned to look over her shoulder and saw him in a crowd of people half a block behind her. Why was this guy following her?

As she quickened her pace, she tightened her hold on the shoulder strap of her purse. Brown hoodie must have quickened his pace too, because he was getting closer. She could hear him behind her; the ice on the sidewalk crunched under his uneven steps.

She had to do something. There were enough people on the sidewalk to give her a fairly good sense of safety. She checked her grip on the strap and reeled around, ready to club the guy with her pocketbook. Instead, she slipped. Her arms windmilled in the air as she fought to keep her balance. Her pocketbook flew out of her hand. His fist landed a hard blow to her stomach. Shocked, she felt the force of his punch knock the wind out of her. Sophie doubled over, gasping, and dropped to her knees. She couldn't breathe.

Fighting for a breath, she tried to yell after the brown hoodie. "Bastard!" All she could manage was a whisper. He'd already disappeared up the block. A passerby stopped to ask if she was okay. He helped her up and offered to call her a cab.

"No, I'm fine." It hurt to take a deep breath. "Did you happen to see the person who punched me?"

He shook his head. "Sorry. Do you want to call the police?"

"No, the guy's gone, and I wouldn't be able to describe him anyway," she said softly. Speaking took effort.

Sophie walked slowly back to the hospital, bent over with her hands holding her belly. She felt a gush of something warm between her legs.

CHAPTER 47

By the time Sophie got to the hospital entrance, it hurt too much to stand upright. She took a detour to the hospital security office and reported that she'd been accosted two blocks away. She'd be back later to fill out a report. Right now she had to get upstairs.

"Can I get you a wheelchair?" the security officer asked.

Not wanting to wait for the help, she hurried to the elevator, praying it would be empty. The pain was getting worse. Bent over, she stepped off the elevator and walked into the NICU. Instantly she felt a searing pain in her abdomen—cramping that felt a hundred times worse than the worst period ever. She ran to the nearest bathroom—the one for the NICU staff. She pulled down her underwear, and just as she feared, there was blood flowing out of her. With each cramp came another gush of blood. She screamed out Kim's name as she sat on the toilet, feeling lightheaded.

She was about to lose consciousness when a nurse came in and caught her from falling face-first onto the bathroom floor. The nurse pushed the emergency button in the bathroom that connected to the front desk.

"I need some help in here!"

Two nurses came rushing in, and the three of them got Sophie into a wheelchair. She started to vomit, throwing up her last meal all over herself and the nurses. They hurriedly wheeled her down the hall, onto the elevator, and to a procedure room on the second floor. They lifted her up onto the examining table.

"What are you doing?" Sophie asked in a daze.

"We're getting a doctor."

Feeling like she was about to faint, Sophie managed to say, "Please, just not Dr. Wagner." Then she lost consciousness.

When she came to, Kim was with her, as well as a doctor pulling off his gloves. Sophie had on a clean johnny and was tucked into a hospital bed. The on-call physician spoke to Sophie and explained that he had done a D&C to stop the bleeding. He put a gentle hand on Sophie's shoulder and explained that he removed a tiny piece of old placenta from her uterus.

"You know, Sophie, that punch was a blessing in disguise. Retained placenta, even a tiny piece like yours, would have eventually caused bigger problems."

There was a quick knock on the door, and without waiting for a response, Adam rushed in. "What happened, Soph?"

She told him about her visit to Rihanna's and the attack on her way home. They looked at each other, neither wanting to say what they were thinking.

Kim and the doctor excused themselves.

Sophie finally said, "Either that guy was out to hurt me, or it was just a random assault."

Adam shook his head. "That wasn't random. He was targeting you."

CHAPTER 48

Sophie and Adam stood together in Pod C.

"Adam, we're getting Danny out of here," Sophie said. "He's obviously not ready to go home, but he can go to another hospital, closer to us and away from Metro. He's stable enough to be moved to a hospital closer to us in Brooklyn."

"Okay, but what's the rush?"

"What's the rush? Take a look at our lives! We have a premature baby through no fault of our own. And now that we're onto Dr. Wagner, bad shit is happening everywhere. I was attacked, your tires were slashed. Next time, it's going to be Danny."

Sophie saw Dr. Patel coming toward them. "Dr. Patel!" she called, raising her hand to flag him over.

Dr. Patel walked over with his arms opened wide. "Hello, Sophie, Adam. I was just coming to see how our little guy is doing. I'm so glad he's getting better. He's a strong boy."

"Yes, he is. We are blessed. Thank you. We wanted to talk to you about getting him transferred out of Metro."

"Oh, I see." His smile faded. "May I ask why?"

"We'd like to have him closer to us. There's a nice hospital in Brooklyn, not too far from our house, that has a level II nursery."

"Ah, yes. I understand." His smile returned. "But it's not up to me. I'll have to talk with one of the neonatologists. As his pediatrician, I can request his transfer, but I can't make it happen. That's up to the attendings."

"Thank you, Dr. Patel. And this doesn't change anything about keeping you as his pediatrician, does it?"

"No, it doesn't change a thing," he reassured Sophie with a pat on her hand. "I'll go find Dr. Morrison now." He gave a slight bow and left.

Transfer would be the next day. In the morning the transport incubator was plugged in and warming up. Kim handed supplies for Danny's ambulance ride to the transport team. Everything was ready. They were just waiting for morning rounds to be done.

It was close to noon by the time rounds ended. Sophie and Adam waited for one of the doctors to bring the transfer papers for them to sign. Dr. Morrison walked into the pod empty-handed. Sophie's heart sank. *Now what?*

"Sophie, Adam, I don't know if you've been outside lately or turned on the news."

In fact, they hadn't turned on a TV in days. Sophie hadn't been outside in at least a day, and Adam hadn't been outside since his drive to the hospital early that morning.

"It's a blizzard out there. I know how much you're anticipating the transfer," Dr. Morrison said, and Sophie braced for what came next. "But it's not going to happen today. All nonemergent ambulance runs are canceled until the snow stops and the streets can be cleared. I'm sorry."

Desperate, Sophie said, "But there must be another way to get him there. We'll drive him ourselves."

Dr. Morrison shook her head. "I understand how important this is to you, but that's not possible either. We can try for another ambulance tomorrow, but I'm afraid they'll be backlogged, and Danny's transfer isn't medically necessary. That also means your insurance isn't likely to cover the cost. I think you'd be better off waiting for his discharge, which shouldn't be too long now."

The team filtered out, leaving Sophie, Adam, and Kim standing next to Danny's crib. Sophie didn't know whether to scream or cry. She was done with crying. She swore she had no more tears left inside of her. So she picked up a pile of Danny's baby blankets and screamed into them.

CHAPTER 49

Mitch put his phone away. He needed some time—time away from the hospital, time away from laboring mothers, and time away from Amanda. Was she getting annoying, or was he falling in love with her? *No, definitely not love*, thought Mitch.

He changed out of scrubs and into his winter running gear and took off at a slow jog, heading west toward Central Park. He settled into his stride, which was interrupted every so often by needing to lunge over a puddle of slush. It felt good to run, and as usual, his head started to clear. He took stock of his life. Metro had come a long way from where it was just ten years ago, floundering financially, almost forced to shut its doors. He had helped turn it into one of the leading hospitals in New York. He hadn't let that slip by his father's attention. He made sure his father read every article about Metro's comeback and the number of times Mitch's name was mentioned. Of course, his father had never acknowledged those articles, instead criticizing Mitch about his life. He always had something to say about his gold digger of a wife and spoiled kids, or his choice of medical specialty. Metro wasn't a worthy hospital in his father's eyes, because of the simple fact it wasn't Columbia University's teaching hospital. Mitch didn't know why he put up with the degradation from his father. But someday, he would show his father that he could live up to the old man's expectations.

Mitch crossed Fifth Avenue and entered the park. Today, he needed this run mentally as much as physically. He could easily cover the half mile over to Central Park West and back and hardly break a sweat.

His wife had been shushed by Mitch's lawyer, warning her to stop threatening Mitch with divorce. What did she want? Divorce or a bigger allowance? She couldn't have both. The kids' tuitions would be taken care of, and each would have a sizable trust fund started very soon. She should be happy with that.

His thoughts shifted to work. He wasn't sure what was happening with the project and was beginning to question what he wanted out of it. The stress was getting to him—constant juggling to keep too many balls in the air at once. Was the risk worth the money?

His father's latest criticism was how Mitch had used his position at WMI to get his best friend from prep school a job at the company. His father called it pathetic nepotism.

"Can't that dopehead get his own job without your help? I'm telling you, he was a no-good kid back in high school, and he's a no-good adult now."

His father was pretty much right. Tommy hadn't amounted to much after being kicked out of prep school and sent to reform school. But Mitch couldn't turn his back on his best friend. He'd just had some bad luck. The least Mitch could do was lend him a hand and get him a low-level maintenance job at WMI.

Once back at the hospital, he dashed up the stairs to the doctors' lounge and changed into his casual clothes—a sports jacket and jeans. He was going for a beer at Evening Rounds. He was off duty until tomorrow morning. He stopped to call his wife to tell her his plans. He'd be staying in their in-town apartment rather than risk the drive home in this crappy weather.

He walked into the bar, hoping to find an unsuspecting young nurse looking for a rich, handsome doctor to go home with. That fantasy burst when he found a group of physician friends sitting around a table.

"Yo, Mitch! Come join us. And bring a round of beers with you." This was followed by loud laughter in agreement.

Mitch ordered beers for the group and a beer and a shot for himself. He settled in with his friends and enjoyed the male bantering that went around the table. War stories of emergency rooms and ORs. Mitch loved it.

He ordered another beer and shot for himself. "Anyone else? Who wants to join me?"

"Thanks, Mitch, I'm headed home. The wife's holding dinner for me."

"Nope, gotta go. I've got a date tonight."

"You? Are you kidding?" A couple of them playfully punched the date guy in the arm.

Still joking around with each other, the men put on their jackets.

"Thanks for the beers, Mitch."

"Catch ya later, man."

Someone else said, "Be good! Don't do anything I wouldn't," followed by laughter.

CHAPTER 50

Mitch wasn't ready to leave the bar. He really didn't have anywhere to go anyway except to his empty apartment a few blocks away.

He sat at the bar and texted Josh, inviting him to join him.

The outside door opened. Adam Young, sporting his Knicks hat and a heavy down jacket, walked in.

"Hey, Adam." Mitch motioned for Adam to join him at the bar. "What brings you in here this dismal afternoon?"

"Waiting to hear from Sophie so I can go pick her up."

"Can I buy you a beer while you're waiting?"

"Sure, thanks. But only one."

"O-o-o-h-h-h-kay." Mitch cocked his eyebrow. He wasn't going to ask.

Mitch ordered two beers and another shot for himself. They toasted and picked up their conversation from the last time. After they recapped the Knicks' past few games, the topic turned to the weather, with more snow predicted over the weekend. It wasn't long before the conversation turned to politics. Thankfully, they held similar political beliefs.

The bar was getting crowded. Nurses and doctors walked in dressed in their puffy winter jackets, tossing backpacks and laptop cases on the tables. Mitch was enjoying a relaxed buzz—a feeling he wasn't used to and, frankly, one he often avoided. He hated losing control, and that was exactly what liquor could do. But he also knew his limit, and he was nowhere close to that yet.

While talking with Adam about the latest subway shootings, Mitch reached into his pocket for a toothpick. Three vials slipped out and fell on the floor.

"Whoops," he grunted as he stooped to pick them up.

Adam got off his barstool and offered to help collect the vials that were, by then, rolling under other barstools.

"Dr. Wagner, why do you have these with you?" Adam asked, reading the labels.

"Because we use them in triage."

"Really? What are they?"

Mitch didn't think this guy would fully understand the pharmaceutical effects and actions of each medication, and he was in no state of mind to give a pharmacology lecture. He kept it simple. "One stops labor, and one speeds labor up."

"How can you leave the hospital with meds in your pocket?"

"Adam, between you and me? I can carry whatever I want out of the hospital. Almost." He held up a pink-capped vial. "Except maybe this one. This one'll get me in trouble if I don't get it back there soon."

"What's it for?"

"It helps mothers to forget all about the pain of labor. It's a wonderful medication."

"I'm not so sure mothers want to forget all about their childbirth experience. Just sayin'."

Mitch took the vials back from Adam, who had been examining the labels. "No, Adam, these mothers don't know what's best for them. They think they want to deliver naturally, no epidural, no anesthetics, but you and I both know they don't know what they're talking about. They think that's what they want, but it's not." He raised his finger to the bartender. "Another round, please." He wondered for just a moment if he'd already reached his limit, then dismissed the idea.

"Actually, Dr. Wagner," Adam answered, "that's not what I

would guess, but I've never been in labor, so how would I know?"

"Exactly." Mitch brushed some strands of hair off his forehead, tucking them into their slicked-back position. "I try to do a good job of keeping triage running efficiently. If it wasn't for Rita and Charlie, I could have that place humming along like a well-oiled machine. But Charlie will never yield that much control to me."

"Who's Charlie?"

"He and Rita—you know the lady who comes through the NICU almost daily? They're the ones in charge. They're in control. I just follow their orders."

Adam took a sip of his beer, not saying anything.

"Part of what I do is keep the hospital in the black." Not sure Adam understood the financial terminology, Mitch added, "You know, making money rather than losing it. Triage and NICU, they make money for the hospital."

"You sound more like a businessman than a doctor," Adam said. "What do the vials have to do with anything?"

Mitch felt the conversation starting to go sideways. He paused for a moment, trying to remember what they'd been talking about. *Right, the vials.*

"Nothing, Doogie Howser." Mitch playfully landed a light punch on Adam's bicep. "The vials mean nothing."

He ordered another round for himself.

The bartender hesitated. "Dr. Wagner, are you sure? Maybe you should take a break."

Mitch glowered at the bartender. "I don't need a break. What I need is one more round. Please."

He turned around to see Josh coming into the bar.

"Joshie!" Mitch called out. "Come join us over here. Have you met Adam?" He slung his arm over Adam's shoulders. "This guy is great. He's the husband of a patient, but he's really cool."

Josh looked at Mitch, then at Adam.

Adam sipped his beer and watched.

"Mitch, what are you doing? What have you been talking about to Adam?"

"Adam, meet Josh, our rep for Kindred Pharmaceuticals. Josh here is the best drug salesman around. Aren't you, Josh? No, I think I'd call you the most typical salesman—you'll say whatever you have to in order to make a deal, and you're full of shit most of the time."

Mitch laughed hard. Adam lowered his eyes.

Mitch took his arm off Adam's shoulders and put it around Josh. "Just kidding, Josh. You keep us rolling. Triage couldn't run without you."

"Thanks, Mitch. You'll have to excuse me. I'm meeting a colleague."

After Josh moved away, Mitch decided it was time to leave. He poured the shot down his throat, enjoying the burn, then turned a little too quickly to slide off the barstool. Adam caught him and helped him steady himself.

"Thanks, Adam. I'll see ya 'round."

As he walked outside into the cold winter air, Mitch paused, trying again to recall the conversation with Adam, but the biting wind stole his thoughts, and instead, he turned his attention to heading home.

CHAPTER 51

Sophie stood in front of Adam. "Earth to Adam. Hey, is everything okay? You're awfully quiet. Is everything okay at school?"

"Yeah, yeah, school's fine."

Sophie worried not only about Danny but about her husband. She was not going to let the two of them become one of those statistics Jody had mentioned. They needed to keep the lines of communication open. "What is it then?"

"I had a beer with Dr. Wagner last night." He went on to tell Sophie about the evening. "I'm still trying to make sense of what he told me. And who's Josh? Do you know?"

Sophie shrugged.

"He sure acted nervous about Mitch spouting off. If Dr. Wagner is responsible for your and other women's early deliveries, who else knows about it? Is anyone in administration involved? He did mention a guy named Charlie and someone named Rita."

Sophie interrupted. "I know who Rita is. She's the one who checks in with Kim and the nurses about the census of the unit. Maybe she's keeping tabs on numbers of babies, which translates to the amount of income for the hospital."

"Well, maybe they're involved too. I don't know. But even if we went to someone in administration to tell them our suspicions, would they believe us? If they'd heard what he confessed to me, would they want to shut him up? Or more importantly, would they try to hush us? Are we even safe?"

Sophie paused to consider the seriousness of what Adam had

just suggested. Were they getting in too deep? Putting their noses where they didn't belong? Probably, but they couldn't just stop now.

"That wasn't really a confession, was it?" Sophie said. "It sounds more like he was confirming what we already think. But only what we *think*. We don't know anything for sure."

Sophie had a ten o'clock appointment with Madeline Cross, chief operating officer of Metro Women's and Children's. Kim had told her that her best chance of someone listening to her and taking her suspicions seriously would be to talk to Madeline.

When she'd called to make the appointment, Ms. Cross's secretary answered the phone, sounding irritated.

"Ms. Cross is a very busy woman, but she's agreed to squeeze you in. Just know, it's time she really doesn't have."

Great. Already I feel like it's a waste of time.

Regardless, Sophie headed to Madeline Cross's office determined to make her case. *She'll either kick me out on my ass, or she'll invite me in to hear more.*

At 9:50, Sophie got on the elevator and pushed the button for the eighth floor. A nurse got on at the fifth floor. The door closed, and the elevator started to move, slowly at first, then very quickly, catching both passengers by surprise. They grabbed the rail on the side of the elevator wall to catch their balance.

Suddenly, the elevator bounced to a stop between the fifth and sixth floors. The nurse started pushing buttons, lighting up every button on the panel. The elevator didn't budge. The nurse started yelling for help, and Sophie pushed the emergency alarm button.

A short while later, there were voices in the elevator shaft telling them not to panic, that help was coming. Sophie relaxed for a minute, until she looked at her watch. It was ten o'clock. The elevator lurched down a few feet.

"What was that?" the nurse gasped.

The elevator made a noise like it was gearing up to start running. Then the noise stopped, and the lights went out, putting the elevator compartment in total darkness. The nurse pulled out her phone and turned on the flashlight.

"Maybe it's just part of fixing the problem," Sophie offered with little conviction.

It was now 10:20. Sophie sighed. Her chances of convincing Ms. Cross to look at Dr. Wagner's delivery pattern were slipping away. What if Dr. Wagner had found out about her appointment? Could he be behind the elevator malfunction? *No, that's being too paranoid. Isn't it?* Now she was too nervous and worked up to speak to Ms. Cross. More time passed. The elevator showed no signs of starting back up.

CHAPTER 52

Sophie had just sat down on the elevator floor when the lights came back on. Slowly, it started to move. Forty-five minutes after they'd gotten on the elevator, it smoothly delivered the nurse to the sixth floor, then Sophie to the eighth floor.

She stepped up to Ms. Cross's secretary and explained why she was so late for her appointment. Could Ms. Cross still see her?

"No," the secretary answered without looking up.

"How about tomorrow then. Maybe the same time?" Sophie asked.

Scowling at her, the secretary took a pencil and wrote Sophie's name in for the same time the next day. "Fine."

Sophie left the office, happy to leave behind the secretary with anger issues. She took the stairs down to the fourth floor.

The next morning, Sophie passed the bank of elevators and climbed the four floors to the administrative offices. As she opened the door out of the stairwell, slightly winded, she saw Dr. Sheldon leave Madeline's office and head the other way. She waited to see if anyone followed him. Nobody else appeared. Sophie continued down the hall to Madeline Cross's office.

"Ms. Cross, as you may know, I spoke with Mr. Buckley about Dr. Wagner's inappropriate touching during my delivery. Nothing has come of that, which is a disappointment to say the least." Sophie paused. "But, right now, I have more pressing concerns about Dr. Wagner."

Madeline removed her glasses and looked closely at Sophie. She picked up a pen, prepared to take notes.

Sophie pulled out her own small notebook, the file that she had started. She told Madeline all she had observed, starting with her own induced labor and delivery. She spent the next thirty minutes methodically making her case against Dr. Mitch Wagner. She spoke of three other mothers and babies in the NICU who were induced and delivered weeks before their due date, despite healthy pregnancies. Madeline scribbled notes. Sophie told her about the baby who was brain damaged, and the mother now partially paralyzed from a stroke. She added that Pitocin was known to increase the likelihood of blood clots, possibly causing strokes. She wrapped up by stating her intention to take this to the state medical board if she didn't get a response from anybody here at the hospital.

"And you are convinced that Dr. Wagner is behind all of this?" Madeline asked.

"Yes, I am."

"Mrs. Young, I hope you're wrong. Dr. Wagner is a well-respected physician in this hospital. He's head of his department. His reputation alone brings patients to our hospital, and Metro has benefited from his loyalty. I can't imagine why he would put all that in jeopardy. Are you sure we're talking about the same Dr. Wagner?"

Undeterred, Sophie continued. "Take a look at his rates of preterm deliveries. Then look at how long they stay in the NICU and the problems they face because of their prematurity. Look at the business those babies bring to the NICU. I know it sounds crazy but—"

"Yes, to be honest, it does sound crazy, Mrs. Young."

Sophie thought for a minute. Should she say something about

Dr. Sheldon's office lab? No, that wasn't why she came here.

She took a deep breath. "He told my husband that the vials he carries around with him, Pitocin and progesterone, are how he helps the hospital make money," she blurted.

Taken aback, Madeline worked to compose herself. "Are you sure you're not just trying to get back at Dr. Wagner?"

Sophie shook her head. "No, this has nothing to do with that. I am not dropping my complaint about his inappropriate touching, but this is more urgent; the lives of mothers and babies are at stake here." She pressed on. "He induces mothers who come into triage to make them deliver prematurely so their babies get admitted to the NICU. Please, I'm just asking you to look into it. See what his numbers show you."

"Okay, Mrs. Young. Honestly, I am struggling to believe that what you're telling me is true, but I'll give you the benefit of the doubt, and I'll see what I find. If it turns out that you are right, we have a big problem on our hands."

"Thank you, Ms. Cross. I appreciate it, and so will the other patients who have babies in the NICU." Sophie added, "Oh, and one more thing."

Madeline sighed, clearly ready to be done with the conversation. "Yes?"

"I was wondering if it's possible to check the Pitocin levels on Dr. Wagner's premature delivery patients."

"Pitocin levels?"

"Yes. If they have unusually high Pitocin levels, wouldn't that help prove that he is causing them to deliver early—by artificial and wrongful induction?"

"That's quite a specific theory you have. But I'll check with the lab," she answered, making more notes. "You mentioned Charlie Buckley and Josh, the Kindred rep. Are you suggesting that they're a part of this too?"

"I don't know. Maybe."

Madeline paused, playing with her pen. Sophie sat patiently, picking at her pinky nail.

"I'll see what I find. But, Mrs. Young, I don't want you to breathe a word of this to anyone, other than your husband. I'm going to need to talk to Dr. Wagner."

"Do you have to tell him it was me who came to you?"

"He has the right to know who his accuser is. He deserves a chance to respond and defend himself."

He doesn't deserve shit, Sophie thought, but she just nodded.

Madeline added, "Sophie, eventually, if this turns out to be true, I'm going to need your testimony and all the proof you have. You will need to present your side of the story."

"I understand. Thank you, Ms. Cross."

Sophie left the office, relieved to know that someone was finally taking her seriously. From the stairwell, she called Adam and repeated the conversation to him.

"Sophie, he didn't say that! He didn't say those vials are how he makes the hospital money. That's a lie. It's only a guess."

"I know, but I had to get her attention somehow. We need her to investigate him."

CHAPTER 53

Sophie had an idea. She took the elevator to the lower floor and the medical records office. When she was let in, she asked if she could see her medical record—the electronic version. The woman set her up at a table with a laptop opened to Sophie's medical record. Sophie scrolled through, seeing the exact same thing she had seen on the paper chart. All the labor and delivery information was the same.

When she got to the last page of the medical notes, there was an addendum: *PTL due to PROM.* She read it again, then googled the acronyms. *Preterm labor due to premature rupture of membranes.* She looked to be sure she had the correct chart. *What is this?*

She went and asked for the paper copy of her chart. She scrutinized every page of her thin chart. Then she saw it. Squeezed onto the last line of Dr. Wagner's admitting note were the same letters: *PTL 2° PROM.*

"Preterm labor secondary to premature rupture of membranes," Sophie said softly to herself. She made sure the medical records woman wasn't watching her and took a picture with her phone. She went back to the electronic record and looked again. The date and time of the entry was the same as her discharge date. She took a picture of that too. She returned the paper and the electronic charts to the woman at the desk and rushed out. She had to show this to Adam.

CHAPTER 54

Triage was cranking. Mitch had two other docs working in triage with him. He was in the middle of examining and admitting one mother, twenty-nine weeks. When he looked up, he saw Adam Young outside of triage talking with Alicia, one of the nurses. She was searching the admitting desk area.

He watched as they talked more. Alicia smiled at Adam, then swiped her badge to open the triage door. Mitch went back to what he was doing. He drew from one of the vials in his pocket and injected it into the patient's IV. He patted her hand and reassured her. When he looked up again, Adam was standing against the wall, six feet away, facing him. As soon as Mitch looked over, Adam turned away.

Alicia came over to Adam. "I'm sorry, Mr. Young. I can't find your wife's planner anywhere. It's just not here. I hope she has another way to reach her clients."

"Thank you for looking." Adam tucked his phone up his jacket sleeve. "It was quite a while ago that she was here. I'm sure she can figure something out."

Mitch called out to Adam. "Adam? What are you doing in here? Alicia, please get Mr. Young out of here. He doesn't belong in here. His wife and baby are upstairs. If he gives you any trouble, call security."

Mitch turned back to what he had been doing, but not until he was sure Adam was out of triage.

CHAPTER 55

Sophie waited for Adam to get back from triage. As soon as she saw him through the pod window, she ran out, and the two of them went together into the empty parents' lounge. The TV blared in the background.

"If babies are being born early by accidentally getting the wrong medication," Adam said to Sophie, "then that's medical negligence, and a couple of lawsuits. But if it truly was unintentional, it wouldn't keep happening. Maybe he'd get away with it once or twice, claiming it was accidental, but not repeatedly. *But if they got the wrong medication on purpose . . . that's a big deal.*"

"That's a huge deal," Sophie said. She pulled out her phone and looked for the video that Adam had sent her. They played the fifteen-second video. The patient was in labor. Her belly was quite small, likely too early to be full term. There were the vials, with the colored caps, and Dr. Wagner's hand on the IV, holding the syringe. Dr. Wagner injected something into the patient's IV. They zoomed in.

The vial in his hand had a tan cap. They watched for the few seconds after he injected. The patient relaxed, with all signs of labor pain gone.

"Wait. What? That was Pitocin. The one that *induces* labor," Sophie said.

"Yeah, that's what we saw on the tan-capped vials Kim showed us."

"But her labor stopped. It didn't get worse. How can that be?"

"Can Kim find out if this mother delivered?" asked Adam.

Sophie found Kim in the NICU and explained.

Kim got on the phone. "This'll be quick . . . Hey, Suzanne, it's Kim." A short pause. "I'm doing good, thanks. Listen, can you tell me what happened to one of Dr. Wagner's patients? It was a woman who was there around noon. We're wondering if she got admitted, or did she go home?"

Pause.

"No, I don't have her name. Don't worry, there's no HIPAA violation," Kim said with a smile. "All I have is the time that she was in triage."

A longer pause.

"Hey, no problem." Kim listened. "She did go home? You're sure. Okay. Thanks, Suzanne. See you later." She turned to Sophie and Adam. "Does that answer your question?"

"Yeah, thanks, Kim."

The two returned to the parents' lounge. Sophie pressed the delete button on her phone. The video was gone.

"Maybe we've got this all wrong," said Adam.

"Or maybe they're switching caps."

CHAPTER 56

After the seventh patient of the morning, Mitch needed a break. He took the stairs to the eighth floor, where he wanted a decent cup of coffee and a little time in the doctors' lounge up there. He was still bothered by seeing Adam Young—and that he was clearly filming what was going on in triage. Mitch knew exactly what Adam saw. He wasn't worried; he was just pissed.

In the stairwell, he heard someone running the stairs, breathing heavily. He looked down from the seventh floor and saw Adam running up from the ground floor. He was doing laps: up two flights, down one, up two, down one. When Adam was between the sixth and seventh floors, Mitch stood in the middle of the stairs, blocking his path.

"Excuse me," Adam mumbled, still focused on the stairs he was climbing as he tried to go around. Unable to get by, he finally looked up to see it was Mitch who was in his way. "Oh, hey, Dr. Wagner," he panted, trying again to go around him.

"Hi, Adam. Can I see your phone?" Mitch asked.

Adam looked up at him. "No. Why?"

"I think you know why. What were you doing with your phone in triage?"

"I was looking for Sophie's planner."

"Well, in that case, you have nothing to hide. Let me see your phone."

Adam hesitated, then slowly pulled his phone from his pants pocket.

"Give it to me!" Mitch's voice bounced loudly off the stairwell walls.

Adam handed it over.

Mitch looked through the photo and video library. He looked through sent texts, sent emails, anywhere on the phone that Adam could have kept the video. Nothing. He wanted to break the phone in half but restrained himself.

He handed it back to Adam. "You have no business being in triage. If I see you in there again, I'll have security personally remove you."

Mitch continued down the stairs.

In the doctors' lounge, Mitch rehashed last night's New York Rangers game with one of the senior residents. The door opened, and he looked up to see Amanda poking her head around the corner.

Mitch jumped up and pulled her back out into the hallway. "We can't be in there together, you know that."

"I need to talk to you. I ran into Sophie Young, and she had a lot of questions about you and all the preterm deliveries."

"What'd you tell her?"

"I told her she was barking up the wrong tree and that she was imagining things. But her antennae are up. She smells something. Maybe we should back off for now."

"No way, Amanda, I don't want to piss off Charlie. They told me I need to fix the damage I've done with that breech baby. We need to be pushing forward, not backing off."

"She's going to be onto you real soon if she isn't already. You need to figure it out."

"Don't worry. I have a plan for Mrs. Young. If she starts getting too close, I know how to get her to back off. I am the doctor, after all. Go on, get out of here."

Amanda crossed her arms, making no move to leave. "Oh

yeah? What kind of plan? How far are you taking this charade, Mitch?"

"You don't need to know the details. You just keep showing up for work, take care of the patients, and do what I tell you to do."

"What happened to the simple project of delivering mothers a couple of weeks early? Why have you let it get so out of hand?"

"Shut up! It's not out of hand. I've got it all under control."

Then Mitch softened and smiled at Amanda. He teasingly touched her nose and gave her a pat on the butt.

"Now please, leave me alone," he said as he went back into the lounge.

He pulled out his cell phone and dialed. He listened for a moment, then said, "We have a problem. Get the message across that they need to mind their own fucking business. And use the good stuff."

CHAPTER 57

Sophie and Adam waited outside the pod while Danny had his third eye exam. When the ophthalmologist was done, he called the two of them over. In his brusque manner, he reported that Danny's eyes were getting worse.

Sophie, fearing this conversation was only going to get worse, called out to Kim. Kim saw the ophthalmologist, sized up the situation, and came over to put her arm around Sophie.

"It's all right, Sophie. I'm here."

They stood next to Danny's incubator.

"You might want to sit down, Mr. and Mrs. Young."

Adam remained standing. Sophie sat, dreading what was coming.

"I'm very concerned about your son's eyes. They're not developing as well as I had hoped. There have been some changes between his second exam and today's exam—changes that aren't good."

Sophie held her breath.

"You should be prepared for the likelihood that your son is going to have some serious vision problems."

Sophie exhaled. "We've been told by the doctors that he'll probably need to wear glasses. That's what you mean, right?"

"I don't think you understand. It's quite possible that your son could be blind."

Sophie felt dizzy. She leaned into Kim, then started to hyperventilate. Adam dropped into the chair next to her.

"Did you say blind?" Sophie squeaked out.

"It's too early to say for sure, but I think it's a very real possibility."

The doctor quickly packed up his examining equipment and left the pod, leaving the stunned parents in Kim's hands.

"How can this be happening?" exclaimed Sophie. "Our son is going to be blind?"

"That's just a worst-case scenario," Kim said, trying to be optimistic. "His eyes aren't done developing yet. They could still be okay. I've seen that happen with other babies."

Sophie and Adam looked at Kim.

"Really? Is that true?" Sophie turned to Danny, put her hands in front of his face, and moved them around quickly, watching for a reaction. He blinked.

"There! Did you see that?" Excited, she said, "He blinked! He can see my hands." She put her hands down. He blinked again. Disappointed, she added, "Or maybe he didn't see my hands at all." She turned to Adam. "Oh my God. He can't be blind. Adam, he can't be blind!"

"Sophie, we have to give it time," Kim said. "Over the next month, six months, even a year, there's time for his eyes to improve. You've just got to be patient. Plus, surgery may be an option too."

"I can't believe this. I can't fucking believe this whole nightmare," Sophie fumed.

CHAPTER 58

Adam and Sophie sat together in the parents' lounge. They talked about all the what-ifs of Danny's life. Lost in their conversation, Sophie distractedly bit her nails to the quick.

Once the conversation wound down and they had run out of things to say, Adam stood up.

"Soph, I have to go. I'm sorry, but I can't keep asking other teachers to fill in for me."

"It's okay. You go. I'm going to call Kate. I'll walk out with you."

At the hospital entrance, Adam gave Sophie a long, deep hug, then jogged off in the direction of his car. Sophie stayed outside, taking a moment to breathe in the refreshing cold air.

She went back into the lobby to call Kate. In tears, she told Kate about the eye exam. The more she talked, the harder she cried. Little kids looked at her with curiosity. Mothers looked at her with concern. Sophie retreated into a corner of the lobby. While talking with Kate, her phone buzzed. She ignored it.

"Sophie. Listen to me," Kate said. "You told me yourself that Kim said there's plenty of time for improvement. You can't give up hope. It's way too soon to know how this will turn out."

"Kate, this is horrible. First, he gets sick and needs to go back on the ventilator. Now this. The doctors talk like it's business as usual, but it's my kid they're talking about. To them, he's just another preemie, but to me, he's my son. My only child, who I love more than life itself." Her phone buzzed again. "I've read about all the complications preemies can have. So far, he's batting a thousand. When will this ever end?"

"I'm coming down."

"You don't need to do that. There's nothing you can do anyway."

"I can be there for you. I'll take a long weekend. I'll call you when I know the train schedule. It'll be Friday sometime."

Sophie's phone dinged with a voicemail. "Hold on, let me see who this is." She saw two missed texts from Adam. "Okay. Thanks, Kate. I gotta go. Adam's trying to reach me."

She hung up and quickly checked her voicemail.

Adam was in the Metro Emergency Room.

Shit, what now?

Sophie jogged to the ER. Adam sat on a gurney, holding an ice pack to his forehead. His face was scraped up, and the dark purple beginning of what was bound to become a black eye had started to show. Grateful to see him, she rushed over and hugged him. He smiled, revealing a broken tooth.

"Oh my God, what happened?"

He told her the story. He had turned down a side street to cut through to Second Avenue, where his car was parked. Caught completely off guard, he was grabbed from behind. He was able to break away and started to run.

"You couldn't outrun him?"

"I could have, if the second guy hadn't popped out from behind a parked car. They knocked me to the ground," he said, grimacing as he gently touched his forehead. "Hence the goose egg. They held my face down on the pavement, scraping it along the gritty ice and giving me the chipped tooth." Sophie winced in sympathy. "Then they rolled me over, and one planted his foot on my chest. He said if I didn't back off, you'd be next." Adam pulled Sophie closer to him. "Then he pulled out a syringe and drew up something from a blue-capped vial. I remember wondering what medication was in a blue vial. Strange what runs through your mind at times like that. Anyhow, I watched him fill a syringe. Then he plunged it into my chest."

Adam stopped talking for a moment.

"Everything went in and out of focus, then the sidewalk started spinning. I don't remember anything after that. I don't know how I even got here. I'm still groggy."

"We're going to the police right now," Sophie said, helping him off the gurney and holding on to him as he steadied himself. She found the nurse to sign discharge papers, and they left.

At the police station, Adam gave his statement. The police were perfectly nice, but not very hopeful that they would catch the two guys who had done this without a better description. The couple then returned to the emergency room to ask if they would test Adam's blood to identify the drug injected into him.

Sophie took Adam home and got him settled on the couch. With Blu cuddled up next to him, he instantly fell asleep.

She returned to the hospital emergency department to see if they'd found the drug in Adam's system yet.

"Yes, Mrs. Young. He had benzos in his system."

"Benzos?"

"Yes. Sedatives that knocked your husband out while also giving him amnesia. But he's lucky. He recovered very quickly."

"Thanks," Sophie said as she left the hospital.

She went home to see how Adam was doing. He was still on the couch but awake. He and Blu were playing tug-of-war with a chew toy. She lifted his feet up so she could sit down at the end of the couch, then lowered his feet into her lap.

"Take a look at this." She pulled out her phone. She showed Adam the picture of the edited page of her chart and explained what she'd seen in both versions of her medical record. "Do you remember seeing that when you looked through my chart?"

Adam thought. "My head's a little fuzzy right now, Soph, but I don't remember seeing it."

"Me neither. I'm sure it wasn't there. He must have added it. Any change on an electronic record automatically has the date and time of entry recorded. He added that information on the day of my discharge. He falsified my medical record."

CHAPTER 59

Friday morning, Sophie was excited to be seeing Kate again so soon. While she waited for Kate to call with an arrival time, Sophie worked on the challenge of getting Danny to drink an entire feed from his bottle. Up to this point, any milk he wasn't able to finish by mouth went in through his nasogastric tube, the narrow tube that went up through his nose and down into his stomach. Once the allotted thirty minutes of feeding time was over, Kim took over to give the rest through his tube.

Suzanne popped her head in and gave a quick wave with her sunny Southern disposition. "Mornin', y'all."

Kim waved back. "Lunch later?"

Suzanne gave her two thumbs-up.

While Sophie waited for Danny's "meal" to finish up, she asked Kim about Christy and Suzanne.

"You guys seem like pretty tight friends."

"Oh yeah. Those two are my best friends. We're like sisters."

Sophie nodded, checking her phone for a message from Kate. Kim continued talking, explaining how she and Christy worked together in the NICU and Suzanne worked both in NICU and triage with dual training in both specialties. They were all friends with Carol from triage, even though Carol was more than twenty years older. She was the mother hen of the NICU-triage sorority and mentor to many.

"But not Amanda," Kim continued. Amanda and a couple

of others tended to stick to themselves. Good team players in an emergency, but otherwise weren't terribly friendly.

"I'd have Amanda any day of the week working next to me in a code," Kim told Sophie. "But girls' night out? Not gonna happen."

Kim, Christy, and Suzanne were particularly close because they'd worked through the days of an overcrowded NICU and a triage unit so overcrowded with laboring patients they were forced to labor in the hallways. There was nothing like the battlegrounds of intensive care and triage to bond friends together.

Still waiting for Kim to finish up with Danny, Sophie called Kate to find out what train she was taking. Her call went straight to voicemail. *She must be on her phone.*

When Kim had finished feeding Danny, she handed him back to Sophie and got ready to go to lunch. Suzanne and Christy stood by the pod doorway waiting for Kim to grab her stuff.

"Hey, Sophie," Christy called over. "Thanks for the amazing fruit platter. Where'd it come from?"

Before she could answer, Kim pulled the two nurses over closer to where Sophie sat. She explained Sophie and Adam's suspicions about Dr. Wagner. Immediately, she had Christy's and Suzanne's attention. "They tried to get a video of him, but it didn't work. Wrong patient."

The threesome, with their heads together, spoke quietly so only Sophie could hear.

"They're looking for someone who can blend in with triage," whispered Kim. She looked at Suzanne. "*If*, and I mean if—because, right now, this is only a theory—but *if* you see Dr. Wagner working with a mother in preterm labor, especially before thirty-four weeks, they're wondering if you could video him with that patient."

She paused to let that sink in.

"Suzanne, you're in there more than Christy or me. But this is totally up to you, no pressure."

"I'll do it," said Suzanne in her Southern drawl. "If videoing Dr. Wagner and his pocketful of Pitocin will atone for my part in the breech delivery, then I'll do it."

It was five in the afternoon, and Sophie still had no word from Kate. There was no voicemail, no missed calls, no texts, not even an email. She called Kate's husband, Rick. No answer there either. *Maybe they're both on their way down here together. But why aren't they answering their phones?*

She called Adam. "Where do you think they are? Kate always has her phone with her. I don't get it."

"I'm sure they're fine. I bet she calls tomorrow."

Saturday morning came, and still no word. This was not like Kate. Sophie called the one neighbor she had met when Kate and Rick first moved to Boston. Kate's car was in the driveway, but the neighbor hadn't seen either one of them. Sophie asked if he could please go and knock on the door.

The neighbor carried his phone with him over next door. Sophie heard him knock, then knock again louder. There was no answer. It was ten o'clock in the morning. Sophie's stomach was in knots; she could no longer make excuses for Kate's silence.

"Please call me if you see any sign of either one of them."

Later Saturday night, her phone rang.

"Sophie, I'm so sorry!" Kate cried. "I can't believe I forgot to call you. The fertility clinic needed Rick and me here in town this weekend. The time is right, my eggs are hot, and they couldn't wait until Monday. I am so sorry. I'll make it up to you, I promise."

Relieved to hear from her sister, Sophie laughed. "Hot eggs?"

JULIE HATCH

Two days later, Sophie got a text from Suzanne: *I worked a double yesterday, and I think this is what you're looking for ;)* Another ding followed immediately, with a video. She and Adam watched the twenty-minute recording on her iPhone.

It was 8:05 p.m. according to the recording. There was a steady buzz of activity and a constant hum of monitors and equipment in the background. Suzanne had just discharged a patient and now had her attention on Dr. Wagner.

Behind Dr. Wagner, the phone camera moved around erratically as Suzanne busied herself with putting fresh sheets on an empty gurney, then getting the phone lined up in the direction of Dr. Wagner and his patient. Suzanne held it at waist level. The camera zoomed in on Dr. Wagner talking with his laboring patient. Amanda was the nurse assigned to the patient. The video showed Amanda putting an IV into the patient's left hand, assuring her everything would be fine.

Adam was pleased with how clearly the sound came through. Even though there was a lot of other triage noise on the recording, they could still make out most of what Amanda said to the patient.

Dr. Wagner came into view and asked the patient how she was feeling. Adam and Sophie couldn't make out the woman's response.

"I understand. There's no need for you to feel scared." He pulled a pink-capped vial from his pocket and injected it into the patient's IV. "This'll help." He held her hand for a moment.

Within seconds, the woman became calmer. Dr. Wagner picked up his pen and the patient's chart as he continued talking to her, asking the typical questions. Yes, she was thirty weeks, and this was her first baby. Perfectly healthy pregnancy. All ultrasounds and blood work were normal, indicating a completely healthy little girl. Dr. Wagner told the patient that he'd give her something to stop her contractions and then send her home.

The video perfectly captured Dr. Wagner's hand on the patient's IV. The camera panned up his arm and to his face so that there was no question whose hand it was. Dr. Wagner pulled a vial out of his pocket. It had a tan cap.

Adam and Sophie hoped this was the real medication, not a switch of the colored caps. Sophie caught herself. She would never actually wish for someone to deliver a preterm baby. She just wanted proof to nail Dr. Wagner. If it was the medication that they thought it was, it wasn't going to do anything to stop the woman's labor.

Dr. Wagner flipped the cap off, inserted a needle with a syringe, withdrew the medication, then injected it into the IV line. He followed this with a very small dose of the pink-capped medicine. He told Amanda to keep an eye on the patient and walked out of the camera's view. The video stayed on the patient as she started to doze off, hand on her belly. The fetal monitor confirmed that the baby was doing well.

"What if it's not even Pitocin?" said Adam. "Shit."

"Sshhh!"

Within seconds, the camera caught the patient's eyes flying open as she lifted her head off the pillow. She yelled out and grabbed her belly. Amanda turned to the patient, asking if she was okay. What was wrong? The patient was panting. Her anxious look had grown to near terror. Then she became racked with another intense contraction. Her face turned beet red as she started to push.

She grabbed Amanda's wrist. "Help me!"

"Dr. Wagner, can you come over here, please?"

It was all captured on video. People started to crowd around the patient's bed, and the view from the phone was blocked, then the video shut off.

Sophie's phone dinged. It was from Suzanne. *She delivered ten minutes later.*

They had all the evidence they needed.

CHAPTER 60

Sophie punched WMI's address into her phone. She had just gotten off the phone with Madeline, who hadn't received the video that Sophie sent. Sophie checked to see that Adam had received it. He had, and he'd downloaded it onto their home computer.

"Sophie, you could be right," Madeline had said. "I'm beginning to get a picture of Dr. Wagner and his numbers in triage. His number of admissions to the NICU are out of balance compared to the other OB docs. The NICU has so many admissions and discharges in one week, even in just one day sometimes, you'd have to really be paying attention to pick up on it. Rita Gonsalves must be involved. She's the one who keeps track of these statistics, and she never said a word to me. As the utilization reviewer for the NICU, she should know exactly what's going on. I'm afraid that I really dropped the ball. Someone should have been overseeing her more closely, and that someone was me."

"Maybe Rita just didn't realize," Sophie replied. "Anyhow, I wish the numbers weren't true, Ms. Cross, but I am glad that someone is finally paying attention."

When Sophie hung up from Madeline, she looked at her sent files and saw the video hadn't gone through. She tapped Send again.

With WMI's Manhattan address pinned on her phone, Sophie began walking. The twenty-plus blocks she had to go would give her plenty of time to think. She put her earbuds in, clicked on Pandora, and cranked up the Foo Fighters. Twenty minutes later she stood at the busy intersection of Forty-Second and Fifth, waiting to cross. As soon as she stepped off the curb, she felt someone grab her jacket from behind, yanking her back up onto the curb. She stumbled, then caught her balance. Her earbuds fell out and landed in a pile of snow. She reeled around to see who had grabbed her like that. As she turned, a car veered toward her. She barely noticed the cold slush that sprayed her legs seconds before she fell to the ground in excruciating pain. The car had bumped her ankle, hard, then blown on by.

Sophie heard a loud thump in front of her. She looked up to see the woman who had been walking just ahead of her catapult into the air and land on her back in the middle of the street. The car sped off as people rushed to help the woman. A crowd swarmed around her, which blocked both car and pedestrian traffic.

"Someone call 911!"

"Give her room!"

"Did anyone get the license plate?"

A cop showed up and was trying to make room for the injured woman while clearing the intersection.

Sophie pulled herself up. "I'm sorry," she heard a man's voice behind her say. He was holding out his hand in assistance. "I didn't mean to grab you so hard. But that car nearly killed you. I was just trying to pull you back to safety." He handed her one of her gloves, which had landed in the snow.

"Thank you" was all that Sophie could muster at the moment. She was in a bit of shock. She could stand on one leg, but the other one throbbed when she put any weight on it. She struggled to push her way through the crowd to get a look at the woman who had taken the hit. She lay on her side with her legs pulled up in a fetal position. She moaned in pain.

"Can I do something to help?" Sophie asked the man standing over the woman.

The man shook his head. He held up his phone. "I'm on with 911 right now. An ambulance is two minutes away."

The crowd started to disperse.

Sophie found her dropped phone lying at the bottom of a puddle. People stepped on it as they trudged through the wet slush. In between legs and feet bumping into her, she leaned down and grabbed her phone, then stood up to hail a cab. Sitting in the back of the cab, she couldn't stop shaking.

That car had been meant for her.

Sophie limped into the hospital, suspicious of anybody who looked at her the wrong way. She went to triage, who sent her to the main hospital emergency room. The doctor there ordered X-rays and Percocet.

When the results were back, she called Sophie into her office.

"The good news is the X-rays showed nothing is broken. The bad news is that soft tissue injuries, like your ankle, are more painful and take longer to heal."

"Great," Sophie groaned.

"Stay off of it as much as possible," the ER doctor told her. She gave her crutches and a boot to support her ankle. "Keep it up, and ice it for the next twenty-four hours. Follow up with an orthopedic doc in a few days."

On her way out of the ER, Sophie allowed herself a slight smile. At least they still had the video, safely stored at home on their computer.

Sophie went straight to the chapel. She was alone. As the tension about what had just happened began to ease, she was left feeling jumpy. She knew in her gut that she had been the intended target and that the poor woman in front of her was an innocent victim. If she went to the police, they'd think she was just another paranoid New York City nut.

Sitting with her wet, trampled phone in her hands, she

replayed the incident over in her head, trying to recall any details. She hadn't seen the driver through the tinted window, and it all happened too fast for her to get a license plate number. She sighed. How had she gotten mixed up in all this anyway? She just wanted to pretend nothing was wrong with Metro Hospital. Maybe she and Adam should mind their own business and just wait for Danny's discharge. But she couldn't just ignore everything. She wasn't going to simply watch and wait. She had to find out more. She had to find a way to end the madness.

CHAPTER 61

The next day brought another preterm labor into triage. Mitch delivered the baby, who was born to a heroin-addicted mother, seven weeks early. Within twenty-four hours, the baby began to withdraw from the opiate. The nurses called Mitch into the nursery and made him stay and watch as the inconsolable baby jittered and shook. Her cry was a high-pitched screech.

"I swear that cry is going to peel the paint off the nursery walls," one of the nurses said.

The nurses tried everything, but nothing helped. She didn't want to be held, but she didn't want to be put down. She wouldn't eat, yet she sucked like mad on her pacifier. Nothing soothed her. The only thing to do was to give her the opiates her body was withdrawing from.

One of the attending neonatologists started her on morphine. Treating the baby's withdrawal with small doses of opiates, then slowly weaning her off, would take time—weeks of time.

Mitch felt bad for the suffering that the baby was enduring, but it was going to happen eventually—whether the baby was born now or six weeks from now. Everyone knew watching a baby go through opiate withdrawal sucked but was unavoidable.

Amanda asked, "Mitch, why in the world did you choose to deliver this one early?"

"I did the right thing by getting her out of that toxic, drug-infested environment. I did the baby a favor."

Amanda walked away, shaking her head.

When Mitch was paged again to the tower of terror, he was surprised to be met not by Charlie but by Madeline Cross, chief operating officer.

"Mitch, do you think you're playing God?"

"Nice to see you too," replied Mitch.

"I don't think this meeting calls for formalities. What possessed you to deliver that thirty-three-week drug-addicted baby? Do you really think it was your right to decide whether the baby was better off out here in the world seven weeks early and withdrawing instead of staying inside her mother?"

"I absolutely believe it was the right thing to do. The baby was wasting away in that uterus."

Madeline sighed. "Just who do you think you are to make a decision like that?"

Mitch stared her down.

"Watch your step, Mitch. People are paying attention."

Mitch took the stairs down two at a time. Stopping on the landing between two of the floors, he made a call. He spoke briefly with the person on the other end, then continued down to the first floor.

CHAPTER 62

It was after midnight, and Sophie couldn't sleep. She had learned the NICU also never slept. It was as busy at eleven at night as it was at eleven in the morning. She got up and headed to the hall with the vending machines. She was craving a Milky Way. She heard footsteps coming toward her from behind. She spun around. The person was backlit, making it difficult for her to see who it was. She turned back and started toward the NICU.

"Sophie."

"Dr. Sheldon! Jesus, why are you sneaking up on me like that?"

"I couldn't sleep either, and I wanted to talk. About the BrainHealth study Danny is in."

"Can't it wait until the morning?"

"No." He guided her out from under the fluorescent lighting. "I'm taking Danny out of the study."

"Why?" She stood against the wall next to the vending machines. Dr. Sheldon was standing so close to her. She moved away a step.

"Because I have all the numbers I need. I have enough data to present to the FDA and for publication. There's no need to keep him in the study. He'll stay on caffeine until he's closer to discharge. After that, you and your pediatrician can decide whether to keep him on it."

"What do the results show?"

"Equivocal. Might help, might not. A little disappointing,

to be honest. I still need to follow up on the babies that enrolled initially, follow them over the next couple of years to see whether their development is better than those who stopped taking it."

"Is that all you wanted to tell me?"

"No, I also wanted to say something about my other project, the one on X-linked diseases."

"Yes . . ."

"Sophie, it's not a big deal."

"Oh really."

He nodded.

"Dr. Sheldon, why are we talking about this now?"

"Because it's important that you understand. You need to know that all I'm doing in the study is tagging the male babies who are positive for the defect. That's it. I'm doing nothing else to them. I'm simply identifying the ones who are an insurance risk for HHI."

"But, Dr. Sheldon, that is so wrong."

"I know you don't agree with it, but it's the way things work. The truth of the matter is if I don't do it, someone else will. I can't fix the system, but I can play along. And the bottom line is, I'm not harming the babies, not in the least. I'm just giving insurance companies information that they would eventually get anyway." He held Sophie's gaze.

She swallowed hard. "Dr. Sheldon, you're only one step away from crossing the line—the line where the insurance companies have the power to decide whether to provide health insurance to these kids or not. How does that, as you say, eradicate the disease?"

He gently held her by the arm. "The reality is, Sophie, that health insurance companies, along with the pharmaceutical companies, are running this country. It's happening right under our noses, and nobody's going to realize the extent of it until it's too late."

"But why do you have to be such an active participant?"

He studied her, not saying a word.

She backed up a step. "What?"

"I want you to see another project I'm working on. Forget HHI and genetic illnesses. I've got something that's going to blow everybody's mind. It's a totally new advancement in neonatology. Mitch and I started it together. And he may have been the brains behind it initially, but he blew it. So now it's my turn."

"What are you talking about?"

"The New NICU. It's a promise for the future of babies. I've got WMI's backing, which is important. I don't need Mitch, and I can't trust him anyway. This is too big a deal." He stopped. "Seriously, you should come check it out someday." He turned to walk away. "I'll tell Rihanna you say hi."

Sophie bought her candy bar and walked to the parents' lounge. She was still trying to figure out what Dr. Sheldon had been talking about as she drifted off to sleep.

CHAPTER 63

Adam picked Sophie up outside the triage entrance and handed her a new phone. They were headed home for a long-overdue night together. The air had warmed up considerably. The snow that remained on the ground had softened. A low level of fog forced Adam to drive extra cautiously. Blu greeted them at the door, excited and happy to see them.

Sophie laughed with delight. "Blu! I've missed you, buddy." She burrowed her face into the fur on his neck.

He jumped up and licked their faces—first Sophie, then Adam, then back to Sophie. He jumped down and bolted out the open door to relieve himself.

Adam poured some wine and lit some candles. Sophie let Blu in and got down on the floor to give him a belly scratch. With half the bottle of wine gone and Blu settled on his doggie bed, Sophie and Adam went up to bed.

Some hours later, Sophie awoke to the sound of Blu barking. The front door had blown open, and a small pile of snow was on the threshold. Blu was frantically barking. Sophie called for him from the doorway.

"Come here, buddy! Blu, come here! I've got a treat," she cajoled. He ignored her and kept barking. His bark turned into a growl. Then he started snarling, something Sophie had never heard from him. She strained to see through the darkness but was only able to make out a figure standing at the edge of the yard. She heard a thud, then a yelp. Blu went quiet.

"Blu!"

She ran to him through the snow, barefoot and with a throbbing ankle. She heard footsteps running away across their yard, then down the street. Blu lay in the snow, whimpering.

She yelled for Adam, who was already out the door.

"What the . . . ?" he said.

"There was a guy! He ran that way!"

Adam chased after him. Sophie heard squealing tires and a car racing off farther down the street. She cradled Blu's head in her lap. There was blood coming from his mouth. "What happened, buddy?"

She noticed a small cardboard box on the ground next to him. She picked it up and helped Blu stand up. He slowly got to his feet and, with his tail between his legs, lumbered toward the house. He stopped and lifted his leg, yelping as he relieved himself.

Sophie went into the house, her frigid feet aching, and tossed the box on the couch.

Adam ran in. "I couldn't catch him."

"Could you see anything? Was he wearing a brown parka?" Sophie asked.

"He might have been, but I can't say for sure."

They checked Blu over from head to toe. His mouth had stopped bleeding, leaving a layer of bloody fur caked around his muzzle. He was in pain, there was no denying that, but he didn't appear to have any broken bones, and other than his mouth, no cuts. They gave him some water and tried to get him comfortable on his bed.

Comfort was not going to be part of Blu's night, which meant sleep wasn't going to be part of what remained of Sophie and Adam's night. Blu whined to go outside, cried when he peed, then came back in. A half hour later, they went through the same thing. This went on through the night.

In the morning, they took him to the vet. After listening to their story, examining Blu, and running some blood tests, the vet told them Blu would be okay. He'd been kicked—kicked hard in his kidneys. Relieved, Sophie and Adam thanked the vet.

"Here's some medication for his pain. Give him plenty of water. He should be fine in a day or two, and if he's not, bring him back. Who did this?"

Sophie and Adam shrugged. "No idea."

"Well, if you ever find the person, they should be arrested."

On the way home, sleep-deprived Sophie and Adam went over what had happened.

"Did you see anything else?" Adam asked Sophie.

"Not a thing. Nobody else was out. It was the middle of the night, not even any cars driving by. Nothing. But I know he was running from our yard."

Adam concentrated on the road.

"Should we go to the police?" Sophie asked. "Report this and maybe ask them to keep an eye on our house?"

"Yeah, I think we should."

When they got home, they helped Blu inside and gave him some of the pain medicine. Sophie got him settled on his dog bed with his favorite blankets.

Adam picked the cardboard box up from the pile of blankets and towels they had used on Blu the night before. "Soph, did you look at what was in the box?"

Inside was a cardboard name placard—the one that hung at the end of Danny's incubator in the NICU. Adam read out loud: "Daniel Fitzgerald Young."

Sophie ran to the bathroom and threw up. When she came back to the living room, she was trembling. She grabbed the card from Adam.

She screamed, looking up at the ceiling. "Who are you? What the hell do you want?"

CHAPTER 64

Wednesday, February 29, was a day that Sophie would never forget. Walking back from spending the night in the parents' lounge, she looked through the windows of Pod C. Three nurses stood over Danny's incubator examining his hands and feet. Sophie had seen this before when Kim was looking for a place to start an IV. But three nurses? Not a good sign. Sophie limped over as quickly as she could. She'd gotten rid of the crutches, but her ankle was far from healed.

"What's going on?"

Kim pulled her aside and told her that Danny was okay but needed a little more oxygen than normal. She explained that he was anemic; his red blood count was low. It was not unusual in NICU babies. Between all the blood tests they drew and the normal physiologic drop in every baby's hemoglobin at about this age, it was to be expected. In Danny's case, though, his anemia was bad enough to cause problems with his oxygen level.

"Basically, Sophie, he needs a blood transfusion."

"A blood transfusion?" Sophie repeated, not fully grasping what Kim was saying.

Kim nodded.

"Okay." Sophie tried to speed up her mental processing. "I'll give him my blood. I don't want him to get some stranger's blood."

"Unfortunately, you can't do that. It'll take too long. It takes days for direct donation, and Danny can't wait days."

"Isn't there something I can do?"

"Not really, Sophie, other than try not to worry. Blood these days is super safe. It's screened for everything—HIV, hepatitis, West Nile, you name it. He'll be fine."

Sophie was skeptical but had little choice given Danny's need for more oxygen. Kim had been gradually dialing up the oxygen concentration just in the last fifteen minutes. She agreed to the transfusion, then called and left a message on Adam's voicemail.

There was another baby in the pod who also needed a transfusion. Sophie saw the same thing happening with that baby—nurses searching for IV sites on the baby's feet and hands, and one of the nurses discussing it with the parents.

The transfusions on both babies took four hours—a slow infusion of only a fraction of a unit of blood. Kim and the other nurse monitored their patients closely, initially checking their vital signs every fifteen minutes.

"We do this," Kim explained to Sophie, "to make sure Danny doesn't have an allergic reaction. But don't worry, he's handling it fine."

Both babies did well during their transfusions.

Until the following day.

Danny started having frequent episodes of apnea. He stopped breathing, causing his alarm to go off, and either Sophie or Kim, or any nurse who was nearby, would give him a firm pat on the back to remind him to breathe. These episodes began happening every ten minutes. Within an hour, his apnea alarms were going off every two to three minutes.

Frustrated and worried, Sophie sat at her baby's incubator, biting her nails. "I thought the blood was supposed to make him better, not worse," Sophie snapped at Kim.

Over the next two hours, Danny needed increasing amounts of oxygen to keep his oxygen levels up, until finally the medical team decided to put him back on the ventilator.

Sophie called Adam. "You've got to get here now. Danny's taken a turn for the worse."

"I'm on my way."

Sophie fumed. She was livid at Kim.

"Is this what the blood did to him? Made him worse? I never should have agreed to the transfusion." She looked around the pod. "And why is that other baby doing so great?" She pointed in the direction of the other baby. "Did he get the same blood?"

"I don't know." Kim tried to comfort Sophie, but all that came out was "I don't know why Danny is doing this. And the doctors don't understand either."

"Maybe it's an allergic reaction? Did anybody think of that?"

"It's not. That would have happened while he was getting the blood, not now," Kim patiently explained.

Sophie took a deep breath in and blew it out hard. "I'm sorry, Kim. I shouldn't be mad at you. It's just . . . just so horrible."

The doctors ran tests on Danny. They ran cultures on his blood, his urine, his spinal fluid. They poked him with needles, examined him from head to toe, and still were unable to come up with a reason why he wasn't getting better.

The other baby showed signs that the blood had helped him. But not Danny. Somehow, the blood had made him worse.

CHAPTER 65

Dr. Sheldon watched Danny's monitors as the numbers drifted down—blood pressure, oxygen saturation, heart rate. It had been thirty-six hours since he'd received the blood transfusion.

"Kim, put him on an open warmer. We need full access. Start another IV and a dopamine drip to help with his blood pressure. We need to get his blood pressure up. Get some help over here."

Kim quickly pulled the supplies together for a dopamine drip and called for extra help. Christy appeared, and the two of them carried out Dr. Sheldon's orders. There were nurses with Danny every minute. Dr. Sheldon and Dr. Morrison took shifts relieving each other, never leaving the pod for more than a couple of minutes. For a while, Danny stabilized, but he still needed a lot of support to keep him alive.

Adam and Sophie sat next to Danny's incubator with their eyes glued to his monitors. They watched his blood pressure drop, then come up, then drop again.

"Is the blood pressure medicine even working?" Sophie demanded.

Kim, who was busy drawing up more meds, checking orders, sending off blood gases to the lab, checking vital signs, and adjusting ventilator settings, answered, "Yes, without it his blood pressure would tank."

His oxygenation monitor shrieked its alarm, and Kim hurried over to turn the oxygen dial, giving Danny close to 100 percent.

She studied the numbers on the monitors and called Dr. Sheldon over.

"His color looks like shit," Dr. Sheldon said. "He's all mottled. His heart can't do the work." Sheldon pulled out his stethoscope and listened to Danny's chest.

Kim called for respiratory therapy to come over and help her adjust the ventilator. "His O2 sats are low, and he's on a hundred percent oxygen."

The therapist adjusted different nobs on the ventilator, watching and waiting for his oxygen levels to improve.

"Sheldon, he's not peeing," Kim said. "I've got a catheter in him, and there's nothing."

"His whole body is shutting down," Sheldon muttered to himself. "Fuck."

Dr. Sheldon left and stood just outside the pod, consulting with a group of doctors. Sophie and Adam could see the drawn looks on their faces and hear the muted tones of their voices.

A lab tech came into the pod searching for Kim. Kim studied the piece of paper and shook her head. Something wasn't right. Kim hurried to Dr. Sheldon, who was standing outside the pod with Dr. Morrison.

The three of them spoke together, then Dr. Sheldon walked slowly over to Sophie and Adam.

In a somber tone, Dr. Sheldon explained that something very strange had happened with Danny's blood transfusion. The blood that he had received was infected with Babesia—a rare Lyme disease–related parasite.

Adam's and Sophie's jaws dropped at the same time.

"What are you saying?" Adam asked. "Are you telling us that Danny's transfusion had infected blood, after reassuring us that donated blood is screened for everything?" He was incredulous. "How can this happen? You're telling us the blood was contaminated?"

"How's the other baby doing?" Sophie asked.

"He's fine."

"I knew I shouldn't have agreed to it. I should have made them wait until I could give my blood," said Sophie.

"Explain to me how this is possible!" demanded Adam.

Dr. Sheldon stood with Kim. "He's got three IV sites, with two lines running into each. We need to start another blood pressure medication, and he needs more fluids. Can you piggyback those to the IVs he's already got going in?"

Kim nodded.

"And we'll increase his morphine and fentanyl." Dr. Sheldon turned to Sophie and Adam to explain that Danny was going on a different kind of ventilator—a jet ventilator—and they didn't want him fighting it.

Sophie and Adam moved out of the way as more people and equipment crowded around Danny's warmer.

"I can't even believe this," Sophie said, clutching Adam's hand. "We had just started talking about discharge plans. Adam, I am so scared."

He held her tight. "I know, babe, me too."

Respiratory therapy brought in a new ventilator that Sophie had never seen. When it was hooked up to Danny and turned on, it did indeed sound like the engine of a 747, though not quite as loud.

Kim couldn't stop to talk. She wouldn't take her attention off Danny for one second. Christy was assigned to work with Kim. His tenuous condition required constant adjustments to equipment and medications. Sophie and Adam held each other, backs against the wall, knowing, with a sick feeling, that there was nothing they could do to help their son.

As more people came to help, Adam and Sophie were pushed farther away from the warmer until they were so far back they could no longer see their baby through the crowd of doctors and nurses. They left the pod to stand outside the door, looking in, observers of their own son's deterioration.

Dr. Sheldon came out to talk with them. "You need to know that the next twenty-four hours are critical." He spoke softly, and his eyes were warm with compassion. "We are hoping to see an improvement in that time. He's on three different antibiotics to fight his infection. They're the strongest we have, and if these don't work, I don't know what else there is. While we wait for the meds to work, we'll give him whatever he needs to keep him alive. Maximum ventilation and blood pressure support—those are the two most important things."

He continued, "I know this is a lot for you guys. It's so damn hard to watch a baby get this sick. But I wanted to level with you about the infected blood, because I don't believe in keeping information from parents. That just leads to more problems later. I want you to trust that we're doing everything we can for Danny. How that blood got contaminated, I have no idea, but we'll find out, I promise. Meanwhile, I want you two to hold on to each other and hold on to the belief that he'll be okay."

He was called back into the pod.

The next shift started with two nurses to relieve Kim and Christy for the night. Sophie and Adam dozed in chairs outside the pod, getting up every so often to check on Danny. Through the night, they saw no change. Sophie felt a glimmer of hope that at least he wasn't getting worse. She knew that if he got worse, there was nothing more the doctors could do.

CHAPTER 66

It turned out, there *was* more that could be done. By the next morning, Danny's condition had gotten worse. His oxygen levels were desaturating despite maximal ventilator support. His blood pressure had stopped responding to the medications he was on. A third blood pressure medication was added. Multiple bags hung off the IV poles—plasma, platelets, clear IV fluid, yellow IV fluid. Sophie counted nine IV lines running into the three IV sites in his arms and feet. There was a single line placed on the inside of his right wrist: an arterial line for frequent blood draws and accurate oxygenation readings, Kim explained.

"Now it's just a matter of time for his blood pressure to respond."

At twenty-four hours, there was no improvement.

"Dr. Sheldon, what does this mean?" Sophie asked. "You said he should be turning the corner by now. What's wrong with him?"

Dr. Sheldon answered, "We just have to wait."

At forty-eight hours, things were bleak. The medication drips and ventilator settings only went up as Danny's infected body demanded more support to stay alive. One minute his blood pressure started to come up; the next minute it dropped. Sophie and Adam stood vigil over Danny, refusing to leave his side, unable to speak the words *what if . . . ?*

"Would you two *please* go lie down somewhere?" Kim said. "You're both walking zombies. I promise I will get you as soon as there's a change."

"No way," they said at the same time.

"You haven't had anything to eat in almost three days. You can't subsist forever on coffee, you know. I'll give you vouchers for food in the cafeteria." Kim handed them a handful of vouchers, which remained untouched on the counter next to Danny's warmer.

Sophie called Kate and told her about Danny's situation. "Kate, I don't know if he's going to make it. I honestly don't know, and it's killing me," she said through her tears.

"I'll get the next train out of Boston."

"No, not yet. You won't be allowed to come in and see him anyway. He's too sick. I'll keep you posted. Just please pray for him."

"You know I will. I'll call you tomorrow. I love you."

At seventy-two hours, Danny was no better, but he was hanging on. The morning rounds discussion on Danny lasted for over an hour. Doctors, nurses, respiratory therapists, and pharmacists all were involved.

Softly, Adam said, "Sophie, remember I told you I can tell when the doctors think a baby is circling the toilet bowl of death? Well, I think that could be our case now." His voice was thick with emotion.

They held each other's hands, desperately clinging to each other and to the hope that something would change. Tears streamed down their faces. Their son was dying.

The one thing Sophie refused to let go of was hope, and she and Adam held tightly to it. Just as Kim had said to Sophie weeks ago, hope is what prevails in the NICU. Eighteen hours later and nearly four days after the blood transfusion, Danny's blood pressure rose and stayed there. Kim stopped one of the blood pressure medications. A small amount of urine came out of his catheter. His color started to improve as his heart started to recover. They switched him from the jet ventilator to the regular ventilator, and his oxygen levels stabilized. He remained on the antibiotics.

Nine days after the blood transfusion, Danny was off the ventilator, and only two IV lines remained. Sophie felt a collective sigh of relief from everybody who had worked so hard to keep Danny alive.

Sophie and Adam's prayers had been answered.

CHAPTER 67

Once Danny had turned the corner and was safely on his way to recovery, Sophie wanted to try again to get him transferred out. She spoke with Dr. Morrison, but her request went nowhere. She spoke with Jody, their social worker, who told her she'd see what she could do.

Days went by, and there was no progress toward getting Danny transferred. She resigned herself to standing guard over Danny for the rest of their time until he was discharged. At least Kim was there for help and support. That was worth a lot.

Sophie and Adam went to the cafeteria to cash in some of the food vouchers Kim had given them. In the corner were Dr. Sheldon and Dr. Wagner, heads close together, deep in conversation. There was a stack of clean napkins in front of Dr. Sheldon, and a scattering of napkins with writing on them spread across the table in front of Dr. Wagner. He was scribbling on the napkins as he and Dr. Sheldon talked.

Sophie and Adam walked past, unnoticed.

"Danny was just a parasite away from dying," Sophie said, picking at her sandwich. "It doesn't make sense. Why was he the only one affected?"

They looked over at Dr. Sheldon and Dr. Wagner, whose conversation was getting heated.

"A lot around here doesn't make sense anymore," Adam

replied. "Why was there contaminated blood in the blood bank, and how did it come to land in Danny's transfusion?"

Sophie nodded toward Dr. Wagner.

"No, it couldn't be," Adam said. "He wouldn't go that far . . ."

"I don't think that anything is too extreme for players like Dr. Wagner. He'll do anything to preserve his reputation. He's afraid of us calling him out. This was the worst threat he could possibly make—Danny's life."

Sophie and Adam turned again to the rising voices coming from the doctors' table. Dr. Sheldon was half leaning across the table, his face two inches away from Dr. Wagner's and turning beet red. Dr. Wagner stood up, knocking over his chair, and walked out. Dr. Sheldon remained alone at the littered table. After a few moments, he collected the napkins scattered across the table, stuffed them in his pocket, and left.

"I wonder what that was all about," Adam said.

As Sophie and Adam walked by the table, there was still a small mess of napkins left behind. They had numbers and calculations and dates scribbled on them. On one of the torn napkins, Sophie read: —*ndling project.*

CHAPTER 68

Mitch stood to the side of the hall talking into his phone, out of the way of the cafeteria traffic and hospital staff.

"What the hell were you thinking, Tommy? I gave you explicit instructions never to do *anything* unless I tell you to. And I *never* told you to go anywhere near the blood bank. What the fuck?"

Mitch listened to Tommy on the other end.

"Shut up. Just shut up!" he screamed into the phone. Now people turned to look. Mitch didn't care. "You're done, Tommy. We're through. Don't contact me again. In fact, why don't you just leave town for a while. I don't want to see your ugly face anywhere near me."

Mitch punched the red button on his phone , ending the call. He squeezed his phone until it made a cracking sound, then with great restraint calmly put it in his shirt pocket. Taking a moment to collect himself, he pulled his lab coat together and buttoned the middle button as he strode away.

CHAPTER 69

Monday, Kim wasn't at work. She hadn't returned from her weekend off. She didn't show up again the next day, or the next. Sophie asked the other nurses if everything was okay with Kim. Nobody seemed to know anything other than she had called in sick. Christy and Suzanne were concerned. They all agreed it wasn't like Kim to be out so many days in a row.

Sophie called Rihanna and asked if Sheldon could find anything out about Kim and why she hadn't been to work. As soon as Sophie hung up the phone, Amanda walked by the pod. Sophie called out and waved her over.

"Do you have any idea where Kim is? She hasn't been at work for the past few days."

"Why would I know where Kim is?" Amanda looked confused.

Sophie grabbed Amanda's arm. "What do you know about Kim?" she asked again through clenched teeth. "Where the hell is she?"

Amanda looked at her like she was crazy. "I don't know." She shook her arm free from Sophie's grip. "Really, I have no idea."

Sophie's phone rang, giving Amanda a chance to escape.

"Sophie, are you sitting down?" It was Rihanna. "Kim was in a terrible car accident. She went off the road while she was driving the Jersey Turnpike. They took her to the closest hospital, stabilized her, then transported her to a hospital in Philadelphia, where her parents live. It sounds bad."

Sophie slumped into the chair, deflated. What the hell happened? As she processed this piece of news, a little flag went up in her head. Her intuition was yelling at her to pay attention. She was certain there was a lot more to the story. Why did Dr. Wagner have to bring Kim into this? Rage burned inside her. *This is getting out of control.*

CHAPTER 70

Madeline called Mitch to her office. She explained that she had asked Rita for her utilization review reports on NICU admissions over the past six months. Mitch searched in his pocket for a paper clip. He didn't like where this was going. He remained standing in front of her desk.

"Mitchell, I saw nothing of concern in this report."

He breathed a sigh of relief.

"At least initially. I think you should take a little vacation, a leave, if you will, until we get this all sorted out."

"Get what all sorted out?"

"I've made an appointment to meet with the CEO of Metro General to review the NICU numbers, triage numbers, and your deliveries specifically."

"Madeline, I'm just doing my job. Administration likes it when patient numbers are up, especially in the NICU. And I'm here to deliver for them." Mitch smirked. "No pun intended."

Madeline frowned at him.

"Seriously, isn't that what we're supposed to be doing, Madeline? Finding revenue for the hospital? That's what all our meetings are about. Revenue."

"Not through artificial means. That's what has been brought to my attention and what I'm investigating. I think you should plan on at least two weeks. Maybe more, depending on how things unfold, and depending on whether we can stop this runaway train that you've put into motion."

"Sure, two weeks off sounds great to me." He shut the door behind him with a bang. *Who told her to look at my numbers?*

He knocked on Charlie Buckley's door and asked to come in. Once he told him what had just transpired with Madeline Cross, Charlie called Rita to join them.

"What are we going to do for the next two weeks, Mitch? What's going to happen to our numbers?" a panicky Rita asked. "What am I supposed to do when the NICU numbers drop off?"

"Relax, Rita," said Charlie.

Mitch knew that Charlie had Rita under control. She collected numbers, and when the numbers fell, she reported them to Charlie. That was her job. Mitch also knew how proud Rita was to carry her supervisor title. As long as she kept track of the numbers, Mitch and Charlie were happy to indulge her in whatever title she wanted.

On his way down the hall, Mitch paged Amanda and asked her to meet him in the hospital lobby. He explained to her that he was taking a break—he wouldn't be at work for a couple of weeks.

Amanda was at first surprised, then suspicious. "Why? Where are you going? I'll come with you—I've got a little vacation time coming to me."

Mitch grumbled, "I'm not going anywhere. I'm staying in the city." As he thought about it, he didn't want Amanda to know that he was under suspicion. "We can enjoy some of this time together. I'll call you tomorrow, and we'll plan a night out. But, right now, you have to take over for me. Charlie and Rita are counting on it."

"No problem."

Mitch smiled. "That's my girl."

Amanda kissed Mitch, then turned to go back to triage. Mitch walked through the hospital doors, out into the noise and bustle of the city. He was forced out, told to leave the place where he was happiest—where he was in control and where all problems had a solution. The hospital was a place of safety and security for him. And, he admitted, a place that fed his ego. How did this happen? Why was he, of all people, the one told to take a leave?

CHAPTER 71

Mitch and Amanda had made a date for dinner in one of the fancy new restaurants near his apartment. As he sat at the bar waiting for her, he considered the night ahead. It was their first real date. Thinking back, the last real date he had been on was when he was single and chasing after the woman who became his wife.

Amanda walked in, looking sexy in a short black skirt, black stilettos, and a tight green sweater that brought out the green in her gray-green eyes. Her hair, normally pulled back in a limp ponytail, was down, freshly shampooed and blown dry, giving it some bounce as it fell to her shoulders. *Wow*, thought Mitch. He smiled as he watched her walk toward him.

He stood and held out his hand to escort her to their table. They ate dinner slowly, savoring the food. They talked a little bit about work but mostly skipped the topics of premature babies and triage.

"You've told me that you're from upstate New Hampshire," he said. "And I know that you are one of the best nurses I've ever met. But other than that, I really don't know anything about you." He laughed. "Isn't that funny? All the time we spend together, and we hardly know each other."

She told him about life growing up in the back country of New Hampshire, with a mother who hadn't finished high school before dropping out to have her first kid, and an alcoholic father who drank away the family's public assistance check. She had grown up ridiculed for her third-hand clothing; her greasy, stringy hair; and as she grew into adolescence, her severe case of acne. She spent many lonely hours in front of the TV to escape her pathetic life. She became fascinated with shows of real-life crimes, brutal murders, and catastrophic accidents. She imagined what it must be like to work with people covered in blood and suffering from life's bad luck.

She stopped talking to take a sip of her drink. "A little TMI?"

"Not at all. I'm intrigued. Please go on."

The one thing she had that nobody else around her had was a high IQ. She was exceptionally intelligent, which must have been a freakish accident, considering the genetic material from which she had been created. Her acceptance into a Boston nursing school on full scholarship was her road out of northern New Hampshire. Her professors soon learned that she was a bright student who caught on quickly and was not the least bit squeamish. In fact, she was quite the opposite. She welcomed the opportunity to work with blood and would happily help her classmates with dissecting their cats in lab. During her clinical rotations, she gravitated to triage and emergency room work.

"To be honest, I liked those areas not so much because I wanted to help people but really for the excitement and adrenaline rush." Quietly, she added, "It fed my need for real-life excitement, filled with victims and heroes."

Gunshot wounds, head injuries, severed limbs—it all satisfied her thirst for the gruesome. It was kind of a sickness. But it was what kept her going.

She looked at Mitch. "Are you horrified?"

Mesmerized, he said, "Not at all. Tell me more."

She took a deep breath and said, "Okay, here goes. Do you want to know my deepest secret?"

He leaned in close.

"I also believed that working as a nurse would be a way to

meet a decent man, a man who would respect and take care of me, something my father never did." She lowered her head as she spoke.

He reached over and lifted her chin up. "Hey, are you embarrassed? You should never be embarrassed about your hopes and dreams." He looked her in the eye. "Never."

Amanda sat up straight. "Sorry about that. That's way too serious for a first date."

She excused herself to go to the ladies' room. Mitch was fascinated. Who knew what lay at the heart of that sexy body and brilliant brain? She returned to the table and leaned over just the right amount to give him an eyeful of what was under her sweater as she sat back down. After dinner and a couple of espresso martinis later, they went back to Mitch's apartment. They had a great buzz going—alert and awake with espresso, relaxed and uninhibited from the gin. He opened a bottle of cabernet. They took off their shoes and got comfortable on the couch. Soon, with most of the wine still in their glasses, they were fully naked, wrapped around each other on the couch. He reached for her breasts. He kissed her neck, making his way down, and paused at her chest. He was beginning to lose himself between her breasts, one hand reaching down between her legs. Too quickly, he brought her to a climax.

"Okay, your turn now," Amanda purred in his ear.

Once they were done, Amanda got up off the couch and wrapped herself in one of his heavy zip-up sweatshirts. She picked up her phone and checked it for messages.

She walked around the living room, admiring the view over the neighboring buildings out to the city beyond.

"This is one nice apartment, Mitch. Where's your family? You keep them stashed away in the burbs while you get to play in the city?"

"No, I call it working in the city. I've got tuitions to pay and a wife to keep happy. I keep this apartment for the month-long stretches when I'm on service and I don't have time to make the commute home."

She carried her phone over and put it under the couch. She lay down next to him. "So, there's your incentive for the census project. Keep the NICU busy and get your bonuses. Is that right?"

"Hey, you know the deal. You're right next to me in the game. Don't you go judging me."

"No judgment here. I do what you tell me to do—I'm just the triage nurse following doctor's orders," she teased. "But seriously, once you go back, are you going to keep doing it?"

"Doing what?"

"Duh, I'm talking about inducing mothers and adding to the NICU census."

"Yeah, I can't exactly stop now. I'm too deep into it."

"I've tried to figure out the details," Amanda said. "Are Charlie and Rita involved?"

"They're just the administrative stamp of approval." He grabbed her ass and pulled her on top of him. "But enough of work talk."

Straddling him, she leaned over and gave him a long, deep kiss.

In the morning, Mitch asked Amanda if she was going in to work. "No, not today. I've got a couple of days off. We can spend some time together if you want."

"That's great, but this morning I need to meet with my lawyers. Can I see you later?" He tossed her a set of keys. "Make yourself comfortable." He walked over and kissed her on the lips, patted her on the butt, and whispered, "Until tonight."

He got to the street corner and realized he was missing his phone. He went back to the apartment. Amanda wasn't in the living room. He looked in the bedroom—not there. "Amanda?" he called out as he walked down the hall. His office door was ajar. He slammed the door open. "What the hell are you doing in my office?"

CHAPTER 72

"I said, what are you doing in here, Amanda?" Waiting for an answer, he scanned the office. Everything seemed to be in order, including his gun still locked in the glass cabinet.

"Nothing. I was just checking out the apartment." She walked up to him and stood inches away from him. She looked up at him with a smile and opened the front of her shirt. She was braless. She gave a little shake and wrapped her arms around his neck, pulling his face down to her chest.

They moved into his bedroom, stripped, and had sex for the third time in twelve hours. Damn, she was good. He moved to get up. She patted the pillow and asked him to stay just a little longer.

"I really do have to go this time." He kissed her on the nose. "I'll catch you later."

The dinners and drinks continued for the next week, each enjoying the other's company more than they'd ever expected. Amanda returned to work once she'd used up her few vacation days. She returned to Mitch's apartment in the evenings after her shift was over. Each night, he greeted her with fresh flowers and a new bottle of wine. For the first time since becoming a doctor, he was able to relax and have fun. She was starting to grow on him.

One night, with two bottles of wine nearly gone, they had another round of particularly rousing sex. Amanda checked her phone briefly, then lay back down with him on the couch. While

THE VERY BEST OF CARE

they cooled off next to each other, they talked about the hospital and how things were running without Mitch there. She asked if he knew anything about Sophie getting hit by a car. No, he hadn't heard about that.

"What about their dog getting attacked?"

"No, I have no idea what you're talking about. Why are you asking me these things?"

"No reason." She rolled away from him and fell into a deep, cabernet-induced slumber.

Mitch lay awake while Amanda lightly snored next to him. Why did she ask about the dog? And Sophie getting hit by a car? Had she been talking with the Youngs? He didn't like it. As much as he liked their time together, he was starting to wonder about her. She used to play it cool with him. But now, here she was, readily available. She'd been quick to take him up on his overnight invitations and his apartment keys. What was she up to?

Mitch watched Amanda sleep. He rubbed the back of his neck, hoping to stop the headache he could feel coming on. He cursed himself. He'd allowed himself to believe he might actually be in love, that they could have a real relationship, even a future together. He laughed out loud. *You idiot.*

Once he was sure that Amanda was sound asleep, he got off the couch in search of his briefcase. A corner of her phone poked out from under the couch. He grabbed it and opened it. It was locked. While he punched in possible codes, Amanda stirred. He paused until her snoring started up again. On the fifth try, he had the code—the last four digits of triage's phone number.

He cringed as he flipped through her phone. She had recorded all their conversations. Then he opened her photo library. There he saw it all: the statements and proof of his financial links to the census project. He also found messages to Josh and calls to an outgoing number that looked like an extension to a hospital line—whose number was that?—as well as other random numbers, most of them attached to her contact list. Friends, coworkers? Family? He doubted she had any family that she was still in touch with. What were these other numbers?

In an instant, he knew his time with Amanda was over. They were done. If he couldn't trust her, then he wanted her gone. Mitch sat in the living room, alone and in the dark. His anger smoldered. How had he allowed this bitch to infiltrate his life? This was what he got for letting his guard down. What was her plan? He stood over her as she slept, snoring into the pillow. He pulled a vial and syringe from his briefcase.

"Here, try this." He injected the liquid between her toes, then put on his jacket, ready to leave the apartment. But first he smashed her phone, leaving the pieces scattered across her naked back.

CHAPTER 73

Amanda woke up feeling fuzzy, like she was still drunk. What was in that wine? She'd never felt a hangover like this one. She got up off the couch.

"Mitch? Are you here?" No answer. She found an empty vial on the coffee table, next to a note that read, *We're done.*

"Wuss," she mumbled to herself. "He was a jerk anyway." Still, tears filled her eyes. Mitch was her one shot at security. Maybe even more. She was a walking dichotomy—one minute looking for the next bloodbath and the next minute looking for Mr. Right. She thought she had found them both by hooking up with Mitchell Wagner. Now he'd gone and ruined it all.

She put the pieces of the phone in her bag in case any of it was salvageable.

"Fucker!" she yelled to the empty apartment. "How could he do this to me? I was only protecting myself."

She'd taken the risk and found herself dancing with the devil. She knew he could incriminate her anytime—she'd done everything he had asked, and now he was going to make her pay. She needed insurance so that if he implicated her in his census scheme, she had proof that he was the ringleader. Her phone had held all the insurance, and now it was all about to blow up in her face.

She collected any jewelry and clothes that she'd left around over the past few days. She picked up the empty vial and syringe, along with his note. She dropped everything in her pocketbook.

JULIE HATCH

Before closing the door, she grabbed the set of keys he'd given her, then she walked out. She knew someone who might be able to help with her broken phone. If there was anything left on it, this guy could salvage whatever hadn't been destroyed.

CHAPTER 74

Mitch's two weeks were up. He got dressed and left for the hospital. On his way through the main lobby toward triage, he passed some friends and colleagues.

"Nice trip?" one called out.

"Hey, Mitch, good to see you. How was your vacay?" called another.

Mitch smiled and gave a wave.

Okay, so they think I was off on vacation, he thought. *That's good.* Yes, everything was going to be just fine.

As he turned down the hallway to triage, Madeline was walking toward him. *What convenient timing.* She was flanked by two administrators from Metro General, the bosses of the "big hospital," as Mitch and others referred to the main hospital.

"Good morning, Madeline," Mitch said in a friendly tone. "Gentlemen." He nodded.

"Good morning, Mitch."

Amid the swarm of people in the lobby, Mitch caught sight of Sophie Young walking toward the exit.

"Mitch." Madeline called his attention back. "We need to meet."

"Okay. Right now?"

"Three o'clock, Wednesday."

"May I ask why? I've done my two weeks of penance. For what, I don't even know."

"We'll talk on Wednesday. In the small auditorium on the

main floor of Metro General. You know the one I'm talking about?"

"Of course I do."

"Good. In the meantime, your privileges are suspended."

Mitch's jaw dropped. In one of the rare times of his life, he was speechless.

"Don't worry, other obstetricians will be happy to fill in for you in triage," Madeline said with a smile of mild amusement.

Still trying to recover, Mitch said, "I'd like to be prepared for this meeting, Madeline. Can you give me an idea of what it's about?"

"Yes. It's a follow-up on what we discussed earlier. Your delivery numbers, specifically those that were premature."

Mitch gave a chuckle. "I trust you've done a thorough and accurate investigation. Because if you have, I don't know what we'll have to talk about. The administration has had nothing but good things to say about my performance."

"That remains to be determined."

"Okay. Then I look forward to our meeting in two days." He turned to leave.

"And, Mitch?" Madeline grabbed his arm. "Stop harassing Mrs. Young."

She walked away, still accompanied by the two men.

So, Sophie had gone to Madeline, Mitch thought to himself. He had hoped he had scared her off from making such a dumb move. Why did Madeline think he was harassing Sophie? He thought back to all his calls to his dopehead friend Tommy. As far as Mitch knew, nobody could make the connection between him and Tommy and Tommy's delinquent friends. Tommy owed Mitch his new life out of prison, working for a major corporation, even if it was among the bottom dwellers of WMI.

CHAPTER 75

Alone in his apartment, Mitch tossed and turned, desperately waiting for sleep to come. When scotch didn't work and red wine just made him irritable, he gave up. Hours before daylight would show, he got out of bed and got dressed. He could go for a run, but it was too dark and cold at this hour; he could go to the hospital, but he wasn't sure there was much point in that.

He stepped out of his apartment building and called Sheldon.

"Yo, why the early hour, bro?" Sheldon answered in a sleepy voice. It was 4 a.m.

"Meet me at Barney's."

Fifteen minutes later, along with the late-night partiers who were still drunk, they sat across from each other in the twenty-four-hour diner that doubled as a bar. Mitch ordered a coffee with double Jameson's. Sheldon ordered black coffee.

Sheldon spun his coffee cup around in its saucer. "Mitch, man, you're in some deep shit."

"Yeah, I'm beginning to figure that out. Amanda's been setting me up. Probably the Youngs too." He reached into his jeans pocket and pulled out three vials, then rolled them on the surface of the table. "Amanda's phone is filled with pictures of my financials, tuition bills, checks from Kindred. I deleted them all before smashing her phone, but I'm sure it's too late. The damage is done."

"So now what?"

"I'm going to wait to hear what's in store for me."

"It's going to be bad."

"Well, then let it be bad." Mitch wrapped a napkin around the vials and rolled them into a tight ball that he batted back and forth between his hands. "I'll disappear for a while and take that six-month vacation I've been wanting. I'll visit Mom, spend a few days with her."

"That'd be good. I haven't talked to her in a while. My bad."

"Don't worry. I'll make up for it when I visit her."

"What if you don't have to leave? What if they just give you a slap on the wrist?" Sheldon watched the back-and-forth game of the napkin-wrapped vials.

Mitch looked at Sheldon as if he was nuts. "Come on, Sheldon. You really believe that?"

"Nah, you're probably right."

"It's all right, I could use the break. I need to get away from the hospital and from the city. And as for Amanda, that bridge is burned." Mitch continued, "Anyhow, enough about me and my impending doom. Let's focus on what's next for you."

"I've had some good numbers on the genetics project. HHI should be happy."

"Have you talked any more with WMI?"

"You mean about my big project?"

"What do you mean *your* project? Last I knew, it was our project. We're supposed to be a team, Sheldon."

"Yes. We are supposed to be a team. And up to this point, we've made a great team."

"What do you mean 'up to this point'?" Mitch batted the napkin ball back and forth harder and faster.

"I mean that if I were a betting man, my money would be on you not surviving this latest fiasco." He paused. "In which case, there's no 'you' in 'our' project."

"Are you serious? Sheldon, man, don't do this. It's going to turn out okay, you'll see. Have you talked with WMI since all this shit came down?"

"Not yet."

"Well, don't. Hold off until the dust settles. I'm asking you. Please, don't write me off, Sheldon. Don't cut me out."

"It's not up to me, Mitch. You've dug your grave." Sheldon shrugged. "We'll see what happens."

Mitch stood up, put the vials in his pocket, and left the restaurant.

CHAPTER 76

Mitch sniggered to himself as he dialed the hospital's social work department.

"Hello, this is Dr. Wagner. I would like to speak with the social worker in charge of the Young family."

"Oh, hello, Dr. Wagner. Jody isn't in today, but perhaps I can help you."

He told her he had concerns and wanted the family investigated for alcohol abuse. He answered some questions from the social worker, then ended the call. Next, he called the NICU to speak with Danny's nurse.

"I'm giving you a verbal order: do not discharge Baby Young until I give the okay. Do . . . not . . . discharge. Got that? Write it down."

"But, Dr. Wagner, you're not the baby's doctor."

"I know that, dear, but I am the obstetrician who delivered the baby, and therefore, I can give any orders I want on his medical care," he calmly stated. "Dr. Sheldon is with me on this. And right now, I'm saying his medical care needs to continue here, not at home. So that means no discharge."

"Even though everything is ready and scheduled? His father has even arranged to take the week off from work," the nurse persisted. "You can't just cancel everything."

"I don't care how scheduled everything is." His voice rose. "I'm canceling the discharge!"

If they can investigate me, I can investigate them.

CHAPTER 77

"Hey, Soph, I'm heading out for a run."

"In this weather?"

"Yeah, I just need to blow off a little steam."

"Okay, babe. Be careful, it's wet."

Adam leaned over and kissed Sophie on the top of her head.

Sophie sat in a rocking chair, holding Danny in her lap. He sucked contentedly on his pacifier with his eyes closed, leaning against Sophie's chest. She caressed the top of his head as they rocked.

"Mrs. Young?" A middle-aged woman Sophie didn't recognize interrupted her brief respite of peace. "I'm Dottie from social work. Jody is off today, and I've been asked to fill in for her on some matters with her families. Okay if I ask you a few questions?"

"Oh. Sure, I'd be happy to answer questions, especially if they're about Danny's discharge."

The social worker hesitated. "I'm sorry, that's not the case. There has been a hold placed on his discharge."

Sophie felt like she'd been hit in the stomach again. "What do you mean 'a hold'? What are you talking about?"

"DSS, the Department of Social Services, has asked that we do an investigation into you and your husband. And your home."

For a moment, Sophie couldn't speak. Then she asked in a tight voice, "What on earth are you talking about?"

Dottie sat down next to Sophie and put a hand on her arm. Sophie yanked her arm away and glared at the woman.

Dottie lowered her voice. "One of the doctors has reported that he is concerned about your husband's propensity for over-indulging in alcohol. He's been seen getting drunk at Evening Rounds, and we need to make sure that, when Danny is ready to go home, he'll be going home to a safe environment. Once we're sure of a safe home environment, then he can be discharged. But for now, we need to keep him here." Her patronizing tone irritated the hell out of Sophie.

"And just so there are no surprises," Dottie added in a quiet tone, "you should know that if for some reason DSS doesn't clear him for discharge, he could be going to a foster home. A temporary one, until things get sorted out."

Sophie started to freak. "You've got to be kidding. My husband does not have a drinking problem. You have your facts wrong!" she said, jabbing her finger in Dottie's face. "I am shocked at what you're saying. I'm beyond shocked!" Her voice rose. "I can't believe you're treating me like this, like a hardened criminal. I have done nothing wrong and neither has my husband. Danny has two loving parents and a very safe and secure home."

She bounced Danny up and down in her arms. "Where's Jody? Jody would never let this happen. She knows us. She's met with us and understands that we are good parents."

"As I said, Jody is off today."

Sophie couldn't believe what she was hearing—how could this be happening? Getting her son home was slipping away. After all they'd been through, why now? Then a light went on.

She brought her emotions back in check. This was not the time for histrionics. How dare he try to stop Danny's discharge? "Who made this complaint about my husband?"

"I really can't say. It's confidential."

By now, Sophie was so worked up that Danny started to cry. She put him down in his crib and asked the social worker to step outside with her, leaving Danny with his nurse.

Through gritted teeth, Sophie forced herself to not blow up at the messenger. "This has Dr. Wagner written all over it. He is holding up our discharge because we're onto him."

Rattled by what Sophie was saying, Dottie scurried back to Danny's cribside and quickly gathered her papers. "I don't know what you are referring to, Mrs. Young. I just know that our department is responsible for ensuring Danny's safety once he leaves the hospital."

With her pile of papers wildly askew, she left.

Sophie saw red. She went to the unit secretary and asked very politely to have Dr. Wagner paged. She waited for his call. Two minutes later, the secretary handed the phone to Sophie.

"Thank you," Sophie said. She turned her back to the staff members milling around the desk. "What are you doing by holding up Danny's discharge? And on the ridiculous accusation of Adam having a drinking problem? I think it was *you* who was drunk the night your lips were flapping. But I haven't said anything to anybody about that. Let social work do their investigating—they'll find out Adam is clean and sober and that you're a lying son of a bitch. Now stay away from me and my son."

"You know I have the ultimate power, Mrs. Young, so why are you doing this?"

"I don't freakin' care about your power. There's always someone higher up than you. And I *will* go above you. I'll take you all the way to the Supreme Court if I have to."

Mitchell chuckled. "Oh, Mrs. Young, you have no idea what you're saying. I'll warn you once more, you don't know what you're doing. You don't know who you're messing with. You'd do best to mind your own business and leave me to mine."

Sophie took a deep breath. *Don't let him get to you.* "Actually, Dr. Wagner, Madeline now knows your business. Adam and I have talked to her about our suspicions, and we have proof. It wasn't difficult to convince her to do some investigating. We've had no problem going up the chain of command."

She slammed the phone down, hoping she hurt his eardrum with the loud bang. Immediately, she questioned what she had just done. Would he punish them further?

Sophie got back to Danny's pod just as the nurse was finishing up feeding him. She lifted him into her arms and put him over her shoulder. She paced back and forth, patting him on his back while thinking about Mitch Wagner. *What if he really does have the power to have Danny removed from my and Adam's home for good? This is so ridiculous.* She bit her lower lip so hard she tasted blood.

CHAPTER 78

When Adam arrived, Sophie was alone in the corner of their section of the pod. With her head down and her arms wrapped around herself, she was rocking back and forth. Adam went to her and put his arms around her. She clung to him. She told him about the delay in Danny's discharge and the investigation of them by the Department of Social Services.

"I can't do this anymore. I hate this place. I miss Kim, I miss Rihanna. I am so pissed at Mitchell Wagner I can't stand it. Danny is doing great right now, but what if something goes wrong and sets him back again? Discharge is set for next week, and now he's pulling the rug out from under us. It's unbelievable." Tears rolled down her cheeks. She sniffled to keep her runny nose from dripping onto Danny, who was busy making funny faces. Probably gas, thought Sophie, which caused her to smile at her little wonder. She looked up at Adam and, in a soft whisper filled with vengeance, said, "Fuck Mitchell Wagner. I refuse to let him win. I'll show him what happens when he tries to screw with this family."

"Hey, what's going on?" Dr. Sheldon came around the corner and into their pod. "You guys should be packing up and getting ready to get out of here."

"Discharge has been put on hold while DSS investigates us," a disgusted Adam explained.

"What are you talking about?"

"It seems as though Dr. Wagner has ordered Danny's discharge to be put on hold." Sophie added in a snarky tone, "Like he can order around everyone in the world."

Adam explained, "The Department of Social Services needs to do an investigation on us, on Dr. Wagner's accusation that I have a drinking problem."

Dr. Sheldon pulled out his cell phone and hit speed dial.

"Mitch, man, what are you doing? Why on earth did you get DSS involved with the Youngs?" He paused, listening. "No way. For one thing, he's my patient, not yours. And I don't know what side of the bed you woke up on today, but you've got it wrong. I have no reservations about sending Danny home."

Dr. Sheldon held the phone away from his ear, rolled his eyes, then winked at Sophie and Adam. "Yes, Mitch. I know where you're coming from. I understand what you're saying, but you're wrong." He paused, listening to Mitch. "Yes, you are. You're wrong to be doing this. Wrong to get DSS involved. And I'm canceling your order for their investigation, if it's not too late, which it probably is. Thanks a lot, Mitch. You've really screwed up again." He punched the button to hang up and jammed his phone in his pocket.

"Hey, I'll do what I can," Dr. Sheldon said to Sophie and Adam, "but now that DSS has been contacted, they can't just drop it. With a doctor's order, they have no choice but to get involved. It's their legal responsibility to follow through on all accusations, suspicions, and certainly, physician requests. Sorry."

Dr. Sheldon thought for a moment, then said, "Don't worry, you guys, I have an idea."

He stepped away from Sophie and Adam and got on his phone. He spoke briefly. All Sophie heard before he hung up was "Thanks, man, I owe you one."

CHAPTER 79

Mitch got on the phone and called Sheldon right back. It rang, then went to voicemail. Frustrated, Mitch dialed again. After the third try, Sheldon picked up.

"What are you doing, undermining me like that in front of the Youngs?" Mitch was searching his pockets for a paper clip to occupy his hands.

"Mitch, what has happened to you? You're not the same guy you used to be. Back in the day, you were an awesome physician. WMI and Metro loved you. It's no wonder you became chief of your department so quickly. You had a gift. Your care of pregnant mothers and especially high-risk patients was unmatched in the city. But then something switched on, or off. Maybe it was with Mom, or your dad, or your wife. You decided to take all that respect and praise and run with it, taking it as a license to deliver any baby anytime you saw fit. Your judgment was off. Your greed for money went unchecked. Was it your father? Your need for his approval?"

Mitch's grip loosened, and he dropped his phone. He leaned down to retrieve it. He couldn't believe his own brother was saying this. He felt sick. He thought back to his ambitions in medical school and residency. He went into medicine genuinely to help people as much as to please his father. "Sissy medicine"—that voice of his father's pounding in his head, challenging him, baiting him, daring him to specialize in ob-gyn. When he initially chose his residency in general surgery, his father was pleased. "It's not orthopedics, but close enough." He'd hugged Mitch, tussled his hair like he was a kid, and patted him on the back, as if welcoming him into the world of real medicine.

"Sheldon, you're right. Once I switched out of surgery and into ob-gyn, things with Dad were never the same. But I was sure I could do it. I could prove that ob-gyn was every bit as good as orthopedics, or surgery, or any other specialty. Then it just happened."

"What happened? What was it?"

"I decided to show Metro that I could turn pregnancies into gold. I knew exactly how to make them the most financially successful hospital in the city." Mitch could hear Sheldon still on the other end, waiting patiently. "And you're right. I took it too far. I lost all perspective."

Mitch sat with his elbows on his knees, his head in his hands. He thought of all the things he wished had turned out differently. He took a deep breath.

"Well, Sheldon, it is what it is. *Que será, será*, and all that horseshit."

Silence answered him over the phone. "Did WMI back you up on this?" Sheldon finally asked.

"No, of course not. I decided to take it in the direction that it went."

"What about HHI?" Sheldon persisted. "Have you made some kind of deal with them? Did they ask you to get involved? Because if they did, I want no part of it. Whatever they do with the information I give them is on them. Beyond that, I'm out. Please tell me you didn't agree to something more that I don't know about."

Mitch hesitated. "No, you're fine. This is all on me."

CHAPTER 80

Sophie could finally focus on getting Danny home. Dr. Sheldon had cleared their names overnight. Sophie and Adam thanked him profusely.

"Hey, no need to thank me. I was only undoing the mess that my half brother created. Now we just need to get Danny ready. He's almost there—a couple more pounds and a few more days in an open crib."

They were so close. She had done her best to help Madeline Cross fill in the holes of her investigation. She had given her all the names and information she had collected in her little notebook over the past three months. It wasn't much, but it should be enough to help. Plus, she had the video.

In preparation for going home, Sophie signed up for discharge class. She needed to hear everything the nurses had to say about how to take care of a preemie baby at home.

The class, it turned out, was straightforward: how to safely bathe your baby, make sure they continue to gain weight, and keep them healthy by staying away from sick people. Sophie knew she could handle all that.

With five minutes left of the class, the nurse turned the meeting over to Josh.

"This is our pharmacy representative. He's here to answer any questions you have about the medications your babies will be taking once you get home. All your babies are on at least one medication, and many are on more than one. Josh is the medication expert."

Josh spoke about the importance of vitamins and special preemie formulas that provided extra calories, vitamins, and minerals that regular formulas didn't. "Some of you may have babies going home on medications for their lungs, or anti-reflux medications. I'm happy to answer any questions you have about those."

Sophie raised her hand and stood up. She wanted all the parents to hear what she had to say, even though she already knew the answer. "Josh, I have a question. What can you tell us about BrainHealth? I think we all need to know about this medication that the doctors have recommended for us to give our babies. Has it been tested on preemies?"

Josh smiled. "Yes, it has, and it's not a new medication. We've been giving it to premature babies for years but under a different name. It's caffeine citrate . . . you all know it as caffeine. We use it to treat apnea of prematurity—a very common condition where preterm babies episodically stop breathing. I believe most, if not all, of the babies going home from this group have been treated for apnea. As their brain matures and develops, they outgrow the apnea and no longer need the medication. Almost all babies are off caffeine by the time they go home."

Many of the parents nodded.

He continued to explain what Sophie already knew, that it was still being researched for use under the name BrainHealth.

"But now, with a new use for the medication, you all have the choice of continuing your children on caffeine, in which case your pediatricians will be prescribing the medication for 'off-label' use. That means that it's being used for a purpose other than what it has already been approved for. Because it's not yet approved by the FDA specifically for this new purpose, you will all be asked to sign a waiver saying you understand that it's still an experimental drug."

He looked back at Sophie. "So the short answer to your question, Mrs. Young, is yes. It has been tested on preemies."

"Josh, I'm not asking about apnea. I'm asking if there has been any research proving that it helps with brain development. Is it safe and effective to use 'off-label,' as you put it? My own baby was in Dr. Sheldon's study on BrainHealth and then was taken out. Dr. Sheldon claimed it was because he had enough numbers and didn't need Danny's participation any longer."

The other mothers in the class were following the back-and-forth conversation. Nobody interrupted.

Josh replied, "The limited studies done so far showed that there were no harmful effects on the study subjects and there was a small improvement in their cognitive and motor development."

"Were the findings statistically significant? Were they studies done by objective researchers who weren't paid to publish certain results?"

Josh was no longer smiling. He looked like he was getting a little warm under the collar. "I don't know the details of the studies. But, Mrs. Young, would you risk the chance that your baby could be missing out on a potential miracle drug for his brain development? I hope not."

Josh made eye contact with every mother and father sitting in the discharge class. "I doubt that any of these parents would decline the opportunity to provide everything they possibly could for their child's health and well-being."

"That's the clincher, Josh. That's what I have a problem with. You are playing on our emotions as parents. You are betting that we will take the risk, pay the cost, do anything, if it can help our babies. I get it. I'm debating the same thing. But until the FDA passes this drug to be used in this capacity, I think we all need to be cautious about what we're giving our children."

The other parents nodded.

More people came into the room to listen to the lively

conversation. One mother raised her hand and asked, "Do full-term infants get this too?"

Sophie sat down.

Josh answered, "No, it's only available to premature babies, because their brains were not fully developed when they were born."

A father asked, "Does it help babies who have severe brain damage?"

"We don't know yet, but any premature infant, with or without brain damage, will be advised to take BrainHealth once they're discharged. Trust me," said Josh as he looked around the room, hands outstretched and open. "The choice is yours. You don't have to give it to your kids. But if you do, you will be doing them a big favor. This is a miracle drug for premature babies who are still developing."

Sophie rolled her eyes. The parents in the audience were beginning to whisper among themselves. She didn't trust Josh and wasn't convinced that the off-label use of this drug was harmless. But she didn't know for sure.

Sophie stood up again. "Josh," she said, "just one more question, and I'd like you to give a straight answer. Can you tell us that quality scientific studies have been done to prove its safety in premature babies and its effectiveness in their brain development?"

Josh hesitated.

Sophie couldn't help herself. "I've looked it up, Josh. Not only that, but I've also talked with Dr. Sheldon about this issue. So far, there are no definitive research results. No proof. Period. You're marketing it as a potential silver bullet when it hasn't been proven to help babies' brains at all."

There was a tense silence as the audience waited for Josh's response.

"Mrs. Young, I'm sure those results will be available very soon."

Agitated, Sophie forced herself to sit back down, relieved to hear another mother ask a question.

"Does insurance cover this drug?"

"Well," answered Josh, "because it's so new to the market, insurance does not cover it currently, though I'm sure that will change soon."

"How much does it cost?"

"Kindred Pharmaceuticals and Metro Hospital are working together to send you home with a free month's supply. After that you'll be able to buy it for around fifty dollars."

"Fifty dollars a month?" someone asked.

Josh cleared his throat. "Actually, that's for a week's supply."

Gasps could be heard around the room.

"What? Are you kidding? That's two hundred dollars a month, times three years . . ." The person speaking calculated on his phone. "That's over seven thousand dollars out of our pockets. That's crazy!"

Others jumped in. "That's highway robbery!"

"You're crazy if you think we can pay that!"

"I can't afford that on my salary!"

Josh raised his voice to be heard over the commotion. "Yes, I know that's a lot of money. I know, I understand." The crowd settled as Josh took command of the room. "But what is it worth to you to provide the best possible future for your children? By being born too early, your babies have been traumatized. Life in the NICU is nothing like what life would have been like if they'd stayed in the womb. Now, here is a drug that could make up for all the damage of being born early. It'll help prevent behavior problems and learning disabilities and enhance their cognitive abilities."

Josh paused, then added, "And I'm sure that well before three years from now, the FDA will approve BrainHealth, and then it will be covered by your insurance."

Sophie watched the other parents. They went from being angry to appeased.

They were buying it hook, line, and sinker.

Sophie's phone buzzed with an incoming text. She ignored it as she stood to speak again, pressing Josh. "Just to clarify, you're saying we should just open our pocketbooks and feed our kids this little pill for the next three years, on the *hope* that it might help them? It feels like we're being held hostage by Big Pharma." Sophie paused for effect. "Tell me, Josh, would you give it to your own child?"

All eyes turned to Josh.

"I believe all premature babies should be given BrainHealth."

Sophie repeated, "But would you give it to your own child?"

Josh replied, "I don't have any children."

Sophie's eyes bore into him. "No children? How interesting." Turning to the nurse leading the class, she asked, "Is class over?" and walked out.

CHAPTER 81

Sophie caught up with Josh as he was leaving the hospital. Her phone buzzed again.

"Can we talk for a second?" she asked, keeping pace with him.

"After what you just did to me in discharge class? I don't know if it's safe to have a conversation with you."

"Oh, come on. I don't bite. I'm just looking out for us little guys, the moms and pops and babes of this hospital."

Josh stopped walking and gave Sophie his attention.

"Do you really believe in what you say about BrainHealth? Do you really think it will make a difference in these babies' lives? Or do you just say what you're told to say?"

Josh shrugged.

"People are so quick to believe the men in the white coats are their saviors. If they say it is so, then it must be true," Sophie said in a mocking tone of voice. "I know, I was one of them. I used to be one of those who drank the Kool-Aid and revered the ground that some of these brilliant doctors walked on."

"You know, Sophie, be careful of what you're saying. Drug companies and hospitals are necessary, and they save lives. What if Danny hadn't had the technology and medications, as well as the doctors and nurses, to save him?"

Exasperated, Sophie said, "Josh, he wouldn't have been born so early if Mitch Wagner hadn't come into our lives. He didn't save us. He created a preemie! You're right. If there had been a biologic reason for me to deliver so early, and Danny's life was in jeopardy, then of course, I'd be grateful for all the technology and medicines. But as it turns out, we'd have been a lot better off if we'd gone to another hospital, or at least another doctor, when I had early contractions. I've said this a million times—this should not have happened. Everybody tells me how lucky I am to have delivered in one of the top maternity hospitals. Maybe that's true, but I will forever believe that it shouldn't have happened in the first place. Mitch Wagner made it happen, and he knows that I know. He thrives on playing God, being in control, and being the master of his little triage universe. And then there's the way he treats women—he's a dick."

"Yeah, it's well known how you feel about Dr. Wagner."

"It's not just me. I know other mothers who agree with me. And I'll bet I could find hundreds more who have the same opinion."

Josh stared down at his feet.

"You know, Josh, you're just a mule. You don't transport narcotics across the border for the cartel, but you are a drug pusher for Kindred. I'm all about exposing the truth—and *helping* families, not robbing them blind. Which, by the way, is what my son is likely to be, thanks to you and Mitch Wagner."

Sophie turned and walked away before Josh could respond.

CHAPTER 82

Sophie knocked on Dr. Sheldon's office door.

"You might want to distance yourself from your half brother. I've already gone to Ms. Cross in administration. Next, I'm going to the FBI with proof of medical fraud. This is big, and Mitch is going down hard. It'll be jail time. He shouldn't be allowed to be anywhere near a hospital or sick people, and nowhere near babies."

Sheldon opened his mouth first in surprise, then to speak. "I—"

"I don't want to get you in trouble," Sophie kept going. "Your health insurance project is beyond my concerns. I don't want to hurt you or Rihanna, so that's why I'm warning you. Extricate yourself from anything associated with Mitchell Wagner."

"Thank you for the heads-up, but have you considered the fallout if you get WMI involved with the FBI? They're big, Soph. If they decide to protect Mitch, it'll be way too much for you to handle."

"Tough. They didn't know who they were screwing with when they chose me to deliver early. It's a fundamental law of nature: don't mess with a mother and her baby. I guess they didn't teach that in medical school." She turned and left.

CHAPTER 83

Sitting in the chapel, Sophie forced herself to take a deep breath. Every day, she was growing angrier. Angry at Metro Hospital, angry at life for dealing her this card, but, by far, angriest at Mitch Wagner. She had to calm down. She was no good to Danny if her blood pressure caused her to blow an aneurysm.

Sophie heard the chapel door open.

She couldn't help herself. She turned to the chapel guy seating himself behind her and asked, "Who are you?" Then, in an accusatory voice, she added, "Why are you here every time I'm here?"

"Don't worry, I'm on your side. I know all about Danny and Blu and everything you and Adam have gone through."

Sophie's eyes widened. "How do you know all this? Who are you?" she repeated.

"I work for WMI. I've been investigating Dr. Wagner."

Her jaw dropped.

"When they caught wind of his census scheme, they sent me here to gather information on what he's been doing."

"That's why I've been seeing you around—in the hospital, on the street, at dinner with doctors."

He nodded. "And you and your family just happened to be caught in the middle of it. WMI had nothing to do with Dr. Wagner's actions. At some point, he went rogue with Josh and Charlie, and the three of them, with Rita's help, started manipulating the number of babies in the NICU purely for financial gain."

Sophie shook her head. "I can't even believe it. You mean you and WMI already know about Dr. Wagner?"

He nodded again.

"Why didn't you stop him?" Anger welled up in her. "You could have prevented me, and others, from delivering prematurely."

"Because we didn't know the full scale of what he was doing until just recently. We thought he was claiming many of the triage deliveries as his own to make his numbers look better than the other obstetricians'. We didn't realize he was actually causing the early deliveries to happen."

"I don't know if I should even be sitting here talking to you. Why should I believe that you are who you say you are? Right now, I feel a lot more suspicious than trusting."

"I understand. But just think about it. You've seen me with Dr. Patel and other physicians of the hospital."

Sophie studied her hands for a few moments. "Okay," she said. "Adam and I have been working to help one of Metro's administrators make her case against him. But it sounds like you've already done all that."

"The more proof we have against him, the better. We expect he will be arrested and have his medical license permanently revoked. WMI wants to use your family as an example of the damage he has done to give to the FBI. That is, if you and your husband will agree."

"I need to talk with Adam, and I need to be sure we can trust you."

"Of course. I understand your hesitation. Do whatever you need to feel confident that I'm who I say I am. But once you do, would you agree to help?"

"Yes. But Ms. Cross, the administrator I was talking about, already has a meeting, kind of like a tribunal, planned for him."

"I've talked with her. She'll complete her investigation and hold the meeting to let him know that he no longer works for the hospital."

Sophie was quiet for a moment, then asked, "What do you know about Danny's contaminated blood transfusion? How in the world was Mitch able to pull that one off?"

"That was an extremely serious offense and apparently even lower than Mitch was willing to go. When we traced the blood that Danny received back to the hospital blood bank, we found that one of Mitch's underlings had gotten himself into the blood bank for the day, under the pretense of being a legitimate WMI employee trained to work there. That guy, whose name is Tommy, insists that Mitch is innocent of the contaminated blood. He had nothing to do with it, and it was all Tommy's idea."

Sophie's phone buzzed with an incoming text. She stood up to leave. "I gotta go. I need to get upstairs to Danny."

CHAPTER 84

Sophie took the stairs, not wanting to wait for the elevator. Why was Danny's nurse texting her to come to the NICU? Running up the stairs, she tried to keep from thinking the worst. She was out of breath by the time she reached the fourth floor. Danny's nurse met her outside the NICU door.

"What's up?" Sophie asked. "Why did you text me to get here in such a hurry?"

"It's Amanda," answered the nurse.

"Amanda? What about her?"

"She's inside. She says she has something important to give you."

Sophie walked quickly to Pod C. With no preamble, Amanda handed Sophie her phone.

Sophie looked at the broken phone. "What is this?"

"It's a broken phone. But there is enough on there to nail Dr. Wagner. I have recorded conversations and pictures of documents tying him to what you've been trying to prove all along. The recording isn't in great shape, but a friend of mine was able to recover most of it. You'll get the gist of what I recorded."

Sophie stared at the phone, then back at Amanda. She didn't know what to make of this. "You recorded Dr. Wagner?"

"Yes, you'll see when you open the phone. I made a copy of what's on there and sent it to Madeline Cross."

"You're kidding." Sophie studied Amanda for a moment. "No, you're serious, aren't you?"

Amanda nodded.

"Why? Why are you helping to catch Dr. Wagner in medical fraud? You worked with him on it."

"Because I know him well enough to know that if he's going down, he'll try to bring me down with him. I'm not doing that. I'm not ruining my life over him. What's on that phone is my insurance—it's my way of showing I am not on his side."

"No, Amanda, you take this. It's yours," said Sophie, handing back the phone. "Keep your proof. I don't need it, and who knows, someday you might."

Amanda took the phone back. "I hope you can believe me when I say I'm sorry." She turned her head and quickly walked away, leaving Sophie to stare after her.

Wow, wonders never cease.

CHAPTER 85

The place had become oppressive. Sophie felt claustrophobic. It was stifling to spend every waking moment in such close confines with all these people who were basically strangers to her. Sophie was sick of the people, the daily walk-through by Rita in her uptight, marmish way. She was tired of always having to move her chair and Danny's crib to make space for new admissions. She was sick of rounds, every eight hours, and having to leave the pod because of HIPAA. She felt like a caged animal. The more she thought about the sterile, controlled environment of the NICU, the more agitated she became.

Then something inside her snapped.

She needed to get out of here—right now. For a minute, she fantasized about hopping a plane to Mexico, just to get away for a few days. Just a quick break. But her son was here, not to mention her husband. She'd never leave either one of them. She knew she wasn't going any farther away than the hospital and her own Brooklyn neighborhood.

Sophie walked past the crowd of doctors on rounds outside of Pod A. She felt so angry at these men in the white coats—young, old, they were all the same. They were so sure of themselves, so confident that what they'd been taught was the right way, the only way. She wanted to scream at them. She wanted to tell them that just because they had MD after their name, they didn't know everything, especially about mothers and their babies. And what about the women in white coats? They were no better, and sometimes worse, because they had a chip on their shoulder, something to prove.

She headed for the chapel, her place of safe escape. She passed Dr. Patel, a vision of steady brightness in her dark, dizzying world. She smiled and stopped to say hi. Why couldn't they all be humble and kind, like him? She squeezed herself onto the crowded elevator and rode down to the chapel level, listening to the joking and laughing between the residents. Didn't they know she wasn't feeling the least bit jocular? How dare they? These kids, with the word INTERN splashed across their hospital IDs, dressed in their starched, too-bright white coats, a symbol of pride to them, looking so smug, now members of an exclusive, elite group of pompous asses. What did they know about having a critically ill child? Had they ever spent three months in an intensive care nursery, not knowing whether their child would live or die? Did they have the slightest clue what that worry and angst felt like?

What was wrong with her? Her head felt ready to explode with anger and frustration. She felt like she was going mad. Was this her father's craziness coming out? Had she inherited a fragment of his psychopathic gene? She wondered if this was how he had felt on his darkest days.

She couldn't talk to Kate or Rihanna, not even to Adam. She felt completely alone, unable to talk to anyone—no one would understand the intensity of her emotions. But she had to hold it together for Danny.

The elevator doors opened, and Sophie burst out ahead of everyone. She fled down the hall, oblivious and uncaring about who she bumped into or the comments about her rudeness. She was sure they were mocking her disheveled appearance, having left the NICU so abruptly with her hair a mess, wearing sweatpants and a T-shirt. She flung open the chapel doors.

What? Who were these people seated here? What were they doing intruding on her safe space? She stormed back out. Where now? She couldn't handle this inner turmoil, so strong that it threatened to destroy her from the inside out. She burned with rage at life for giving her such a shitty blow. This whole bloody experience was a nightmare. She felt herself dropping into the abyss of depression.

Then she thought of Jody, who might be the rescue she needed from this downward tailspin. She needed to tell someone these out-of-control feelings before she completely lost it.

CHAPTER 86

She knocked on Jody's door. Jody opened the door and right away saw Sophie's distress. Jody led her to the couch, where Sophie plopped herself down. She put her head in her hands and let go. She cried uncontrollably as she let it all out—all the thoughts and feelings she'd worked so hard to keep in check all these weeks. She hated feeling this way.

"And don't tell me how lucky I am to have delivered here in this state-of-the-art hospital—I don't need to hear that right now," she said between sobs.

"I had no intention of saying such a thing," said Jody in a gentle tone. She passed Sophie a box of tissues. Sophie pulled a handful out to wipe the thick mucus dripping from her nose. Minutes passed as her emotions rose and fell, softening briefly, then building up again to cause another release of tears.

When the storm had settled, Jody took Sophie's hand and began to speak. She spoke of a better life for her and Adam and Danny, after the NICU. She talked about all the NICU success stories. She told her about the follow-up clinic—the clinic where graduates of the NICU celebrated their milestones, their birthdays, their nursery school graduations. She spoke of the compassion and love the nurses had for those kids, and the strong connection between staff and families and between the families themselves. Sophie listened. She noticed the pictures around Jody's office of former NICU babies with their parents and their siblings—all smiles and love.

"These families have faced very tough, challenging situations, like you and Adam. They've come out on the other side of it stronger than they thought possible. The experience of having a premature baby was the hardest thing most of them have lived through. But they survived. Just as you will. They have a different kind of appreciation for their kids, and for all of life, that other parents don't have."

Sophie wasn't anywhere near feeling any gratitude.

Jody suggested they go visit the CCN—chronic care nursery.

"Why does everything in medicine have an acronym?" Sophie tried to joke.

They took the elevator to the seventh floor. Before opening the door to the unit, Jody explained that this was where chronically ill kids went when they left the NICU but wouldn't be going home. It was where they stayed until a bed in a long-term facility became available.

"Like a nursing home for kids?"

"Yeah, pretty much."

Whoever was in charge of decorating the CCN had tried hard. There were colorful pictures on the walls of bright red balloons and smiling blue teddy bears. The lighting had been updated with soft lightbulbs and wall sconces, helping to add a feeling of warmth. The floors had been done over with hardwood laminate. But the effort had fallen woefully short. The metal cribs had bars that were spaced for safety regulations. They looked like cages, Sophie thought. The walls held a coating of old grime, and the curtains needed washing. The room was still an old, forgotten section of the seventh floor.

Sophie felt a tightness in her chest as she looked around the room at the handful of kids living there. There was a young child with a tracheostomy. She was attached to a corrugated hose that ran from a small ventilator machine to the trach hole in her neck. Her throat rattled with mucus with each breath. Drool ran down her chin. A stuffed animal lay in the girl's arms, but she had no interest.

In the next crib over, lying quietly with his eyes closed, was a toddler dressed only in his pajama bottoms. A red rubber tube protruded from his overly distended belly. There were multiple scars on his abdomen, and the skin around the base of the tube was angry red and excoriated. A machine next to his crib slowly dripped formula into his tube, one drop at a time.

Another child, maybe four years old, lay on her crib mattress. Her back severely arched backward. She appeared to be looking behind her, except that her eyes weren't focused on anything. She held a blank stare. Her legs and arms were contracted and contorted into unnatural positions. The whole place was heartbreaking.

Jody leaned toward Sophie and said quietly, "She has cerebral palsy."

There were a few other children, ranging in age from infancy to toddlers. She heard the whooshing sound of humidified air blowing into the tracheostomy and the mechanical clicking of the machine delivering drops of formula into the gastric tube. Cardiac monitors blipped and beeped continuously. She heard an infant cry and the low voices of the nurses trying to comfort the baby. Beyond the sights and sounds, the smell of ammonia permeated the air—not from a cleaning agent but from wet, soiled diapers. Sophie felt overwhelming sadness by the institutionalization of the unit. The decorator had tried, but there was only so much one could do.

"The staff works hard," Jody said. "They love these kids, but it's tough. It's an emotionally demanding job, as you may imagine. Nobody talks about these children who have been put aside. Nobody other than the staff who work here."

A physical therapist massaged the tight, spastic limbs of the CP girl. A nurse was trying to spoon-feed an older toddler, who gazed off to an empty corner of the ceiling. There were no parents.

"They are wards of the state because their parents, unable to care for them, have relinquished their parental rights."

Sophie felt tears collect in the corners of her eyes. She saw the point Jody was trying to make. She should be glad that Danny was doing as well as he was.

"Why are they on monitors if they're out of intensive care?"

"The state is accountable for these kids, and the hospital is responsible for their welfare. A tragic accident happened several years ago when a baby died in his sleep. He got tangled in his feeding tube in the middle of the night—so now all kids have to be on a monitor. But remember what I said about the kids in the follow-up clinic who are doing well? There's research being done to improve the care of preemies all the time. Unfortunately, there will probably always be a few like these kids who still suffer bad outcomes."

"Were all these kids premature?"

"All but one."

Sophie and Jody left the CCN as a group of medical students were led in by one of the attending pediatricians.

The two women got on the elevator together.

"How are you doing?" asked Jody.

"I don't know, Jody. That was pretty depressing. But I guess you got my mind off my own dark thoughts. Thanks for that. And you reminded me of an important meeting this afternoon. One I can't miss."

"Well, you come back anytime, okay?"

"Yes, thank you." Sophie continued to ride to the ground floor.

CHAPTER 87

Once on the ground floor, Sophie went outside and wrapped her flimsy sweatshirt around her. She'd walked a couple of blocks when her attention shifted away from her troubles for a second time. A protest march was going on outside the family planning building, creating an energetic charge in the air. She stopped to watch.

The demonstrators carried signs, and they shouted out their messages: "Pro-choice," "Pro-child, Pro-choice," "Mind your own uterus!" Sophie smiled. Now this she could engage with. She grabbed a sign that was stuck in a snowbank and started marching. She took a quick selfie and sent it off to Adam.

There were men marching too. She joined the parade of people marching back and forth on the sidewalk. She felt a bond with the protestors, a sense of comradery fighting for women's rights. The energy of this greater purpose was contagious. She forgot about Danny, the NICU, and Dr. Wagner for just a few minutes as she joined in. On the other side of the crowd, she saw Dr. Sheldon and Christy. Even Carol was out here marching. Sophie waved. She cheered when she saw employees holding signs with the WMI logo and shouting to protect women's rights. She was swept up in the spirit of the demonstration—loud and passionate.

Sophie was still reveling in her emotional high when the police showed up. They told the marchers to move on, that they were blocking the sidewalk. She started to leave when some of the demonstrators shouted back at the police. Loud voices yelling their protests led to violent pushing and shoving. She tried to duck out of the crowd, but the crowd closed around her. When she fell to the ground, she shielded her head as people stepped over her.

She stood up, only to be knocked harder in different directions, everywhere but where she wanted to go—which was away from the crowd. More police came and started arresting the demonstrators. Sophie tried to get away. She pushed with all her might to get out of the crowd that had become too dense to penetrate. She was stuck in the middle of a group of the rowdiest demonstrators. The cops pushed some of the demonstrators into a police van, and Sophie was swept in with them.

At the police station, the booking officer told Sophie she would likely be released once everyone had been processed. The clock read two o'clock. There was only an hour until Mitch's hearing, and Madeline was counting on her. Her recording and testimony were required to nail Mitch. Without those, Madeline would have no choice but to let him go. She reached for her phone to call Adam.

"Damn it!" They'd taken it from her. Her mind raced. Another thought gripped her. What if DSS found out about this? Would it go on her record? Had she just risked Danny going to foster care? What had she done?

She took a couple of deep breaths and tried to calm down. She told herself that everything was going to be okay. With as much calm as she could muster, she spoke to the officer behind the desk. He told her she was free to go once she'd signed some forms. She waited for the officer to collect the paperwork, which seemed to take forever. She watched the clock as she scribbled her name at the bottom of the three pages that required her signature. Next, she found the officer who had her phone, and ran out of the station. She ran as fast as she could, jumping snowbanks, skirting the puddles of slush, and dodging pedestrians. She had to slow up to cross the streets but otherwise ran like she used to run when escaping her drunken father. She burst through the hospital doors and looked for the clock. It was 3:05. *Shit*. With no time to change her clothes, she ran to the auditorium. She texted Adam: *On my way*.

CHAPTER 88

Mitch had prepared for his meeting with Madeline. He was dressed in his most conservative suit, complete with his finest Italian leather shoes. He combed his hair back one more time, then entered the auditorium. Two security officers stood by the door.

Madeline sat in the front of the auditorium and indicated for Mitch to take a seat at the table. He looked around, surprised to see an audience. He nodded to several fellow obstetricians as he walked to his seat. Some pediatricians and a smattering of NICU and triage nurses sat in the auditorium seats. A few medical students and interns filtered in. He saw Sheldon and Rihanna seated together. Then his eyes landed on Adam with an empty seat next to him.

He heard whispering from the small audience. He didn't understand why there were people here for his meeting with Madeline. Rita and Charlie were conspicuously absent. He felt a bead of perspiration on his forehead. He searched his empty pockets for something to occupy his hands. He clasped his hands together and examined his fingernails before picking up his head to look directly at Madeline.

Madeline stood to speak. "For now, I will address you as Dr. Wagner, but I believe, very soon, you will no longer carry the title of doctor."

Mitch's stomach lurched. *This is it.* This was what he'd been dreading.

Madeline glanced at her watch, then at the empty seat next to Adam. She began to read from the papers in front of her. "I have decided to revoke your privileges at Metro Women's and Children's Hospital based on our investigation of the following allegations: fraud, malpractice, misogyny, assault, falsifying medical records, and animal cruelty. I've just learned that I'll be adding kidnapping to those charges."

There was a collective murmur in the audience.

Sophie burst through the door at the back of the auditorium and took the seat next to Adam. Madeline gave her a slight nod and a relieved smile.

"You have deceived us all by breaking the Hippocratic oath of 'Do no harm,'" Madeline went on. "Rather, you have caused great harm to numerous babies and parents. Those families, whose lives will never be the same, have lost trust in this hospital and perhaps the entire medical system. But you've also brought a great cost to society. Some of these babies have been so damaged by their premature birth that they will end up costing hundreds of thousands, if not millions, to meet their medical and special education needs as they grow.

"And the emotional cost to each family, I can't even put a dollar value on it. The child with severe brain damage, the mother who is half paralyzed from a stroke—their medical care will likely be in the millions. And that's just the financial cost of these abhorrent acts you carried out. I counted twelve wrongly induced preterm deliveries over the past two years. The number of complaints that have come forth about your inappropriate touching of your patients is at least that high. The emotional damage you have done to these women cannot be quantified. Your actions are reprehensible, Dr. Wagner. A woman's trust in her physician is highly personal and should never be violated. Her emotional bond with her child is priceless, something *you*"— Madeline pointed her finger at him—"have fractured by causing them to be born prematurely. These mothers were robbed of a normal nine-month pregnancy, delivery, and first year of life with their babies. And they will never get it back. You robbed them of some of the most precious time between a mother and her child."

Mitch sighed heavily, but he refused to yield. He held his head up as he kept his eyes on Madeline.

"It is beyond my authority to have you disciplined fully, as I believe you deserve. That is up to the authorities. All I can do is take away your privileges to practice here at Metro. You have lost the respect of this hospital and its administration, as well as the staff, and you owe everybody here an apology. The nurses, who respected you and your work, no longer stand behind you, and I doubt any of them will ever choose to work with you again."

Mitch thought about Amanda. He was sure he could make amends with her. She had said it, right? They were two peas in a pod. Where was she anyway? Did she know about this so-called meeting? He listened to Madeline prattle on with numbers and documentation. She referred to the video, assuring anyone who doubted her that there was no doubt of what Dr. Wagner had done. Then Sophie Young stepped forward. She spoke for five minutes about how she and her husband had pieced together their proof of what he had done, and how her family had been affected.

Madeline turned back to Mitch. "Your case will go in front of the state medical board, and they will decide what to do with you. The police will officially charge you with the laws you have broken."

When Madeline finished speaking, a hush fell over the room. Mitch didn't break eye contact with Madeline.

"Do you have anything you'd like to say?" Madeline asked him.

"Yes. You have no idea what you've done."

The auditorium door opened. Backlit in the doorway stood

Amanda. She looked at Mitch and smiled as she held up her phone.

Suddenly, there was a deafening crack of a gun. Mitch dove for the floor.

"Get down!" shouted one of the security officers.

Everyone in the room took cover under their seats, arms protecting their heads, hands over their ears. Two more loud bangs followed.

"It's coming from the family planning hallway!" shouted one of the security officers.

Then silence. Nobody in the auditorium moved. Feet raced past the auditorium; panicked voices shouted. The sounds fell into the distance of the clinic hallway. After several minutes, the security guards instructed people to get up and move out quickly.

Mitch left with the crowd, scrambling to get away. He searched for Amanda. There she was up ahead. He ran to catch up with her. When she saw him coming toward her, she turned and bolted.

CHAPTER 89

The next morning, Adam dropped his phone on Sophie's lap, opened to the CNN website. The headline read: *Manhattan Doctor Fatally Shot.*

> Breaking News – March 28, 2012, 4:37 PM EDT
>
> A Manhattan doctor was shot and killed at New York's Metro Hospital. Earlier in the day, Dr. Champlain had performed an abortion on the girlfriend of the gunman. She was eight weeks pregnant.
>
> New York Police Commissioner William Brady said thirty-eight-year-old Steven Campari of Jackson Heights came into the family planning section of Metro Hospital, located in a building adjacent to the main hospital. He was able to access the clinic via a hallway that connects the clinic to the main hospital. According to witnesses, Mr. Campari stepped up to the main desk and asked to see the doctor who had terminated his girlfriend's pregnancy. The nurse at the desk pressed a silent alarm button to alert hospital security and the police department of a possible threat.
>
> The gunman then pulled out his handgun. People started yelling and hiding from the gunman. Dr. Champlain attempted to escape down the hallway to the safety of the hospital. The gunman shot him in the back as he was running away.
>
> Police arrived and fired at the gunman, who sustained

life-threatening injuries. He died in the ambulance on the way to the hospital's emergency room.

Questions of security at Metro Hospital have become an issue lately. While there are security officers stationed at the main entrance, there is no metal detector that may have alerted security personnel to the concealed weapon.

The article went on about the doctor, his family, and all the staff, who would greatly miss the beloved physician.

Sophie swiped right to the next story. *Prominent Obstetrician Charged with Medical Fraud.*

She took in every word. When she was done, she handed back his phone while holding up her other hand to high-five Adam.

"Adam, we did it! Mitch Wagner has been arrested and charged. WMI has washed their hands of him, claiming they had nothing to do with his actions." Sophie exhaled a long breath of relief.

Sophie's phone rang. Her face lit up with surprise when she answered. It was Kim. Sophie started peppering her with questions. When she realized Kim wasn't answering her, she stopped to ask, "Where are you?"

Kim answered in a quiet voice.

"Kim, what's the matter? This doesn't even sound like you. I've been so worried about you. Rihanna said you'd been in a terrible car accident. Suzanne said that when she talked to your parents, they told her that you'd gone away on some kind of a volunteer trip."

In a hushed tone, Kim answered, "I can't talk about it. Not now. But I'm okay. I'm coming back."

"Why can't you talk? What's going on?"

"Just stay safe and keep Danny safe. Keep your eyes open and your guard up."

"What are you talking about? Kim, it's done. Mitch is gone. He's going to be put away."

Click.

"Kim? Kim, are you there?"

There was only silence on the other end.

Sophie and Adam met Rihanna and Sheldon at Rihanna's apartment. They talked about the outcome of Mitch's hearing and the shooting. Sheldon cracked open a bottle of champagne, then explained to the other three what he knew.

"Even though everybody has wondered if WMI was behind Mitch's actions, it wasn't them. They're a good company. It's Mitch who was the bad egg. He caused all the problems for you guys." Sheldon looked at Adam and Sophie. "The attack on Adam, the car hitting Sophie, the slashed tires, even the attack on your dog—he was the mastermind behind everything. He was able to do it all with the help of a couple of outliers who worked at WMI. Mitch's high school stoner friend, along with some other lowlifes, were happy to do whatever Mitch paid them to do."

Sophie and Adam clinked glasses.

"It's a bittersweet win," Sophie said. "I'm glad we nailed him, but I would trade it all for having never entered Metro Hospital in the first place."

Adam squeezed her hand.

Sheldon went on to explain that WMI had heard about Mitch's census scheme but didn't know exactly what it entailed. All the threats and attacks were Mitch's way of telling Sophie and Adam to back off. Leave him to do his thing, and Danny would be okay.

"Why didn't he help get us transferred, get us away from him?

If we had been able to transfer, he could have kept doing what he was doing in triage with no danger of us catching him."

"Because the ever-controlling Mitch wanted to keep an eye on you two. He'd rather force you into silence than let you out of his sight."

Her intuition had been right. Sheldon was the good brother; Mitch was the evil one. Charlie, Rita, and Josh were both or neither; they flew in whichever direction the wind blew. It was Mitch—misogynistic, miserable Mitch—who had caused her life to forever change. He had taken away three and a half months of her life, time she could never have back. That was the hard one to swallow. The pain of missing that time with Danny left a visceral ache.

She looked around the room at her husband and her two new friends and felt content for the first time since this whole debacle had started.

Sheldon spoke again, raising his champagne glass. "I'd like to toast to a new and better future."

"Here, here," they all replied. Even Isabelle cooed from Rihanna's arms.

Dr. Sheldon cleared his throat, getting Adam and Sophie's full attention. After a dramatic pause, he announced, "Rihanna and I are getting married."

Sophie grabbed Rihanna and hugged her. "Congratulations!" Whispering in her ear, she added, "Welcome to the United States, Mrs. Vandewater."

"Congratulations, you two," Adam said, shaking Sheldon's hand. He then took Sophie's champagne glass from her hands and set it on the table. "I hate to interrupt the party, but we have to go."

Sophie glanced at the time. "Oh yes, we do. Thanks so much, and congratulations again. We'll see you guys later."

CHAPTER 90

Back at the hospital, Sophie and Adam climbed into the waiting limo. The driver welcomed them and told them traffic wasn't bad and that they should be at the WMI home office in forty minutes.

"Forty minutes? I thought their office was in Midtown."

"Mrs. Young, you must be thinking of their regional office. Their home office is in Westchester—you know, 'Westchester Medical Industries'?"

"Oh, right," she answered the driver. A wary but curious Sophie whispered to Adam, "I still don't understand why they want to meet with us. Really, I'd rather be spending my time packing up Danny and getting him home. We're so close."

Adam held Sophie's hand. "I have no idea, but it's got to be something good." He ran a hand along the leather limo seat. "Maybe something like that magic pill you wanted, the one that would take you back in time." He gave her a wink. "We are due for some good luck."

The driver pulled up to the entrance of WMI. The building sat high on a hill overlooking Long Island Sound. The grounds, covered in snow, were expansive. The driver opened the limo door and escorted them through the entrance. They were ushered upstairs and taken into a spacious waiting area. Magazines were carefully laid out on the large table in the center of the room: *Nature, The New England Journal of Medicine, Journal of Health Care Management*.

A large man swept into the room. His big smile and even bigger presence offered them a welcoming and hearty hello. "I'm Mr. Baker, assistant director of WMI. Come on into my office."

They followed him in.

"Please, make yourselves comfortable. Can I get you some coffee?"

"No thank you," Adam and Sophie answered simultaneously. They settled into two chairs.

"It is a pleasure to meet you both. The reason I invited you was to offer you a personal apology for all you and your son have been through."

Sophie braced herself, distrustful of most people she'd met over the past several months. She did not want to be patronized or to allow this man to think that her experience could be erased with the wave of his executive hand.

As if reading her mind, he said, "I know my apology may not mean much, given what you've been through. I apologize on behalf of WMI, because we are responsible for what goes on in Metro Hospital. We don't accept responsibility for Dr. Wagner's egregious actions, but we are sorry for all the harm he has brought to you and the other families."

Adam and Sophie looked at him, unsure of his point.

"Which is why my boss and I would like to offer our help in bringing a group lawsuit against Dr. Wagner. None of this heinous damage can be undone, but he can be forced to pay for all the past and future medical bills you are bound to incur."

Sophie didn't know what to say.

"I see you're at a loss, or maybe you don't trust my peace offering. I assure you, WMI is behind this one hundred percent. Dr. Wagner should have to pay for the damage he has done. The state licensing board and the FBI will punish him as they see fit. But as far as I know, nobody has talked about bringing justice to the families. Financial justice."

Sophie opened her mouth to speak but couldn't find the words.

"Shall I give you a chance to think about our offer?"

"No, sir!" exclaimed Adam. "We don't need to think about anything. We'll take any help we can get in paying Danny's medical bills. Thank you so much."

Mr. Baker stood to leave as they all shook hands. "Wonderful then. Our legal counsel will be in touch with you in the next couple of days to get this rolling. Again, my sincerest apologies."

Waiting for the elevator down, Sophie and Adam simultaneously looked at each other in amazement and silently mouthed *Whaaaaaat?* to each other.

During the limo drive back to the hospital, they talked about what this windfall would mean—they couldn't believe it. And to think that they had thought the worst of WMI.

"They aren't just buying us off, are they?" asked Sophie, suddenly unsure about what they'd agreed to. "Are they paying us to not say anything?"

"I don't think so, Sophie. WMI may be a big corporation with a reputation to maintain, but this isn't about them. It's about Mitch Wagner, the one bad apple."

CHAPTER 91

Sophie and Kim finally had a chance to meet away from the hospital. Kim sat on a bench in the park, her jacket unzipped on the unseasonably warm day, a hint that spring wasn't far away. The blue in her hair had faded, but her silver dangle earrings danced in the breeze.

"Oh my God, Kim, I am so happy to see you!" Sophie exclaimed. The two hugged. "I was afraid I'd never see you again."

They both started talking at once, then laughed.

"You go first," said Sophie.

Kim began her story.

"That Thursday morning, I hailed a cab to get to work. I was running late, and taxi was the quickest way to get there. I got in and gave the driver the hospital's address. After a few blocks, I realized he was going in the wrong direction. I thought the driver was taking me the long way to the hospital just to rack up a higher fare. I watched the Uptown buildings disappear behind me. Then my phone rang—it was Rita telling me that the cab driver was taking me to a nursing conference downtown. I remember thinking that was strange since she hadn't mentioned anything about it before. I should have known as soon as I heard her say '*we* grabbed the last spots for the conference' that something was up. But I had no idea."

Kim paused, then continued. "I asked her if my supervisor knew I wouldn't be at work that day, and Rita assured me that she did. The cab dropped me at a hotel in Lower Manhattan. I was handed what appeared to be a typical conference name tag, complete with a lanyard, and was led into the hotel. Next thing I knew, there were two guys holding my arms, taking me upstairs to my room. And that's where I stayed for the next three weeks."

Sophie gaped at Kim. "Are you kidding me?"

"I wish I was." She looked off in the distance for a few moments, then returned her attention to Sophie.

"No. There was no conference. There were no other nurses. It was me and these two thugs with guns for three weeks. There was no way for me to leave, no way for me to call anybody. They cut my phone service and internet so I couldn't make any outgoing calls or receive any calls, not even voicemail. No email, no web browsing. Every meal was hotel food delivered by room service. My days consisted of the same thing every day over and over—video games, hotel HBO movies, and endless rounds of Sudoku. Rita sometimes called on one of the guys' phones, reassuring me it wouldn't be too much longer. Every time she called, I begged her for an explanation.

"I asked the guys holding me hostage why they were keeping me there. They shrugged and gave me blank looks. I didn't know what was happening back at the hospital. I had horrible thoughts about Danny and you and Adam. Nobody would tell me a thing. I think they were waiting for Danny to be discharged home, away from the hospital, away from exposing Mitch."

She stopped talking. After a minute, she resumed. "I know it doesn't make much sense, but hearing from Rita every so often reassured me that I'd be okay. I guess once Rita saw the writing on the wall that Mitch would be caught, she told the guys to bring me back and to make sure they scared me enough to not say anything. They told me if I breathed a word of what had happened, my parents and my brother would pay. You're the first person I've said anything to. Now, of course, everybody knows everything, so it doesn't matter. I'm safe."

"We were told you'd been in a car accident," explained Sophie. "When Suzanne tried to reach you at your parents' house, she couldn't get through."

"And my parents were told I was away on a nursing volunteer trip out of the country. Somehow, Dr. Wagner made sure my parents and my nursing friends and roommates never put two and two together."

Sophie stared at her in amazement. "That is just too unbelievable," she said, shaking her head.

"Now tell me all you know," Kim said.

"At first, I was convinced WMI was behind Mitch's scheme and that they were connected to Dr. Sheldon's lab experiments and Josh's pushing BrainHealth. I was sure WMI was the driving force behind it all."

"Yes! You're right!" said Kim. "The people at WMI are the ringleaders. They own the hospital, which means they own all the people that work at Metro. They own Kindred, HHI insurance company, and a host of other medical businesses. I think Mitch Wagner was their puppet and that Sheldon Vandewater was doing their shady work."

"No, Kim, you've got it wrong. That's what I thought too. Adam and I went to meet with WMI. They've washed their hands of Dr. Wagner. They're not protecting him. In fact, they've offered to help us start a lawsuit against Dr. Wagner for medical expenses for Danny and all the other babies who were wrongly born too early. They're a good company, Kim."

Kim took a minute to absorb the information. Sophie could see her trying to make sense of everything.

"Well, then who kidnapped me? Who's responsible for keeping me hidden away all that time? It's gotta be WMI."

"I don't know. Dr. Wagner had his own den of hooligans. They worked at WMI but in low-level positions and, for the right price, would do whatever Dr. Wagner asked. WMI has fired everyone they found to be associated with Mitch Wagner."

"What about Sheldon and his lab? Even Rihanna didn't know what he was doing. You're the only one who saw anything, and you never said a word."

"That's because Dr. Wagner threatened me if I said anything. I couldn't risk telling you because I didn't know what he would do."

They sat in silence for a few more moments.

"I guess it makes sense," Kim said. "I just wish they'd left me alone. Why did they have to drag me into it?"

"Because Dr. Wagner knew that you were onto him as well and would help me bring him down. He needed you out of the way. I'm so sorry you went through what you did because of me."

"No, Sophie, don't apologize for Dr. Wagner's actions." She laughed. "They must have thought I could do a lot of damage. I had no idea I was that important." Kim gave Sophie's arm a squeeze. "I'm just glad everyone is okay, and you'll all be home soon."

CHAPTER 92

Sophie and Rihanna waited to cross First Avenue. Sophie grabbed Rihanna's hand, and they stepped into the street when there was a break in traffic, behind a city cab and in front of the M4 bus before it pulled away from the curb. They jogged safely across to the other side.

Rihanna pointed to the steel door on the street level of the family planning clinic. Sophie tried it, expecting it to be locked. Surprisingly, it opened. They stepped in, allowing their eyes a minute to adjust to the dimly lit entry. They took the flight of stairs down one level and through another heavy metal door that led into a tunnel. The narrow tunnel with old, cracked concrete floors sloped downward. The walls were lined with metal ventilation ducts. It smelled dank and musty.

"Are you sure we're in the right place?" Sophie whispered.

"Why are you whispering? Nobody's here," whispered back Rihanna. They giggled nervously. "Yes, I'm sure. He told me to come visit him, and I'm sure he said this was the place."

At the end of the tunnel, they came to a glass-door entrance. Etched on the outside of it in large letters was THE FOUNDLING, and in smaller letters, WMI.

They tried the door. It was locked. Rihanna banged on it, the noise echoing loudly through the tunnel. Sheldon appeared at the door, surprised, then happy to see the two women.

"Hey, you made it!" He kissed Rihanna.

"Does this have anything to do with those baby boys and your insurance company project?" Sophie looked around his shoulder, suspicious.

Sheldon burst out laughing. "No, no, no."

The two women waited for an explanation.

"This has nothing to do with HHI," he said, still laughing. "This is totally different. What's happening down here is going to change the world of neonatology. Mitch and I nicknamed it the New NICU, but as you can see on the door, the real name is the Foundling."

He held the door open for them. "I'm glad you decided to venture down here. Not the most inviting of places, but it works."

"'Not inviting' is an understatement. I feel like the morgue might be right around the corner," Sophie half joked, moving closer to Rihanna.

"Quite the contrary," an amused Sheldon answered.

"What is this Foundling place?" asked Sophie.

"Remember that day in the cafeteria when you saw me arguing with Mitch? I accidentally left behind some torn-up napkins with writing on them—important writing. Some of my best ideas get written on napkins." He chuckled. "When I went back to retrieve them, they were gone. I figured you and Adam had picked them up."

Sophie and Rihanna were following Sheldon as they listened. Sheldon walked over to a wall and turned up a bank of light switches. The room was the length of a city block. The lighting was low. Soft music played in surround-sound style. Under the music, Sophie heard the deep lulling rhythm of a heartbeat. Small cameras facing different directions lined the corners and walls of the massive room.

"Welcome to the future NICU." Sheldon smiled.

Sophie saw large barrel-shaped containers positioned throughout the room. There were twelve of these tubs. Each one stood about five feet high and two to three feet across. Heavy curtains separated them. Next to each one was a large machine that hummed at a low volume, wrapped in insulation so that its sound was muffled. It reminded Sophie of the ECMO machine that kept the NICU babies alive. There were no alarms, no beeping of monitors.

Sophie grabbed hold of Rihanna's hand. They walked together up to one of the tubs. Looking over the top of it, they could see it was filled with a viscous fluid. With a gasp, they both drew back. Submerged in the liquid was a baby.

CHAPTER 93

The baby's eyes were closed. He looked serene as he floated around the barrel like he was in a bathtub. Weightless and with plenty of space around him, he moved his arms and legs as if he were swimming. He was small, only slightly bigger than Danny was when he was born.

Recovering from their initial shock, the two women stepped up to the tub again, this time more cautiously. Taking their time, they looked again.

"He looks so calm and relaxed," Rihanna said softly.

"I know," said Sophie. "It's like he's back in his mother's womb." The whole place held a feeling of tranquility and safety. *Reality check, Sophie—this is screwed up!* Then the next minute, she wondered, *Or is it a medical marvel?*

Sheldon interrupted the moment. "I'm going to let Dr. Hennessy explain things to you."

A young doctor stepped out from behind a desk.

"Peter, this is Sophie Young," Sheldon said, "and this is my fiancée, Rihanna. I'm so glad you all get to meet at this auspicious time."

"Dr. Hennessy . . . that name sounds familiar," Sophie said. "Do you work in the NICU?"

"Actually, I started working at Metro about six months ago in the anesthesia department. But when WMI offered me a position here, I gladly accepted it. Let me show you around."

Sophie and Rihanna looked in the next barrel, which was empty. They whispered back and forth to each other.

"What is going on?"

"What are they doing?"

"This is crazy!"

Sheldon cleared his throat and turned his attention to Dr. Hennessy, indicating for the ladies to do the same. They followed Dr. Hennessy as he led them through the room and around each barrel. Sheldon followed behind. Two of the twelve tanks were occupied. Dr. Hennessy explained the mechanics of providing an artificial womb for underdeveloped fetuses.

"The machine, designed much like the ECMO machine you've seen in the NICU, functions as a placenta. Each fluid-filled tank serves as an artificial womb. The tanks are filled with a synthetic amniotic fluid, which over time, we modify to be more like natural amniotic fluid through cellular enhancement. The baby's two umbilical arteries and single vein connect to tubes that connect to the ECMO-like machine. Blood is circulated through the machine, where waste is removed and then replaced with clean, oxygenated blood and circulated back into the fetus.

"The age of the baby must be right—eighteen to thirty-ish weeks. Younger than seventeen or eighteen weeks is too small for the tubes and most of the equipment. Between eighteen and twenty-three weeks is ideal, when we can most help the brain, lungs, and liver to develop in a perfect environment."

Sophie listened, hanging on every word and trying to understand the full scope of what Sheldon and Dr. Hennessy were doing.

"We have technical hurdles we're still working to overcome," Dr. Hennessy went on. "We need to get the babies here within minutes of birth so that we can keep their lungs from fully expanding. It's the ECMO machine that breathes for them and keeps them alive, not their lungs." He looked to Sheldon to take over.

"Yes, that is our biggest challenge," Sheldon continued. "Timing is everything. But once we're able to do that, once we get them connected to the imitation womb, then we're in business. The fetuses float unencumbered and without the pressure of gravity weighing on their fragile skin and bones. Noise is minimal, and whatever noise does reach them is muffled. Everyone who works here is instructed to speak in calm, soothing voices. There is no unpleasant stimulation. There are no needle sticks, no tubes down their throats with ventilator pressure damaging their lung tissue, no bright lights in their eyes, no sudden loud noises—there is nothing like the current state of the NICU, which you both know so well. This is as close to replicating life in the womb as technologically possible."

Sophie's mind raced. "Where do these babies come from? Is this a WMI thing? Is this even legal?"

Ignoring Sophie's questions, Sheldon continued to lead the small group through the maze of vessels.

Stopping at one of the tubs, he looked in. "Do you remember Anna?" he asked Sophie. "Of course you do. This is her baby. She's almost fully mature and is doing quite well."

Sophie was blown away when she peered into the tub. "This is Anna's baby?"

She even looked like Anna. Her heart filled with love for this poor baby who lost her mother before her life even began.

Sheldon paused, allowing Sophie to absorb what she was seeing. "Anna's baby was saved, all thanks to the Foundling project."

"What's going to happen to her?" Sophie asked, still gazing at the baby in the tub.

"I'll get to that in a minute. But first, your questions. Yes, it's WMI who is helping to fund this project, and technically it's still experimental. We've had one success, and WMI is pushing us to get more results, faster.

"But let me back up a minute. You should know Mitch no longer has anything to do with this project. We started it together a couple of years ago. Mitchell is brilliant in many ways, and together we developed the idea. But over that time, he changed, and as we all know, he is no longer fit or able to participate in the project." Sheldon's voice got louder. "I'm taking over and leaving him out of it. He would poison it and find a way to turn it into a dark project if I allowed him to be involved, and I refuse to let that happen."

He stopped and lowered his voice. "That's the argument you and Adam witnessed in the cafeteria," he said to Sophie. "I told Madeline everything I knew about Mitch's census scheme, and, as we all saw, she sent him away. WMI fed him to the wolves. I don't know what's going to happen to him, but the Foundling will not be a part of his future."

He moved on to the next two tanks. "Look here," he said, his voice softening. "This baby was born early to a heroin-addicted mother. Here, she's able to be weaned off the heroin gently, sparing her the miserable experience of opiate withdrawal. This peaceful, nontoxic environment is perfect for all fetuses but especially those who have been drug exposed. All the babies in here are free from toxins, alcohol, nicotine, stress hormones, medications, air pollution—all the substances in a mother's system that can potentially harm her baby.

"This tub here," he said, stepping over to the next vessel, which held fluid but no baby, "was where we had the baby that I think you were worried about, Sophie. His mother took off the first night after he was born, never to be heard from again. No family, no emergency contact information for us to follow up with. Unfortunately, we didn't get him here fast enough, and he didn't survive."

They walked through the maze of the remaining unoccupied tubs.

"Upstairs in the hospital, I oversee the medical care of thousands of premature babies every year. But down here"—he swept his hand through the air—"we'll be saving babies who never would have lived."

"This is amazing, Sheldon," said Rihanna. "I can't believe this is what you've been spending all your time on. Now things make more sense."

Sheldon put his arm around her, pulling her to him.

"It sure is like nothing I've ever seen before." Sophie looked around the vast room. "I am so glad to see that Anna's baby is alive. And now I know what happened to that other baby who had mysteriously disappeared."

Sheldon watched her. "But?" he asked.

Sophie chewed her lip, thinking about what she wanted to say. "It's playing with Mother Nature in a way that maybe she didn't intend. My heart is glad to know that some babies can be given a chance, but my head is questioning the ethics of it."

"I asked myself the same thing initially. Is this the right thing to do? I quickly came up with the answer that yes, it is. As long as the people in charge are committed to using it ethically."

Sheldon continued, "Placental abruption, miscarriage, premature rupture of membranes, all the things that can go wrong midway through a pregnancy—we now have a solution for those moms and babies. We all know it's best for a baby to remain inside of mom for as long as possible." Sheldon reconsidered. "Well, maybe not in an environment saturated with heroin and fentanyl. But otherwise, when staying inside the mother is not possible, this is the next best option."

"So what's going to happen to Anna's baby?"

"The two babies here now will go up for adoption. They are wards of the state. Anna's baby is in state custody because there is no living relative able to take her. The mother of the heroin-addicted baby has lost custody because of the damage she did to her baby in utero, but if she manages to rehab and pull her life together, the baby may go back to her eventually. But that's a big maybe."

Sophie wondered to herself what she and Adam would have done if their only choice had been to adopt from here. Would they still have adopted? "Anyone who sees what's going on here is going to ask you the obvious question."

"And what's that?" asked Sheldon.

"Are you profiting off these orphaned kids?"

"Sophie! I'm insulted. Of course not! I'm Mitch's half brother, not his evil clone. WMI controls the operations. Try to look at it from my perspective. It's a solution for children entering an already overpopulated and overstrained social system. No matter how you look at it, it is the best thing for these babies. They are so much better off here than if they were born too early and put in the NICU. There is no black market here. WMI won't allow it, and anyhow, that's not me." Sheldon paused again. "If you think about it, we're reversing the damage Mitch has done. He purposely delivered babies early. I'm working to save those same babies."

Everybody was quiet for a few minutes, lost in their own thoughts.

Dr. Hennessy spoke. "Everything is automated. A human is here twenty-four seven, but the monitoring and necessary adjustments to the equipment are done automatically. The more we can leave these babies alone in their artificial wombs, the better off they are . . . Oh, another thing," he added. "They're currently using this technology in Europe. My guess is that pretty soon it will be in every major hospital in the US."

"Ten years?" Rihanna questioned.

Dr. Hennessy paused, then said at the same time as Sheldon, "Well, maybe twenty."

Sheldon continued, "What you see here is a pilot study—our first trial run. I'm not in this for the money. My purpose is all about helping sick babies survive. That's it. And now that I'm a father, I can't imagine what it must be like to lose a child."

Rihanna cocked an eyebrow in mild surprise.

"Let's go upstairs," said Sheldon. "We've got more to talk about, but it doesn't have to be down here." He pulled on his jacket. "Peter, you got this for a couple of hours? I'm heading out for a bit."

"Sure, I'm good," he answered.

"Call me if you need me. Just remember to use the landline. There's no cell service down here."

Sheldon walked with Rihanna and Sophie back through the tunnel. When they got outside, Sophie took a deep breath, relieved to be out in the fresh air.

"We have to keep Mitch out of this," said Sheldon. "If he does jail time, then it's not an issue until he's out. But if he gets out on bail or is given a lenient sentence of community service or something, I'm going to need to figure out how to keep him away. Right now, he thinks he's still in charge. He won't be able to handle the idea of not being included, let alone not in charge."

Sophie considered this as she gave them a wave and headed back to the hospital.

CHAPTER 94

Mitch was on his way from the police department to his apartment. After his "meeting" with Madeline Cross, he had been arrested, booked, and released from police custody. There were two conditions: he needed to return for his arraignment Monday morning, and he had to stay at least five hundred yards away from any medical facility. That meant Metro was off-limits to him for now. But that would soon change. He would be found not guilty and would return to the position he had held at Metro for years. Even better, he would go back to the way he practiced medicine when he first started working at Metro, when things ran smoothly. Back to when he and Sheldon got along well, and people thought he could do no wrong. It wasn't too late. He and his wife could go to counseling. This time they'd make it work. He would be around more for his kids. They still had such bright futures ahead of them.

He snapped out of his daydream and brought himself back to his current reality. What were his options? He could run. He'd have to break all ties here and would constantly be looking over his shoulder. Could he do that? The idea of living in new places around the world sounded exciting, but the idea of being a fugitive was not so appealing. Or he could stay and face the consequences. What about his father? He would have to face him, and Mitch thought he might rather go to jail than face his father.

Nearing his apartment, he saw a handful of reporters on the sidewalk in front of his building. He snuck around back, stepping on broken glass and bumping into garbage cans in the dark alleyway. Once in his apartment, he grabbed a small duffel bag and threw in a couple of shirts and pairs of underwear. He took all the cash from his safe, as well as account numbers and passwords he would need to access more money. He eyed the gun, locked in its cabinet. Deciding to leave it behind, he picked up his passport and spare pair of glasses and added them to his duffel. He left the building the same way he went in.

Mitch spent the night in a hotel close to Midtown, one that didn't charge the ridiculous rates that Upper East Side hotels did. He didn't know how much money he was going to need in the weeks ahead. He needed to call his wife and explain he wouldn't be home for a while. She would have already read about it in the papers. He doubted she was losing any sleep over his fall from grace.

The next morning, Mitch woke with renewed hope. He made an appointment with one of his former bosses at WMI and walked the distance to their Midtown office. He spent the better part of an hour pleading his case, even at one point asking forgiveness. Could they please consider letting Mitch hire their top lawyers? He could pay; he'd pay them well. He needed solid representation if he was going to beat this rap. By the end of the meeting, it was clear to Mitch that WMI was done with him. They washed their hands of him, then wiped those hands on his own shirttail before giving him a good kick in the ass out the door. He was on his own. No way was he going to jail. It made him sick to even think about being locked up alongside common street thugs and drug dealers.

With no plan yet, he went into a barbershop. Thirty minutes later, he emerged with a buzz cut, his beard shaved off, his mustache intact, and wearing his spare pair of glasses with round tortoiseshell frames.

A new look couldn't hurt, especially if he decided to run.

Mitch ducked into a coffee shop and ordered a cup of coffee. He needed a plan. How had he managed to fall so low? He had seen it coming. Or had he? Maybe he was so full of himself he couldn't fathom the idea of actually getting caught for what he was doing, let alone arrested and charged. He blamed Sophie Young. If she had never come into triage that day, he'd still be practicing medicine and running Metro's obstetrics. It was her fault that this had happened to him. He pounded his fist on the table, making the diner dishes rattle. He threw a twenty-dollar bill on the table and barged out the door.

He called Sheldon's cell, then headed to Rihanna's, where Sheldon was staying.

Sheldon greeted him at the door with a solid hug. "I like the new look, bro. But why?"

Mitch shrugged.

"Don't tell me you're planning on leaving town," said Sheldon.

"Hey, Rihanna," Mitch said as Rihanna joined Sheldon in the doorway. "I hear congratulations are in order. I'm really happy for you guys." He stepped up and gave her a hug.

"Thanks, Mitch."

"Could you give Sheldon and me a few minutes?"

"Sure." She held Isabelle in her arms and went into the kitchen.

Mitch and Sheldon moved into the nursery to talk.

CHAPTER 95

Sophie's phone rang. She draped a burp rag over her shirt, then lifted Danny onto her shoulder.

"Hello?"

"Hey, it's me," Rihanna whispered.

"Why are you whispering?"

"Mitch is in the other room."

"What's he doing there? I thought he was arrested."

"He was, but they let him go on his own personal recogni-something-or-other."

"Recognizance," Sophie said in disgust. "How did that happen? Don't they know what he's done? What's wrong with them?"

Rihanna cupped her hand around the mouthpiece and spoke quietly. "He said that he's supposed to stay at least five hundred yards away from any hospital. They're talking so quietly I didn't catch everything, but I did hear Mitch say something about going back to Metro."

Sophie jiggled Danny as she paced. That feeling of impending doom was back.

Rihanna was talking. "Sophie, be careful. Just because he's supposed to stay away from the hospital doesn't mean he has to stay away from you."

"Thanks, Ri. I doubt he'll try anything with me. But I appreciate the heads-up."

After she'd hung up with Rihanna, her phone buzzed with an incoming text. It was Amanda telling her where to be in an hour.

CHAPTER 96

Mitch and Sheldon talked quietly. They didn't want to start arguing again. Mitch needed help with a plan.

"Why don't you just chill out and wait for your arraignment?"

"I can't do that. I feel like a caged animal waiting to be eaten."

"You have to show up at court on Monday. If you don't at least do that, you're screwed."

Mitch brushed his hand across his newly buzzed hair. "Shit, Sheldon. I don't know." He stared at the floor. "I've got to figure this out."

"Figure what out? What don't you get? You need to go home and wait for the arraignment."

Mitch leaned forward with his elbows on his knees. "You wanna know what you could do to help?"

"Sure, anything."

"Promise me when I get out, we can go back to working together as a team. You and me, working on the Foundling project. That's the only way I'll be able to get back on track. It'll be my second chance. Please, Sheldon. Work with me. Give me something to live for."

"You're jumping the gun, Mitch. We don't even know if you're going to jail. We don't know if your medical license will be revoked, and if it is, when it will be reinstated. There are a lot of ifs, Mitch."

"Okay, but let's just say I'm free to practice medicine again in, say, two years. Will you let me back in on the project? You know you'll need me."

THE VERY BEST OF CARE

Sheldon felt the pull of Mitch's silver tongue trying to persuade him. "I don't know, Mitch. I'm not making any promises."

"What do you mean 'no promises'? We're blood brothers, Sheldon. We've always had each other's back."

"That was before you crossed the line. Before you went to the dark side. If you weren't my brother, I'm not sure I'd even like you anymore."

"Ouch."

"Sorry, but it's the truth. With a fiancée and a child to watch out for, I can't mess around with shady operations. And I know for a fact that if you joined me in the project, it would turn shadier than the shadow of the huge maples in Central Park. You'd poison it."

"Double ouch."

"Do you deny it?"

Mitch shrugged. "Okay, I get it. I know when I'm not wanted around."

"Don't go playing the victim, Mitch. I love you for the brother you are, and you're welcome in my home anytime. But that's where it ends."

They were quiet for several minutes. The only sounds were baby noises coming from the kitchen. Mitch stood up, shoulders back and head held high. He walked to the kitchen to say goodbye to Rihanna, then came back and stood over Sheldon.

"I'm not going down, Sheldon, and I'm not going away. I just hope you're here for me when it's all over."

"See ya, man."

Mitch hesitated with his hand on the door handle. "Hey, you know what? I'd like to check out what you've done with the Foundling since I saw it last. If I can have an image to hold in my head, to keep me going, it'll be a lot easier to face the judge."

"That's a bad idea, Mitch. You've been told to stay away from the hospital. Nothing's changed since the last time you were

300

there. If you're caught anywhere near Metro, they'll arrest you again. It's not worth it, Mitch. Forget about it."

"You don't have any babies there yet, do you?" Sheldon didn't answer.

"I need to see it."

"I'm telling you it's a terrible idea."

"I'm going anyway. You coming?"

Sheldon shook his head. He got up and held the door open. "Good luck, Mitch."

CHAPTER 97

Back on the street, Mitch called Amanda on the slim chance she'd pick up and talk to him. Maybe they should try again. Her phone rang and rang. He thought about what would happen if he went to trial. A sizable fine, no doubt. Jail time maybe. White-collar jail, like where Martha Stewart did her time, might not be too bad. For a couple of years? Golf club jail? He needed a damn good lawyer to get him that. He had plenty of friends who had been sued, and their lawyers had gotten them off. He calculated the cost of his actions over the past few years in triage. What started out as a financial bonanza was quickly becoming a financial liability. Personal gain? None whatsoever. He still hadn't gained acceptance from his father, and now, his father would quite possibly disown him.

"Hello?" Amanda answered her phone.

"Hey. Guess who."

"What do you want, Mitch?"

Hearing her voice brought back memories of triage, the thrill he got as soon as he set foot in there. He remembered the charge he felt working on the census project. Sheldon was right; he had crossed a line, and he knew he could never go back to playing by the rules. This was a dangerous feeling, and he needed someone who could understand.

"I'm wondering if you want to help me out."

"Why?"

He could see she wasn't going to warm up to him easily. "Meet

JULIE HATCH

me across the street from family planning, and make sure you're five hundred yards away from the hospital."

"Like I said, why?"

"Just do it." *Click.* He knew she'd be more likely to cooperate if he played the tough guy barking orders. Cajoling and reasoning didn't work with Amanda. She liked it straight to the point with no sugarcoating.

Thirty minutes later, he was waiting for her in the doorway of a deli across from the family planning clinic. When he looked up, he saw the back of Amanda's head. He'd know that thin dirty-blonde ponytail anywhere. He pulled her into the doorway.

CHAPTER 98

They stood together and watched across the street. People went in and out of the clinic. He pointed to the steel door of the lower level.

"There's a lab downstairs over there called the Foundling. Do you know what *foundling* means?"

She scowled at him. "Of course I know what that means. It's a term for kids who have no parents."

"No, you're wrong. Those are orphans. Foundlings are kids whose parents have abandoned them."

Amanda crossed her arms over her chest.

"Google 'artificial womb,'" Mitch said.

She looked at him questioningly.

"Go ahead, do it. It's what Sheldon and I were working on. Actually, Sheldon was working on it, and now he's trying to keep me out of it. But I've been thinking, Amanda. I think if I can get back to my life either doing a minimum sentence or without going to jail, I've got a plan. It's something we can do together."

"I think I can forgive you for drugging me," Amanda said.

"That's a bit random. Why are you bringing that up now?"

"Because it's important to forgive if you're going to stay in any kind of a relationship, professional or personal."

"Okay, well, for that matter, I'm not sure I can forgive you for sending incriminating photos and recordings to Madeline. Why'd you do it? Why'd you double-cross me?"

"Because if you got caught, I knew you'd try to bring me down with you."

"Okay, great. So now we've cleared the air on that. Can we move on?"

Amanda nodded.

Mitch explained what he and Sheldon had started together with the Foundling. "We started with the idea of saving babies whose mothers were drug addicts or who delivered them and never had any intention of keeping them, leaving them at the hospital. But then we started thinking about all the babies born extremely premature, before twenty-eight weeks, and all the damage they suffer. There are so many babies who need help."

Amanda scoffed. "That's ironic, coming from you."

"Just hear me out. Think of all the spontaneous abortions, babies infected with chorioamnionitis—the list of things that can go wrong during pregnancy is a long one, and think of how many fetuses are lost because of these conditions."

"That's Mother Nature keeping things in balance."

"No, it's not. That's just shitty luck. These artificial wombs, which will fill the Foundling lab, will keep these babies, more like fetuses, alive. Do you want to know how it works?"

"Sure, I'm curious."

Mitch explained, in detail, how the artificial womb worked.

"That all sounds great, Mitch, but get real. Sheldon and WMI won't let you anywhere near it, not now. I'd be all in, but I'm not the one going to jail. My next move was going to be to go to California, but for this, I would definitely stick around."

"Let's go check it out," said Mitch, looking again across the street.

"Now? You're not even supposed to be here."

He took her across the street and unlocked the heavy steel door. They descended the stairs, landing them in a tunnel somewhere below the building of the family planning clinic.

"This is lovely," said Amanda, making a face as they made their way through the dark, dank tunnel.

"Just hold on."

After a minute of walking, they came to the set of glass doors with THE FOUNDLING etched on it. Mitch put a key into the lock and turned it. It didn't work. He jiggled the key and tried again. He took it out, then put it back in. It still didn't work.

"Hmm, that's strange." He tried another key, then another. None of them worked. He banged his fist on the glass, hard enough to hurt his hand but without leaving a crack in the glass.

"He must have changed the locks. Asshole," muttered Mitch. He pounded on the glass again, this time yelling, "Asshole!" to the locked lab.

They left and walked back through the tunnel. Amanda talked the entire time about this new project. She was excited.

"Mitch, we can go back to being a team. I'll help you with this, but we'll do it our way. We don't need WMI or Sheldon. We've got each other. We're both smart and enterprising. You and I both have the same vision. Your brother may see it as a way to save babies and help families. But you and me? We see an opportunity to make a whole lot of money. I promise you, I'll be here for you whenever you're ready."

Mitch needed to hear this. He smiled and took her hand as they walked up the stairs to go outside.

CHAPTER 99

Sophie stood across the street from the steel door. Crowds of people passed in front of her. She bobbed her head back and forth, trying to keep a clear view of the door. She waited. She checked her phone for any missed texts or calls.

Just as she thought her toes would go numb, Mitch and Amanda came out the door. Sophie held up her phone to take a picture of Mitch exiting hospital property. It turned out the photo wasn't necessary. Four cop cars pulled up with lights flashing.

Sheldon and Rihanna walked up and stood next to Sophie. She didn't need to ask what they were doing there, just as she didn't need to ask Adam when he showed up. They all watched as the cops cuffed Mitch and loaded him into the back of the cruiser.

Sheldon watched, saddened, as his half brother was taken away.

The two couples shouted a thanks to Amanda, who was walking away in the direction of downtown. Without looking back, she gave a wave over her shoulder.

CHAPTER 100

"You know, Adam, parenting is going to be so vanilla compared to the last three and a half months. Are you ready for that?" Sophie asked from the back seat. She sat next to Danny in his infant seat. The snow on their neighborhood streets was mostly melted.

Sophie's phone rang. "Hey, Kate! Yes, we're on our way home. Finally." Pause. "A baby shower would be awesome! We talked about that before, didn't we? Like a lifetime ago." Sophie laughed. "Let's talk tomorrow and plan it for the next time you come down." She clicked off.

It was dusk, and the streetlights were on. Every time they drove under one of the lights, Danny squeezed his eyes shut.

"Hey, look at this."

"What?" Adam asked, looking in the rearview mirror.

Sophie put her hand on Danny's head like a visor, shading his eyes. He stopped closing them to the flashes of light and kept his eyes open. She put her face in front of his and watched as he turned to look at her.

"Oh my God! Adam, stop the car. You've got to see this!" Sophie cried, bursting with happiness.

ACKNOWLEDGMENTS

It all started with a conversation on a busy, chaotic day in the NICU. Exhausted after too many admissions of babies born too early, one of us joked about how the senior VP of nursing must be outside drumming up business for the hospital by dragging pregnant women in off the street.

Many years later, I decided to take that idea and write a medical thriller. My sincere appreciation to all who helped me make that happen: Thank you to my publisher, Brooke Warner, and her amazing team at She Writes Press; my editor Steve Parolini, Noveldoctor; and all the supportive fellow writers I've met along the way. Thank you to all my early readers and critique partners for helping get this book to the point of submission and eventual publishing.

Thank you to the bookstore More Than Words in the South End of Boston for pulling together and supporting More Than Writers, my writing group that is so much more than just a writing group.

Special thanks to all my nurse practitioner colleagues for their commitment, hard work, long days, longer nights, endless hours on rounds, and dedication to giving the very best of care to every NICU baby. I offer my heartfelt thanks for the camaraderie—the laughs and the tears that we shared through all the thick and the thin. Thanks to the labor and delivery nurses I worked with throughout the years, without whom the labor and delivery units would be lost.

Many thanks to my siblings, my three sons, and my friends for all the encouragement along the way.

Deep gratitude to my husband, David Olson, for his unwavering support and belief in me and this book.

Finally, many thanks to all you readers, without whom this book could not exist.

To stay in touch and learn more, go to juliehatchbooks.com.

ABOUT THE AUTHOR

Julie Hatch is a master's-prepared pediatric and neonatal nurse practitioner with a passion for kids' health and well-being. She spent over thirty years working in pediatric and neonatal intensive care. Ten years ago, she left Western medicine to earn a master's degree in traditional Chinese medicine and open her own acupuncture practice. At the same time, she began writing medical fiction, drawing on her experiences from the front lines of intensive care. This is her debut novel. Julie lives with her husband on the south coast of Massachusetts.

Looking for your next great read?

We can help!

Visit www.gosparkpress.com/next-read
or scan the QR code below for a list
of our recommended titles.

SparkPress is an independent boutique publisher delivering high-quality, entertaining, and engaging content that enhances readers' lives, with a special focus on commercial and genre fiction.